# Legacy of Dragons

by

Rex Sicka

PublishAmerica
Baltimore

ISBN: 1-60836-871-8
PUBLISHED BY PUBLISHAMERICA, LLLP
www.publishamerica.com
Baltimore

Printed in the United States of America

# Dedication

To three generations of fabulous women who have inspired my personal journey; my wife Heidi, my mother Glenda, my granddaughter Chante. Thank you for empowering my dreams.

# Chapter (1)

For the third time Stan opened the leather bound folder to view his newly acquired college diploma. He brought the folder close to his face and breathed in that familiar new car leather smell. With his eyes closed the scent was reminiscent of the leather interior of his Father's new Mercedes. The ancient script lettering, accented in all four corners with authentic gold leaf, radiated real power to the recent graduate. In this moment, the four years of fear, doubt and hard work, finally, felt worth the effort to Stan. His Mother had suggested framing the diploma for display, but Stan would have none of it. Stan intended to keep this record of his achievement with him for reassurance in those moments of doubt. In two years Stan intended to have an MBA from Harvard Business to bolster his resume. Then, and only then, would the two documents be proudly displayed on the wall of his Wall Street office. Even his Father, the demanding and imposing Stanton Wainwright II, would then be impressed, though it wasn't always so. Stanton the Elder had become incensed when Stan balked at leaving the Seattle area after graduation from Prep School. Stan wanted to remain in the area to attend the University of Washington but his Father had been adamant about him attending an Ivy League University. Stanton insisted entry to Harvard Business would be more difficult with a degree from, as he called it, a run of the mill university. In all probability, Stan's Mother had intervened on Stan's behalf because his Father eventually relented. The few victories Stan had won in his conflicts with Stanton were probably attributable to his Mother's influence. Of course there were stipulations imposed by Stanton before he surrendered. Stan was to maintain a 4.0 grade point average. Extra curricular activities were subject to Father's approval. Class selections as well as a declared major were decisions to be made, no questions asked, by Stanton alone. Stan agreed and adhered to the terms of the agreement with only a handful of minor infractions and one major slip up. The major event had nearly been a deal breaker. The confrontation that particular event spawned had been rewound and played many times in Stan's mind. Confrontation was actually a mischaracterization because confrontation requires there to be opposing forces. On that particular day, Stanton the Elder bellowed while Stan the Younger cowered.

Stan had just completed mid term exams during his junior year at the University. It was a day like any other day. Stan was home, working at the computer in his room. Stanton had burst through the door of Stan's room which, in and of itself, was a rare occurrence. Normal interactions between the two took place in Stanton's study where the air of intimidation hung heavily. There was no greeting as his Father charged into the room. Stanton's booming, scalding voice filled the room before the door was completely open.

"This is totally unacceptable, Stan! I did not invest my time and money in your education so you could drink beer, skip classes and boff some simpleton waitress. I put my name and reputation on the line pulling strings assuring your acceptance into Harvard. I didn't do it so you could humiliate me by sleepwalking through your studies because you have a hard on! If rubbing your pathetic little dick against your co-ed is more important to you than your education and family legacy, you need to tell me now so I can cut my losses. I invest only in success, nothing else. Your mid terms are not a success, they are deplorable! I will never accept this level of effort from my employees and I will not accept it from you! I signed every check, I greased every palm, I yanked every chain. I demand the same effort from you. I have never been vague about the path to success so if this girl, Hannah, has detoured my plans you need to declare yourself. You can melt away into a mundane existence in the suburbs with the other three hundred million ordinary people. I know everything about your Hannah. I know who she is, what she is and where she comes from. She is not a person who could stand behind a man on a financial fast track. You will make many decisions which will influence your life. This is one of them, so get on with it. Make your choice and do it soon. I have no patience for failure and I have no desire to stand back to watch it. There are a handful of people with the capability and opportunity to rise to the heights I aspire for you. Aside of those few, stands the rest of the world. Choose your world, Stan." Stanton had spun around, slamming the door as he left leaving no opportunity for excuses and explanations, not that Stan had any. Stan had listened to his Father's rant, wide eyed and frozen in place. He was terrified Stanton would venture far enough into the room to see the computer's monitor which displayed an e-mail Stan was composing to Hannah.

Stanton's reaction was not surprising. The surprise was his Father had discovered Stan's relationship with Hannah in the first place. Stan had gone to extreme measures to keep the two worlds separated. Stan had always manipulated their encounters so he could meet Hannah at the restaurant, bar or library giving him plausible deniability. Stan knew he would be naïve to believe his Father wouldn't find out about his secretive affair. No one has better intelligence gathering capabilities than an investment banker. Stan remembered only too well the stories his Father told about the father of modern intelligence agencies, the banker Mayer Rothchild. Rothchild understood the value and profit potential that could be realized by utilizing information. Stanton's favorite Rothchild story involved Mayer's manipulation of the events at the Battle of Waterloo where Napoleon had surrendered to Wellington. Rothchild's spies brought the news of surrender to Mayer a full day before the king, himself, received the news. Rothchild released false reports of a Wellington surrender creating a selling panic in the London Financial Markets. Rothchild calmly and systematically tripled his holdings the following day for pennies on the dollar when the factual news arrived in England. Information is a pivotal tool in the creation and retention of great power. No wonder modern intelligence services (CIA, MI6, Moussad) are the evolutionary product of centuries of experience in intelligence gathering. Stan shouldn't have been surprised his Father knew all about Hannah, his minions were everywhere.

The week following their confrontation had been a horrible time for Stan. In an attempt to avoid telling Hannah of Stanton's ultimatum, Stan had resisted all urges to see her. Stan could not stop himself from reflecting on all the glorious stolen moments he and Hannah had shared in the previous few months. Stan saw his life in shades of gray. The all of Stan's existence was merely as a piece of his Father's plan. Hannah had given Stan a glimpse of a life in the light; no script, no expectations. There was no hidden agenda offered up by Hannah, only a soft, comfortable place to escape, if only for brief moments. There were so many nights Stan couldn't get to sleep. His mind would race, his heart would palpitate with nothing more than the expectation of spending a moment with Hannah the following day. The day Hannah directed their relationship into the physical realm was the day Stan realized everything he had been feeling went well beyond obsessive newness to something unique, wild and wonderful. Whenever her image floated through his thoughts, his body ached to be near her. When Hannah laid down beside him, language was useless. You can't describe a perfect moment. Words are impotent to convey an inner caress. Stan had known from the very beginning of the relationship, eventually, he and Hannah would be confronted by destiny. The fantasy and reality in his life were on a collision course. Stan had known from their first encounter she would never pass the scrutiny of his Father. She wanted to be a Marine Biologist and save whales, for Christ sake! The fact she was working her way through school, by herself, wouldn't impress Stanton. That would merely highlight her meager social standing to his Father. Family legacy didn't open doors for Hannah, she opened doors herself.

Stan had seriously considered sharing the secret of Hannah with his Mother, but had decided against it. Although he believed his Mother would understand his feelings, Stan could not envision his Mother as anything but his Father's wife. No matter how much sympathy she felt or how much compassion she expressed, first and foremost she was Mrs. Stanton Wainwright II. She would have told his Father. The position of the first wife of finance came with responsibilities and obligations not to be ignored. The price of status and station is unwavering, unquestioning loyalty. If his Mother could recall the intensity of young love from her own life it would never cause her to jeopardize her present for the sake of Stan's.

Stan had shoved the realities of the future into the shadows of his mind until that fateful day when Stanton stormed into Stan's face and ripped reality into the light. Stan, eventually, arranged to meet Hannah at a restaurant they had frequented, hoping the comfortable familiarity would somehow make his task easier. Hannah's words had floated past Stan's ears, totally uncomprehendable. His only thought was an overwhelming urge to grab hold of her, pull her close to him and tell her everything would be alright. But it wouldn't be alright. From this day forward his life was going to change. Hannah had noticed and noted Stan's distance. In some sort of Freudian reaction, Stan instigated a disagreement. Maybe anger would make the words he had to say roll more easily from his tongue. It didn't. Hannah made Stan feel even worse by refusing to fight. She didn't even get angry. Hannah had looked into Stan's eyes for a suspended moment before she softly spoke,

"We both knew this day would come. I've always known this would be the day I'd know your heart. Now I know." Hannah stood up, never taking her eyes off of Stan. She reached across the table and gently stroked Stan's cheek, "Goodbye Stanton." She turned quickly and walked briskly away, never looking back.

That debacle had occurred a year and a half ago. He hadn't spoken to Hannah, nor would he have even seen her if he hadn't watched her waitressing from the shadows across the street from the diner where

9

she worked. Visions of Hannah tortured Stan for months but time slowly lessened the pain. Stan reacted by burying himself in his studies while he methodically buried his feelings. There was no longer any reason to search for a judgment of right or wrong, only to set aside his feelings for the sake of a future.

Hannah wasn't with him today. This was the summer of Stan. In a couple of weeks he and two friends were going to Europe where anything was not only possible, it was highly probable. The trip was just a portion of his graduation gift. The other was the new automobile that would be waiting for Stan in Massachusetts. Stanton wanted for his son to arrive on the campus in Cambridge in a style befitting a Wainwright.

His Father's voice boomed from the intercom interrupting Stan's daydream, "Stan, come to the study. I need to speak to you."

Stan quickly replied," I'll be right there, sir."

Stan immediately headed for the other wing of the house where his Father's study was located. Stan had always disliked the study. The cold and foreboding room left Stan feeling vulnerable and helpless. He chalked it up to the power of intimidation or was it the intimidation of power?

Stan knocked at the door and waited for his Father's voice.

"Come in."

Stan entered into the familiar surrounding where he had been scolded and schooled by his Father for so many years. The stern face and barrel chest under the shirt and tie were all Stan ever saw in Stanton's lair.

Stanton looked up from his desk and motioned to the chair in front of the desk, "Have a seat."

Stan's eyes focused on Stanton, trying to find a hint of his intentions as he took a seat.

Stanton began, "You look like your riding high. That's good, you deserve it."

"Thank you, sir."

"I rented a townhouse, off campus, in Cambridge. You will have a service to care for your needs; cleaning, groceries, maintenance and such. Use your credit card for expenses but don't be foolish with my money. Pay your own way and let others do the same. I haven't decided on a specific car for you as yet. Your Mother tells me I am out of touch in regards to the style of auto that would appeal to a young man, so it will have to remain a surprise. On another note, I have something else I want you to do before you leave for Europe. Actually, it's something your Mother wants you to do. I'm not sure whether I was badgered or convinced into agreement. I want you to fly to West Virginia and drive your Grandfather back to Seattle. He broke his leg falling off of that ridiculous motorcycle again and Emma says he is struggling to care for himself. He refuses to get on an airplane. My guess is he is simply losing the few mental faculties he still possesses."

Stan struggled to find his voice, "What about Europe?"

"This will only take a few days. Your Mother thinks this will be the last chance for you to know her Father. He's in his seventies now and quite frankly, I'm surprised he made it this long. It's no secret he and I have never seen eye to eye. He's just another in a long line of left wing throwbacks who never evolved beyond the sixties."

Stan's mind frantically searched for a previous engagement that could free him from his Father's request, "I haven't seen him since I was twelve years old. I didn't know what to say to him then. I hardly know him. What could we possibly talk about?"

"You'll figure it out. The business world will be full of people you will need to deal with. Whether you like them is inconsequential. You need to pack. Your plane leaves at 8:45 tomorrow morning. Just do it for your Mother. There will be plenty of time to sort things out once you get the old coot here. Emma thinks he can live with us, but I believe we would all be better served if he went to an assisted living facility. In any event, I'll see you in a few days."

Stan knew debate was useless. The plans were made. They always were. Ready or not, Stan was going across the country for a journey with a virtual stranger who was possibly senile, probably helpless and most definitely someone he would share very little in common.

Accepting his fate, Stan asked, "Do I need to rent a truck or is that taken care of?"

"I'm told he is packed, loaded and ready to go but you'll have to assess that when you arrive. You can't call him; he refuses to own a phone. Like I said, his body has made the trip but his mind is stuck somewhere in the past."

# Chapter (2)

You couldn't call Stan's mood a funk, because the entire length of the flight to Atlanta he had molded his mood into more of an angry daydream. The connecting flight to West Virginia found Stan composing a mental list of all the reasons he should not have been obliged to baby-sit an old man he barely knew. Stan mentally replayed the conversation with his Father, which he commonly did, but in Stan's mind he could replay it his own way. Stan's response in his replays were always powerful. He should have said, 'Why don't you get one of your lackeys to move him? Why me? It's not only unfair; it's a complete waste of my time. Three days in a truck with a senile old man is not going to enrich my life. Strolling through the Louve will enrich my life. Destitute people from the backwoods of West Virginia have absolutely nothing relevant to add to the life I intend to lead. He needs a nurse not an economics major. I don't want to do it. I won't!' That's what Stan should have said. 'Yes sir, I'll take care of it' is what he actually said.

Stan very seldom challenged his Father. It was not in Stan's best interest to resist his Father's will. Stanton had all the money and power, besides he scared the shit out of Stan. At least with a continent between them, Stan was free to embrace his angry resentment.

The plane touched down snapping Stan back to the present. He knew there was only thirty minutes for him to get to his connecting flight. He checked the gate number on his ticket before following the other passengers into the modest terminal. Stan disembarked at gate 'B'. He looked toward the other end of the terminal. He couldn't imagine the building was large enough to contain alphabetical gates extending to a gate 'W', where Stan's plane was boarding. He walked briskly toward the other gates. Reaching the far end of the terminal left Stan in front of gate 'F'.

'Perfect' thought Stan.' I'm not even in the right building. What a great start!' .

Stan located an information desk and was informed gate 'W' was in a building adjacent to gate 'A'. Stan spun around; saying nothing to the attendant and hurried back in the direction from which he had just come. He was already tired of carrying his bag. It didn't have a shoulder strap or even wheels so Stan had to muscle the bag everywhere he went. He hustled out of the gate 'A' exit where he stopped dead in his tracks.

'What other building?' The only other structure was an airplane hanger. Stan hurried to the only visible door at the front of the hanger. There was a bumper sticker sized sign on the door saying simply 'Air Appalachia'. Stan shook his head in disbelief as he entered the hanger. Surprise stopped Stan once again as he surveyed the nearly empty building. There was a stairway leading to an unlit office and three rollaway tool chests against the far wall and nothing else. Stan walked briskly to the only other door which appeared to lead to the tarmac. Stan stopped again after exiting the hanger, not from surprise but because he suddenly felt like he had entered a time warp. The plane before Stan was right out of the closing scene of the classic movie 'Casablanca'. The metallic skin of the plane glistened in the afternoon light. The tail section of the seventy five year old plane was proudly stenciled 'Air Appalachia'.

'Probably in crayon', thought Stan.

"Are you Stan Wainwright?"

Stan spun around, startled by the voice of the man who had quietly walked up behind him. The man held up his hand,"Sorry, I didn't mean to scare you."

Stan quickly regained his composure and reclaimed the mood he had worked so long to groom, "You surprised me, you didn't scare me and yes, I am Stan Wainwright. I'm looking for gate 'W'."

The man gave Stan a wink and a nod, "You found it."

"Where are the other gates?"

He chuckled, "Aren't any. Silly isn't it. The FAA forced the airport to accommodate us, so they stuck us out here for punishment. Personally, I like being out here so the joke is on them. I just went and called to make sure you had made your connecting flight. Anyway, we're ready to go. We were just waiting for you. You have any other bags?"

Stan shook his head no.

"This way then."

Stan followed the man onto the plane. The man pulled the steps up and secured the door behind them, "Sit wherever you want. I'm Wesley; I'll be your pilot. It's a short flight but it's pretty scenic. Nice mountains 'cept the ones the miners topped. If you're hungry I hope you brought something 'cause I got nothing." With that he turned and headed for the cockpit.

Stan took a window seat, setting his bag in the seat beside him. Wesley was true to his word, the flight was short and scenic. Stan was seriously taken aback by the sight of the mountains being mined. They actually did take the tops off of the mountains. Stan thought the open pit mines resembled atomic blast sites.

'That's the price of energy,' Stan thought.

The flight was surprisingly smooth and ended softly and uneventfully at a rural airport near Oakdale. Wesley opened the door and folded down the steps immediately after bringing the plane to a stop. Stan grabbed his bag and exited with the handful of other passengers he had barely noticed. The terminal was a one room affair consisting of two unmanned ticket counters and one car rental desk where an elderly woman was seated reading a paperback. The only other signs in the building were for baggage claim and Greyhound bus.

Stan walked to the car rental desk, "Excuse me; I'd like to rent a car."

The woman looked up from her book and smiled broadly, "Round trip or one way?"

"To Hope, one way."

The woman shook her head," I'm sorry, but there is nowhere to turn in the car in Hope."

This was not going to improve Stan's mood. Sarcastically he asked," Where is the closest place to Hope where I can turn in a rental car?"

The woman smiled and shrugged her shoulders,"Well, that would be here."

Stan looked blankly at the woman for a moment, "Then how can I get from here to there?"

"Greyhound is about the only way from here. It should be by here in about an hour."

Stan summoned his best sarcastic tone, "No specific time, just about an hour?"

Sarcasm was lost on the woman. She lifted her book as she replied, "Thereabouts."

Stan picked up his bag and turned to leave before realizing the Greyhound desk was unmanned. He turned back, "How do I get a ticket for the bus?"

She sat down her book, "I can sell you a ticket. There's never anyone at the bus counter."

Stan asked as he was purchasing a ticket," Is there anywhere to get something to eat?"

"Sorry, we used to have a lunch counter but there wasn't enough business. They even took out the vending machines. It's a couple of miles to town so you will never get there and back in time."

'You have got to be kidding,' Thought Stan. "Why is the airport so far from town?"

"They built the new airport way out here to make room for the growth. Then the Whisper Mine closed down and poof, no more growth. Go figure."

Stan took his ticket and sullenly sat down on one of the arbitrarily placed benches. The only other person Stan saw with the exception of the woman at the car/bus counter was the pilot, Wesley, when he crossed the terminal on his way home. Stan's mood was sliding quickly to a dark new high in lows,' This is just great! I'm working my way down the evolutionary transportation ladder. Next I'll be on a mule train!'

Stan had nothing to read, so he aimlessly watched the paint peel for an eternity which was an hour, 'thereabouts'. No planes, no buses, no taxis, just one lone woman reading a Sidney Sheldon novel. 'Don't these people realize there is a world out there where you can do things and interact with other people. I'd go insane if I had to live here. I'm going crazy just being here.'

About an hour finally passed. An hour Stan would never get back. He had made use of the time by slowly stirring the dark mood stewing in his mind. The first diversion of sight or sound was the airbrakes of the Greyhound bus snapping Stan back to the present. Stan picked up his bag and headed for the bus. The woman behind the ticket counter caught his attention, waving for Stan to come to her. He took the few steps out of his way to where she sat.

The woman held out a sandwich in a Ziploc bag, "Why don't you take my sandwich? You're not going to find anything in Hope either. It's just a post office and a Grange Hall."

Stan was stunned but he was also hungry. He looked quizzically at the woman as he took the sandwich from her, "Thank you. That is very nice of you."

She waved him off, "It's nothing, I'm going home soon." Her eyes went back to her book.

Stan glanced back over his shoulder at the woman before he exited the terminal and boarded the bus. The driver had a huge smile on his face as he took Stan's ticket.

"Come on aboard. It's a good thing Gladys called dispatch 'cause I usually don't stop here."

Stan handed him the ticket and took a seat. The driver closed the door and rolled back onto the roadway. Besides Stan there was only one other passenger, a young soldier in the very rear of the bus. Stan quickly devoured the egg salad sandwich which was either extremely tasty or he was extremely hungry. Stan scoffed at the lack of food services but at the pace these people lived, they probably didn't require much nourishment.

The two lane road wound up a canyon which was either very familiar to the driver or he delusionally believed the behemoth he was driving was a sports car because he negotiated the sharp turns at speeds forcing Stan to firmly grip the armrests. The view he enjoyed from Appalachian Air was out of the question on the speeding bus. Stan's eyes were glued to the road which he hoped the driver's were also.

The bus topped a summit and barreled across a high mountain meadow. It came to a screeching stop in front of two antique buildings. The driver smiled as he opened the door, "This is your stop, young fellow."

Stan's feet no sooner touched the ground when the door closed and the bus accelerated away, disappearing over a rise in the road. He watched the bus melt into the horizon before he turned to take stock of his present situation. Stan could see no sign of human activity as he made his way to the post office building. Stan stepped inside to find an elderly man sitting quietly behind the counter reading a Louis L'Amour western.

Stan shook his head, 'Is that all these people do? They should be the smartest people on the planet. Of course how educated can you get reading western adventures and trash novels.'

Stan approached the counter, "Excuse me. Is there a taxi or a shuttle? I need to get to my Grandfather's house."

The old man let loose with a cackle, "Sure thing, young fellow. Just like the Big Apple, step outside and yell 'taxi'. It's rush hour." He let out another cackle, "I'm sorry; I don't mean nothing by it. Who's your grandfather, anyway?"

"Ty Hanstead."

A look of recognition spread across the man's face, "That's right, he told me you wuz comin'. Ty lives three, four miles yonder. You should have stayed on the bus. It goes right by Ty's place. I can give you a ride after the mail truck gets here but that might be an hour or two. Other than that, you walk."

' Here comes the mule train' was Stan's first thought, "Walking will be fine. Will I be able to recognize his place?"

"No problem. Ty likes to say he lives beyond Hope on Wall Street. You can't miss it."

Stan picked up his bag. The postmaster motioned to him, "Would you mind taking Ty's mail? He hasn't picked it up in a while."

Stan sat down his bag and grinned menacingly, "Do you always release U.S. mail to just anyone?"

The man chuckled, "I don't believe you came all the way up here on foot just to steal ole Ty's mail."

Stan's mood released its grip for a second allowing him to flash a genuine smile while he stuffed the mail into his bag. He thanked the man, grabbed his bag and started down the road. There was no traffic. He happened upon an occasional driveway, but Stan never saw the houses connected to the driveways. Stan trudged on, switching his bag from hand to hand every few hundred yards. The sun was getting very low in the western sky when he rounded a small bend in the road revealing a road sign. Proud as can be, atop a wooden post was an authentic street sign. 'Wall Street'.

Stan's eyes lingered on the sign. He sat his bag on the ground for a short break before switching arms.

He snickered, "Wall Street, I've finally arrived." Stan picked up the bag he had learned to hate and started down the driveway. His mood had simmered out during his hike. He was tired, hungry and upset only because they were not already on the road which was his original plan. The cabin was just beyond view from the road. It was a simple structure with a screened in porch stretching the length of the front of the cabin. Ty was sitting in a wooden rocker on the porch, reading. Stan half expected to find Ty with a ponytail and a long white beard, but he was surprisingly clean shaven with short cropped white hair. Ty smiled from ear to ear when he spotted Stan. He stood and limped to the screen door, meeting Stan just as he arrived. Ty was tall and thin. He was wearing a walking cast extending to just below the knee on his right leg. The pant leg was cut off just above the cast.

Ty held the screen door open, "Stan three! It is great to see you."

Stan stepped onto the porch and sat his bag down for, hopefully, the last time. He extended his arm to shake hands but Ty grabbed his hand and forcefully pulled Stan into a bear hug.

Ty held Stan firmly for a moment before releasing him and stepping back to get a good look, "You look good. Come on inside, you're probably hungry. I've been simmering a pot of gumbo all day."

Stan realized he had not said anything in response as yet. Ty picked up the bag and limped into the cabin. Stan followed into the expansive interior of the cabin. The cabin was one great room. The kitchen area was down one wall while a couch and two chairs faced a woodstove on the opposite wall. Everywhere else were nearly full book shelves. Stan looked appraisingly around the room, impressed at the level of neatness until he suddenly realized all these items should be in packing boxes.

Ty sat Stan's bag by the front door and limped to the kitchen. He motioned to the table, "Have a seat. I'll get you a bowl." Ty filled two bowls from the pot on the antique cook stove. He sat the gumbo on the table, "You're not a mute are you? You haven't said a word."

"I apologize. It's been quite a day, that's all. It's good to see you, too."

Ty's piercing blue eyes were fixed on Stan as he sat down to eat, "Your Mom said you just graduated from U-dub. Good school. I was class of "56."

"I didn't know you were a Husky."

"Hell, yes. I still have purple and gold underwear."

Stan's hunger directed his attention to the steaming gumbo. He scanned the room as he ate, "Looks like you read a lot. What are you reading now?"

Ty's forehead wrinkled, "Right now I'm working on 'The Elegant Universe' by Brian Greene. I'm still trying to get my head around this time/space continuum concept. My conceptual thought process isn't what it used to be but I still have lots of questions. It's the answers that confuse the hell out of me."

Ty got up to retrieve two glasses and a bottle of red wine. He sat back down and poured two glasses.

Stan was still devouring his meal, "I was starved. The only thing I've eaten today was a sandwich a lady at the airport gave to me."

"Did you come in on Air Appalachia?"

"Yes, I did. It was a nice flight."

"Wesley's a good pilot. He sure loves that old plane. That plane is in better shape now than it was when it rolled off the line in the thirties. You should have told Wesley you were coming to see me. He could have given you a ride, he's my neighbor. I should have mentioned it to him but I didn't think about it until just now." Ty shrugged and picked up his wine glass.

Stan took a pause from his gumbo. He looked at Ty and shook his head. He quickly scanned the room again, "Mom said you were packed and ready. It looks like you have more to pack."

Ty looked around, "No, everything I'm taking is in the van ready to rock. I would have driven myself but I don't have any touch on the pedals with this cast. Every time I hit the brakes I end up with everything on the dashboard."

"What about all this stuff? Are you just leaving it?"

Ty nodded, "Yeah, this all stays. I have everything I need."

"Don't you at least want to put this stuff in storage?"

"That's not necessary. There's this family, the McKinneys, they've been squatting in a cabin on the other side of the hill behind Wesley's place for a few years. They're going to move in. They're real nice people."

"So you sold it furnished?"

"I didn't sell it. They couldn't afford it. I gave it to them."

Stan was shocked. He studied Ty's face for any sign he was joking. Ty was as calm as if he had just said he was giving away an old bicycle, "You've got to be kidding! You gave it away? That's crazy!"

"Why? If you really think about it, property ownership is crazy. I got one for you I've thought a lot about, Stan. Imagine what a task it must have been for the first representatives of the European colonial powers. These guys had to come over here and try to explain to people who had lived here for eons that some rich guy on the other side of the planet now owned all the land. What a tough sell that must have been. It's no wonder they decided to just kill everyone. That ownership thing was never going to sell. This land will be here long after I'm gone so what did I really own. Besides I didn't pay much for it anyway. I got my money's worth."

"But Grandpa, for the last few centuries, property has been worth something."

Ty grinned, "You're absolutely right and it'll be worth a lot more to the McKinney's than it is to me."

Stan kept his eyes on Ty, still expecting him to start laughing, but there was no flicker of joke in Ty's eyes. Stan decided Ty might very well be crazy. No one gives away their house.

Ty continued, "I left most of the books. The McKinneys have four kids so, hopefully, they will use them. I've brought some. I read most of them but with my memory, some of them still surprise me." Ty poured another glass of wine, "To help us sleep."

Stan asked, "Speaking of sleep, where do I sleep?"

Ty pointed to the back wall, "You can have the loft, up the ladder. There's just a bed up there, but it's the warmest place in the house. I can't get up the ladder very easily with this silly cast so I've been sleeping on the sofa."

Stan drained his wine glass and stood up, "Maybe I will hit it. I'm pretty tired and we should get an early start tomorrow, don't you think, Grandpa?"

"Call me Ty. I feel old enough. We can become friends before you have to claim me as family."

Stan went to the ladder extending up the back wall.

Ty called after him, "You're right about early though. Brutus is stronger in the morning air."

Stan stopped cold. 'Brutus better not be a mule', "Who's Brutus?"

"That's the name we gave the van. Good night, Stan."

Stan started up the ladder, "Good night, Ty."

Stan shook his head as he climbed the rungs, 'Ty, Brutus and Stan three, I hope I'm up to this.'

# Chapter (3)

Stan sat bolt upright in bed to the sound of Ty pounding on the ceiling beneath him.

"What do you say we get going, Stan? Coffee is on."

Stan rolled out of bed and put yesterday's clothes on. Ty was sitting, quietly drinking a cup of coffee when Stan got to the bottom of the ladder.

"Did you sleep okay?" Ty didn't wait for an answer, "There are clean towels in the shower room if you want to clean up before we leave."

The term 'shower room' left Stan slightly bewildered, "What's a shower room?"

Ty noticed the concern on Stan's face which forced a grin, "It's on the back porch but don't worry, we have hot and cold running water. It's septic systems we don't have. This ground doesn't perk up here so we're still pioneers with bodily functions. The out house is up on the ridge. It's cold in the winter time but the view is awesome. You don't need a magazine up there."

Stan retrieved some clean clothes from his bag and went to check out the shower room. The shower enclosure was attached to the back of the house on the rear porch. There was a gated entry on the side of the enclosure. The walls came only to shoulder height where it was screened in up to the roof. Stan enjoyed a shower with a view but it was the view from the outhouse that was really unique.

When Stan returned from his scenic tour of the bodily function facilities, Ty was waiting on the front porch with Stan's bag, "You ready to rock?" Again he didn't pause for a response, "Every time I start a cross country trip I get butterflies. I crossed the first time in 1953. Man, I was young. I was going out into the world to find myself. It's kind of a funny concept if you really think about it. I mean, how would you recognize yourself if you didn't know who you were before you left." Ty picked up his back pack and started towards the barn, "I think anytime you go somewhere to find yourself; you're going the wrong way. Did you ever hear about the kid who was still living at home with his parents long after he got out of school? He came home one day and all of his belongings were packed and on the front lawn. His Father looked at him and said, 'You've been looking for yourself for years now. Obviously you're not here.'"

Ty stopped in front of the double doors on the barn. Stan motioned toward the house, "Don't you want to lock up the house?"

Ty chuckled as he opened the double doors, "If you can find a door lock, feel free to lock it."

The flowered Volkswagen Microbus with peace signs from Stan's imagination didn't materialize when the doors were opened. Brutus was a very old, faded baby blue Ford Econoline van. Attached to the rear of the van was a gray primered, enclosed trailer.

Ty smiled proudly and held out his hand to present the van, "1966, but we didn't get her until '70 or '71. Once we made friends it's been a great ride. I got almost three hundred thousand miles out of the first engine. This one barely has a hundred." Ty turned, trying to read Stan's expression, "Don't worry, Stan. She might need a paint job but mechanically she's tight. I even had Wesley over to check her out. She's got good rubber, new brakes, belts, hoses and wheel bearings. I even put in a bigger radiator."

The new parts were some relief but Stan was struggling to see something more than a forty year old truck. He pointed at the trailer and said, "Do you think it can handle the extra weight?"

"No problem. That's what the bigger radiator was for. She might be a little slow up hills so you will just have to kick back and enjoy the view."

Stan checked out the interior while he stowed his bag behind the driver's seat. It was simple with a raised, padded bed platform in the back. The walls and ceiling were nicely done with a light colored paneling. The bed and floor were covered with a plush, light gray carpeting.

Ty got into the passenger seat, "Stan, you have that deer-in-the-headlights look about you. You really expected to see Big Stan's vision of me, didn't you? I hope you're not disappointed I don't have hair down to my ass and a pair of Lennon glasses. And I'm sorry Brutus doesn't have shag carpeting and flower power painted on her sides. Big Stan sees what he expects to see."

"You're right; Dad thinks you're a hippie throwback."

"Hippie! That's great. Big Stan has been freeze dried. The only thing left of hippies are a few ideas."

Stan studied the dash to familiarize himself with the lay out, "Do you have the keys?"

"The key is in it. It won't come out."

Stan fiddled with the shifter, "I've never driven a car with a column shift."

"It used to be called a three-on-the-tree. You'll get used to it. She's got a manual choke, too, next to the ignition. Pump twice, pull the choke, no throttle and she'll fire every time."

Brutus started, as stated, and shortly settled into a smooth idle. Stan put the van in gear and slowly pulled out of the barn. When he reached the road he turned to Ty and asked, "Which way?"

Ty pointed, "Take Highway Thirty Three to Homer and then take Seventy Nine West to Charleston."

They pulled onto the road. Stan pointed at the radio, "Is that an actual eight track?"

"Yeah, it is. That tape has been stuck in there for years. It doesn't play anymore. Too bad, I still love Pink Floyd. No matter, I talk enough to avoid those awkward pauses."

"I've got a question. Aren't trucks like boats? Aren't they supposed to be named after women? What's with Brutus?"

"Brutus seemed like the perfect name when we first got her because every time I depended on her, she stabbed me in the back. We've been friends for a long time now so I think she accepted the name."

Ty studied Stan's profile, "So, have you decided whether this is a chore or an adventure?"

"Truthfully, I haven't decided what it is yet."

"Truth, if you're looking for truth you're going to be disappointed. There is no absolute truth, only perspectives."

"You think your truth is different than mine?"

"Sure it is. Einstein was right. Everything is relative to where you view it. Let's say you are floating on a raft in the middle of the Pacific Ocean. The water is dead calm and there is nothing but water in every direction. On the horizon you see someone sitting in a raft just like you. The raft drifts towards you, floats past and disappears over the other horizon. His perspective on the motionless ocean would be identical to yours. You could both, truthfully, report someone had floated past but the actual truth is in the current below the surface. Anyone who says he has your truth is lying to both of you."

Ty's eyes followed the entrance to a mine as they passed, "No matter how many times I see the mines, they still blow me away. Did you see them from the air?"

"Yeah, I did. I was surprised they actually take the tops off the mountains. They look like bomb sites. I thought the mines were underground."

"They are. These mountains are catacombed with mine shafts but open pit mines are cheaper to run. That's the latest technique. Energy corporations don't recognize the word 'nature' in natural resources. The bizarre part of the story is the ironic situation the people in these mountains are forced into. They find themselves in a position where they are working against their own best interests. The mines poison the water and the land but they are the major source of income for the people. Quite a dilemma." Ty pointed to an approaching strip mall,

"Why don't you stop at the market before we get to the interstate so we can get some food and ice for the road?"

Stan marveled at how quickly Ty could change his train of thought. Ty could go from philosophy to devastation to lunch at warp speed, sometimes in the same sentence.

Stan pulled into the lot and parked Brutus. Ty grabbed his back pack as he exited the van.

A young male employee of the chain store stepped in front of them before they reached the first aisle of the store. The employee was about the same age as Stan. The clerk was wearing a kelly green vest with a prominent store logo and a large name tag on the lapel.

The young man addressed Ty, "Excuse me sir, but you will have to leave your back pack at check stand five."

Ty smiled at the young clerk, "No thanks, I better keep it with me. I'm liable to forget it at check stand five when I leave the store." Ty started to step past the clerk, but the young man held out his arm and stepped in front of Ty.

"Sorry sir, but it's store policy. No back packs. It's posted on the front door where you came in."

Again with a smile, Ty responded, "I didn't realize I was required to read the front of the building before I shopped here. Was I supposed to read everything? Does everyone have to do that?"

The politeness left the clerk's tone as he began to lose his patience with the old man, "I don't make the policies. We have a problem with shoplifting."

Ty's smile stayed in place as he leaned forward to better see the man's nametag, "So Fred, I take it you are accusing me of being a thief." Ty pointed at a woman walking down the aisle," I noticed you didn't ask her to surrender her purse at check stand five."

"The policy is for back packs."

Ty slipped the pack off his back, held it by the straps and said, "I'll carry it and we'll call it a purse." Ty again began to step around Fred.

Fred blocked Ty once more. Fred's face was beginning to flush, his eyes narrowed, "I have to insist! Policy is policy."

Ty continued to conceal any trace of aggravation. Still smiling he said, "Don't most shoplifters hide things under their clothes? Why don't you collect their clothing? You could even make your customers hold their hands in the air so you can see them at all times."

The flushness was spreading on Fred's face and neck, turning quickly from pink to crimson, "I don't have time for this, are you going to give me the pack or not?"

Ty held the pack out but quickly pulled it back, "I'll need a receipt, Fred. You've made a believer out of me about the dishonesty of your patrons. I want to make sure I get everything back."

Red faced, Fred began anxiously shifting his weight from foot to foot, "You don't get a receipt! No one is going to rip you off!"

Ty leaned in closer to Fred, "You don't know me and I don't know you so why can you accuse me of being a thief but I'm supposed to blindly trust you? Doesn't seem very equitable to me."

"Listen here, mister! This store is part of one of the biggest chains on the east coast. Employees are thoroughly screened and trained. Everything is monitored. Nobody is going to touch your stuff!"

Ty's smile grew, "Oh, I get it. Corporations can be trusted, it's the people you can't trust. "Ty paused looking intently at Fred, "You might want to get out of the stock room a little more often, Fred."

Fred was ready to start bursting blood vessels, "Are you going to give me the back pack or am I going to have to call the manager?"

"What do you need a manager for? Are you afraid you might have misunderstood the intent of store policy?" Ty held out the back pack. He leaned forward and softly added, "There's nothing in it anyway. I'll come find you when we're ready to leave."

Ty limped nonchalantly down the aisle. Stan had been watching the confrontation completely dumbstruck. He focused for a moment on the stunned, seething clerk before he hurried to catch up with Ty. When he caught up, he softly said, "Why in the hell did you do that? I thought you people all loved each other."

Ty shrugged, "I do love people. Its automatons and morons I have no patience for."

Stan convinced Ty not to page Fred over the intercom after they had finished shopping and it was time to retrieve the back pack.

Once they were back in the van, Ty asked, "Did that embarrass you?"

"A little bit. It was pretty unnecessary, don't you think?"

"Probably, but it was entertaining. I thought the little robot was going to explode."

Stan chuckled, now that it was over, "The picture is beginning to take shape. You're fiscally irresponsible, partially crazy and occasionally an unwarranted asshole. Well let's make some miles, you ornery old fart!"

Ty laughed, "Cool! I was beginning to think you didn't have a sense of humor. In this day and age you have to be able to laugh or you'll end up crying yourself to sleep every night."

Stan pulled back onto the roadway, "Why do people like Fred bother you so much?"

"I guess it bothers me anyone would accept things unconditionally without asking themselves if it makes any sense. Hell, there would still be slaves if people never questioned authority."

"Wow, Ty. From morons to slavery in one sentence. That was a giant leap. Maybe you didn't get the memo, but it wasn't inquiring minds that ended slavery, it was the Civil War."

"You might have been misinformed, young Stan. Check the dates. The Emancipation Proclamation was signed into law in January 1863, almost three years after the start of the war. Slavery was the public face legitimizing the war which was primarily a struggle between powerful northern industrialists and equally powerful southern agriculturists. It was an economic war. The only humanity existing in that time belonged to the people, not the governments."

"Even if that's true Ty, what does that have to do with questioning authority?"

"It's not just questioning, it's about enforcement. You need to start with the law of the land, the Constitution, and I need to add that even with the inherent flaws of the Constitution, I think it might be the greatest legal document ever written."

Stan interrupted, "That surprises me to hear you say that."

"Why? Think about it, Stan. The Constitution had for the first time, and probably the last time, in recorded history given the sovereign power of an entire country to its people. That was huge! It was revolutionary! Government wrote the laws but the people held the power of enforcement. Read state and city charters. Read the words on all law enforcement vehicles. 'To serve and protect'. The courts and law enforcement agencies enforce the laws of the people. Go back to the Civil War. Southern politicians had dominated government for a long time and through their pressure got the Fugitive Slave Act signed into law. The people, through the jury system, refused to enforce the law. The jury's simply released the people accused of violating the law. The government and the courts had no choice but to repeal the law because the people refused to enforce it."

"That can't be right. No one can arbitrarily and openly defy the law. They would be aiding and abetting criminal activity. There would be anarchy."

"You're wrong, Stan. The people had that power and they still do but no one knows it. I have another great story for you. There was this judge in the early part of the nineteenth century. I don't remember his name but it doesn't matter. Anyway, at the end of the trial he was presiding over he instructed the jury, exactly as they do today, by saying, 'You interpret the facts and I will interpret the law.' At that time the spirit of the Founding Fathers and even some of the founders themselves were active in government. The judge was quickly removed from the bench. Jury's still have the right to interpret the law but judges long ago quit instructing jurys about their true power. To this very day, any jury has the right to say, 'That may be the law but we disagree with the law'. The accused would be set free and the government would have no recourse."

"Maybe you're right, Ty. I don't know. But what did you mean by the inherent flaws of The Constitution?"

"The Constitution placed extraordinary power with the people but the list of qualified people was narrowed down to include only white, male property owners. It was a short list but it was a great idea. I just noticed Stan, why don't you have a cell phone? I thought all you young people had cell phones."

Stan marveled again at Ty, from slavery to cell phones in a heartbeat. "I forgot it at home. It was on the charger and I was in a hurry to get to the airport. I could have used it a few times yesterday."

"To call who? Not me. I haven't had a phone in thirty years."

"You're kidding me. How did you get by without a phone all these years?"

"I never saw the need. I managed to talk to everyone I needed to. What do you say we stop for an early dinner? There should be a phone there so you can plug back into the world."

"That's a good idea. I should call Mom and tell her we are on our way. That last billboard said there is a Holiday Inn ahead. Is that okay?"

"Sounds good."

Shortly after arriving at the Holiday Inn, they seated themselves at an empty table in the busy restaurant. The waitress promptly appeared with the menus, "I'll be right back to take your orders."

Ty replied without looking up from the menu, "I'll wait right here."

The waitress glanced over her shoulder, grinning at them as she walked away. Stan looked sheepishly at her and shrugged his shoulders. It didn't take long for her to return to take their orders. She was a stereotypical waitress. She wore a light gray uniform dress with white nurse's shoes. She had a large name tag on the lapel on the left side of her uniform. Two oversized pockets were filled with menu pads, pens and pencils. She was likely in her late forties but that didn't preclude her from leaving the top two buttons of her dress unbuttoned displaying a more than ample cleavage.

"I'm Else; I'll be your waitress. What can I get you fellas?"

Ty smiled broadly as he handed her his menu, "Pretty name." He nodded at her nametag, "Did you name them both or just the one?"

Else flashed a guarded grin at Ty, "Behave yourself. Don't make me get security."

"I'm harmless, Else. I appreciate beautiful woman but I'm too old to chase them."

Stan interrupted," Can I get a teriyaki chicken burger, rice and an iced tea?"

Ty added, "I'll have a grilled tuna sandwich, french fries and coffee. And Else would you fill the ketchup, also?"

Else reached across the table to pick up the half full bottle of ketchup before turning to leave, "I'll be right back with your drinks."

Ty watched Else walk away. Stan watched Ty watching Else," Is it your mission in life to see if you can embarrass me? Why didn't you just stand up and look down her shirt?"

"That would be rude but I didn't have to. Why do you think I asked her to fill the ketchup? I don't even like french fries. Besides, it's not my fault. I didn't unbutton her dress. I just enjoyed the view. Man, waitresses work their asses off and they don't get paid shit. Else lives on her tip money. I don't blame her for using what she's got to increase her income. I didn't disrespect her, I just noticed. We both win. She'll get a nice tip and I got to see her tits. That's free market economics at its glorious best."

They finished their meal with the exception of the french fries. The fries were still a good investment, though, because Else had replaced the ketchup bottle to the same spot in front of Ty.

Ty reached for his wallet," What's the damage?"

Stan picked up the check, "Dad said I should pay for everything. It's on his card."

Ty replaced his wallet, "I guess I'll have to learn to let Big Stan bad mouth me if he's going to feed me. I'll get the tip."

"That's fair, you got the show. I'll get the check and then I'm going to call Mom. I'll be right back."

Stan's phone call went directly to the answering service," Hi, Mom. Sorry I haven't called sooner. I left my phone at home on the charger. We're on our way. Everything is fine. I'll call when I can. Love you."

Else was cleaning off their table when Stan returned," Did you see where my Grandfather went?"

Else pointed towards the lounge, "He went into the bar."

"Thanks." Stan dejectedly headed toward the lounge. They didn't have time for this. They should get back on the road. Stan could clearly hear the roar of the bar patrons over the blaring jukebox music before he opened the door. The large room was packed. Stan stretched his neck trying to spot Ty in the room full of partiers. He started working his way through the crowd but he didn't see Ty until he was through the room and almost to the bar against the back wall. Stan saw Ty's white head at the bar at about the same time Ty spotted him. Ty signaled for Stan to join him.

Ty leaned close to Stan in order to be heard over the roar of the crowd, "I saved you a seat, have a drink."

Stan leaned close, "We don't have time for this. It'll take two weeks to get home at this rate."

Ty looked shocked, "Two weeks! Man that would be the fastest I ever crossed the country. Time is all we have, my boy. Have a drink. Besides my friend Ray, behind the bar, says they are going to have a live blues band tonight. That's as good as it gets on the road. Try a microbrew."

Stan watched Ty turn to resume his conversation with Ray the bartender. Stan ordered a beer and settled onto a bar stool. He could tell this was another battle he wasn't destined to win.

# Chapter (4)

Stan was nursing his second microbrew while he watched the amazing Ty who seemed to have the uncanny ability to interact with virtually anyone. Stan was quite sure Ty had never met any of these people but an outside observer would be easily convinced Ty was celebrating at a reunion of old friends. Ty and Ray exchanged barbs like a couple of frat brothers. The two young cocktail waitresses innocently scolded Ty even as they encouraged his harmless flirtations. There were four coasters stacked in front of Ty to remind Ray of the number of beers patrons had already paid for. Ty was incredible. He engaged anyone and everyone who passed his way.

Stan purposely avoided any of the conversations, hoping Ty would notice his quietness and feel guilty about stopping their progress. Ty wasn't doing guilt.

Stan tapped Ty on the shoulder, "I'll be right back. I need to find the restroom."

Ty turned away from the diminutive urban cowboy he was having an intense conversation with, "Go Stan, set the beer free." He turned back to the cowboy with the huge ten gallon hat sitting comically atop of his five gallon head.

When Stan returned there was an attractive woman sitting on his bar stool being consoled by Ty.

"Barbara, this is my grandson Stan. He's escorting me to Washington because my daughter thinks I getting senile and I might get lost. I like being lost, it's the most efficient way to see places you've never been." Ty motioned behind him, "Barb's boyfriend is a dickhead. He treats her like shit. He's over there power drinking with the other Neanderthals. They look kind of like a bunch of gorillas in flannel, don't they?"

That comment put a smile on Barb's face.

Stan picked up his beer, "Maybe, but they look like drunk gorillas to me."

Stan stood sipping his beer while Ty continued to comfort Barb. Stan glanced occasionally at the Neanderthal table in case one of the drunken simians came to claim his property. The band was setting up. Stan hoped he could steer Ty out of the bar after the music started or at least after the first set.

Ty put his arm around Barb when she could no longer hold back the tears, "I just don't understand him, Ty. I try so hard but whenever he's around his friends he treats me like a piece of trash. I don't understand. He says he loves me and then he treats me like shit. I don't know what to do."

"There's nothing you can do because you didn't do anything wrong. When he's around his friends his macho gene gets engaged. When he's drinking it gets worse. Barb, he's just trying to convince the other alpha dogs you belong to him. It's hard to blame him for that, I mean, look at you woman. You are absolutely gorgeous. When you walked across the room, every male eye in the house was following you. Your boyfriend just doesn't know how to show you how proud he is. Male ego! It's the most illogical and dangerous thing on the planet. Believe me Barb, it's not you, it's him."

Barb managed a weak smile. She softly touched Ty's cheek, "Why couldn't he be more like you?"

"Young guys pound their chests and howl at the moon because they don't know any better. It's one of life's cruel ironies. By the time men are smart enough to appreciate beautiful young women we're too old to be of any use to them."

Stan was unconsciously nodding in agreement with Ty's council to Barb when he snapped to attention as a flannel billboard suddenly appeared behind Ty.

"That's my girlfriend you've got your hands on, old man."

Ty slowly turned his head to look up at the monster towering over him, "Barb just needed someone to talk to. It sounds like you're being an asshole."

Attempting to look as large and menacing as possible, the gorilla glared at Ty, "You best be careful who you call an asshole, you old fuck. Now get your hands off my girl."

Ty chuckled, "Your girl? Maybe I should have checked her for a brand."

The gorilla moved in closer. His voice got louder, "Don't give me any shit old man or I'll stuff your ass in a garbage can!"

Ty kept his eyes on the simian. His smile stayed in place, "So you're an equal opportunity asshole. You like to intimidate women and old men. How impressive."

"Back off!" The giant looked over at Stan who was frozen in place, "I don't think poindexter is going to protect you."

The blood instantly drained from Stan's face while the butterflies pulled his stomach into his throat. Stan's mind reeled with an array of thoughts all ending with him being beaten senseless in Backwater, Kentucky.

Ty stood to face the big man. Ty was close to the same height but he was easily seventy or eighty pounds and fifty years shy of being the man's physical equal, "I don't need anyone to protect me from a blowhard like you. I doubt you're going to get laid tonight, so why don't you go fuck yourself."

Stan nearly fainted! He possibly spotted in his underwear. The only thing racing faster than Stan's mind was his heart. He saw the faces of the other gorillas, intently watching the scene, giving Stan visions of a massacre of epic proportions.

The asshole attempted to put his hand on Ty's chest to push him onto the bar stool. Ty brushed his hand away," I don't want to fight with you, but I will. If you want to dance with a one legged old man, then go for it. Otherwise get out of my face. I'm old enough to know what you are." Ty sat down and picked up his beer, never taking his eyes off the big man.

The asshole grabbed Barbs arm, "Let's go, I'm sick of this old puke. I have half a notion to thump him just for drill."

Ty stood back up," Listen badass, I'd hate to see you waste a perfectly good notion. You probably don't have many."

Stan jumped between Ty and the asshole just as there was a deafening crack. Stan nearly jumped out of his skin. He was sure it was the sound of the first blow of the beating he was about to take. To his relief it was Ray striking the bar with a bat.

"Knock it off! All of you!" Ray looked directly at the asshole's friends who had quickly filled in behind him, "Sit him down or get him the hell out of here! Now!"

The friends of the big man quickly and forcefully directed him back to their table. The asshole glared menacingly at Ty the entire way back to his seat.

Barb touched Ty's arm, "Thanks Ty, but I better go."

Ty replied compassionately, "You take care of yourself, sweet thing. "Ty watched Barb walk back to the Neanderthal table before turning back to Ray, "Thanks Ray. My eye sight isn't what it was but I do believe he would have kicked my ass."

Ray shook his head, "I don't know about that. I'm not sure he was convinced. I know I'm not."

Ty picked up two of the coasters from his stack and handed them to Ray, "How about a couple of beers for me and Stan. Did you see him jump in there to protect me? The boy is part bulldog."

Stan sat back down, "Well, this bulldog almost peed himself."

Ty and Ray roared. Ty slapped Stan on the back, "Breathe Stan. It's all over. Pretty exciting wasn't it?"

Stan was floored by the statement, "You're insane! Exciting? I was terrified. Why did you do that? We could have been killed. Do you have confrontations everywhere you go?"

Ty scoffed at Stan's reaction, "Not at all. Like I said automatons and morons. This guy surely qualified. Stan, he was never going to hit me. Real bad asses don't announce when they are going to kick your ass. He was trying to convince himself, not me."

Stan took a long pull from his beer, "So is your sociological theory ever wrong?"

"Sure, nothing is ever fool proof."

Stan pressed, "What happens then?"

"I'm not much of a fighter so I usually get my ass kicked."

"That's really comforting. Does that mean anytime you misjudge some one's character, I can reasonably expect a beating?"

Ty laughed and slapped Stan on the back again, "Don't worry Stan, I read this guy right. He won't be back but I'll bet you a beer he gets thumped tonight if Barb can't get him out of here. Let me tell you a quick story about my Dad before the band starts. He was like most men of his generation, the strong silent type. He was pretty critical and he very rarely offered advice, except one piece I have never forgotten. I was just starting high school when we moved to the Seattle area. My parents rented a house down towards Tacoma. That's where I started school. I hated it. I didn't know anyone and it seemed like every guy in the school wanted to kick my ass. My Dad really got on me about moping around the house. He said nobody wanted to beat me up, they were just testing me. My Dad's advice was to punch the next guy who tested me. He said not to worry about being on school grounds. Dad said it didn't even matter if I was in a class room. I should keep swinging until they pulled us apart, which he guaranteed would happen fast. Dad said I might get suspended but he bet me a dollar to a donut no one would mess with me again. He said boys don't really want to fight, they just want to know who will. The very next day in history class this big guy, Charley, was messing with me. He used to kick my books out from under my desk, shoot spit wads on my back and generally harass the new kid. When the bell rang I picked up my books and headed for the door with Charley right behind me, hurling insults at my man hood. As soon as we were through the door and into the hallway I dropped my books, turned around and hit Charley as hard as I could. I did it just like Dad said, I kept swinging until they pulled us apart. It's kind of funny, besides that first punch I have no idea if I even hit him again. We both got suspended but Dad was absolutely right, the taunting stopped. In fact, that was the only fight I had in four years of high school. Dad was pretty smart about some things. I never did buy him that donut."

"Well, it's nice it worked out for you but I don't think I will add it to my list of life skills."

"Have you ever been in a real fight, Stan?"

"Not really. I had a couple of scrapes in grade school and once at prep school. It was kind of like yours. It got broken up fast and we never finished it."

"I'm surprised, you didn't even hesitate coming to my defense. You've got a lot of heart."

The band began playing which interrupted Ty. He turned around to enjoy the music. They sat quietly drinking their beers. The music was much too loud to allow normal conversation. It quickly became apparent why the band was playing in a lounge in Backwater, Kentucky. Their sound wasn't horrible but they clearly weren't destined for the big time. The people danced, hooped and hollered, applauded and generally enjoyed the show none the less. Ty's prediction for the asshole came to fruition halfway through the band's first set. Another young man, easily a head shorter than the gorilla, knocked the big man to the ground and proceeded to bounce the moron's head off the floor numerous times before he was pulled off. The other gorillas led the asshole out the front door with him screaming non stop threats and obscenities at the man who had just cleaned his clock.

The band took a break giving Stan a chance to speak to Ty, "Are you ready to go? I'm not driving anymore tonight so maybe we should get a room."

Ty shook his head in agreement," Sure, but why get a room? I've got sleeping bags. Why don't we crash in Brutus? Then we can get an early start. We can get a room tomorrow to get some showers."

"That's fine with me. We definitely need to cover more ground than we did today. Maybe I can get you to take a break from your social machismo theories so my heart can have a break."

Ty flashed a huge smile before he spent the next twenty minutes saying goodbye to his newfound friends.

# Chapter (5)

The side door of the van slid open waking Stan. Ty was standing there holding two cups of coffee.

Stan sat up and took a moment to orient himself, "What time is it?"

"It's about six thirty. If you want to deposit last night's beer, we can get going."

They were on the road in fifteen minutes. Stan was becoming comfortable with the three-on-the-tree shifting but every time he tried to get Brutus past fifty five miles per hour she would start vibrating uncontrollably.

Ty casually stated," Remember, Brutus is old like me. If you don't try to make her do things she's not capable of doing, she runs like a Swiss watch. Her sweet spot is about fifty five."

"That's great but the speed limit is seventy. These big trucks are going to blow the mirrors off."

"So what, the mirrors just show you what you've already seen, anyway. Relax. Tell me, Stan. Do you have a girl in Seattle?"

"Not anymore. We split up last year."

"Oh, what happened?"

"It was kind of a mutual thing. We both knew we weren't suited for each other. Dad didn't like her at all. I tried to keep her a secret but you know Dad, he has spies everywhere. He and I had a huge blow up when my grades started slipping. He forced me to make a choice. I tried to talk to her about it but she just said she had expected it all along and walked away."

Ty was studying Stan's face, "Do you think it's a little strange I asked you about your girlfriend and you told me what your Father thought of her? What was her name?"

Stan was quiet for a moment before he replied in a low tone, "Her name was Hannah. She was really something. We were together for about six months. She was the first person to ever understand anything about me. She was the only one who ever wanted to. I still wonder if I made a huge mistake but mostly I try not to think about her. There's nothing I can do about it anyway. In September I'll be in Massachusetts so I'll probably never see her again. In time maybe it won't feel so real."

"But it was real and it happened to you. It sounds like you really cared for Hannah. Do you think you loved her?"

"I don't know. I don't have any basis for comparison. I know I've never felt that way before." Stan paused,"Or since." Stan looked over at Ty, "How about you, do you want to share any of your love stories?"

Ty grinned, "Well, you know how hard it is to get me talking."

Ty's attention was drawn to a pickup truck with two large American flags flying behind it as it passed, "We're definitely getting into the heartland. Have you ever seen so many American flags in your life?"

"Do you have a problem with people showing their patriotism?"

"Not at all, I applaud patriots. Its symbols I have trouble with. One time Belle and I were anchored out in the Gulf Islands. This huge bald eagle was diving on this frantic little duck and her babies. Now that was symbolic. Belle jumped into the dinghy and escorted the mother duck and her remaining babies to shore. I chalked it up to the brutality of the natural world. Mother Nature doesn't judge and she doesn't play favorites. When it rains, bad people get just as wet as good people."

"Was that Grandma's name, Belle?"

"People called her Belle, but her full name was Belinda. It's a shame she didn't get to meet you. She would have loved you. She could spot someone with heart in the middle of a crowded concert hall. I met her at Evergreen College in 1960. I was an associate professor and she was a nursing student. The first time I ever saw her was in the student union. She was giving vaccinations. In those days everyone lined up to get shots and boosters. It was like an assembly line. I don't know if it was love at first sight but I can tell you for one of the few times in my life, I was speechless. Belle was breathtaking. I read her name from her nametag and had one of my friends in administration switch her file so I could be her faculty adviser. She had to have known what I had done but she never said a word. Belle and I had more counseling sessions than anyone in Evergreen College history. She graduated that year and we moved in together. Those were some of the greatest days of my life. You know what I mean. I was in the right place at the right time and all was well in the world. We fit so good. But it wasn't all wine and roses. Belle pushed me hard. She didn't like lingering doubts. She wanted resolution to everything. Even trivial stuff I would have been happy to let slide. She was tough. She saved me." Ty's voice trailed off. His eyes were fixed on the horizon.

Stan glanced at Ty. He noticed Ty's eyes were filling with tears, "Are you okay? You don't have to talk about her if it upsets you."

"It's okay. Not a problem. I do get a little choked up sometimes. You know, I never saw my Father cry, not even at my Mother's funeral. Until I met Belle, I thought that's what men did. Belle introduced me to my own emotions. She could have me blubbering like a three year old."

"What did you mean when you said Grandma saved you?"

"I don't mean in a literal sense but in a life sense. I'll tell you something Stan, but you can never tell your Father. Big Stan needs to keep believing I'm a flake, it's the only way we can co-exist without hurting your Mother. Anyway before I met Belle, my views on politics, economics, religion and most everything else were not much different than Stanton's. You need to understand I came from blue collar roots. I was the first one in my family to even go to college. You would have gotten a kick out of my Dad. He loved to introduce me to his friends as the Professor. That's what I wanted to do, though, teach and publish. I was going to be a world renowned writer and educator. I was going to be the distinguished Professor with the elbow patches on my houndstooth jacket. Well, Belle read my writing and she listened to my plans and then she did what she always did. She told me the truth as she saw it. She challenged me. She called me a coward. Belle said I was composing a life story that wasn't even mine. She said my thoughts and dreams were merely a compilation of what I believed others expected of me. Belle told me my writing was unreadable because it lacked any spark of passion. She accused me of pandering to the intellectual crowd by using the quotes and thoughts of the great thinkers. She thought I was borrowing thought and trying to spin it into something original. She was right. The price for memorization is conformity. Blind acceptance is a death knell to your own mind."

"You talk about her with a smile on your face but it sounds like she was ruthless."

"Not ruthless, just honest. It didn't stop me from being furious with her. I accused her of having no faith in me and of sabotaging my career. But, eventually, I sat down and read all my stuff. By dogged if she wasn't right. I threw it all away. I pouted for a long time and didn't write anything. I remember when I decided to write again I asked her what she thought I should write about and she laughed at me. She said 'how the hell would I know, you're the writer.' Just like before, I was trying to pick someone else's brain. But Belle had some really profound thoughts. Man, you think my heads all over the place, Belle would blow you away. One time we were both sitting on the couch reading and she looked up from her book, not really at me, and said 'in the absence of greed would there be a need for the rule of law?' Then she went back to her book. Another time we were driving past a school and she said 'If wisdom comes with age why are most people happiest as children?' I thought she was brilliant but she was right. They were her thoughts not mine. Belle told me once she loved my mind and she didn't want to live with a Hollywood facsimile of it." Ty paused for a moment, tearing up again, "Man, I love thinking about Belle, tears and all. If you try to hide your emotions you run the risk of putting them to sleep. I cried like a selfish baby when she died. I felt like she abandoned me. I didn't think I could navigate without her. Even when she was gone she forced me to find my own way."

Stan decided to try and direct the conversation away from the sentimental. He asked, "Did you and Grandma always live in Seattle?"

"We did until 1967. We bought a little sailboat for a summer adventure up the Inside Passage. Your Mom was five years old at the time. We wanted to get away from the madness for awhile. Vietnam was heating up and the whole time felt like we were headed down a dark road. It probably feels like that in any country when the leaders sacrifice people's lives for their own ambitions. Anyway, we made it to Ketchikan, Alaska. We ended up staying there for two years. I lost my job but Belle had no problem finding work as a nurse. I put my college degree to use by working in a fish processing plant. I'll tell you what, two winters in Southeast Alaska is a long time. They measure rain by the foot and daylight in the winter is only a few hours so we went back to Seattle. Belle went right to work but I didn't have a clue what I wanted to do. I was searching for my inner author but I was struggling. One day I came home and there was a motorcycle sitting in front of the house. Belle bought me this beautiful BSA 441 Victor. It was awesome! Man, it had a yellow and chrome gas tank, chrome fenders, and a chrome exhaust. I was blown away. I had talked about traveling on a motorcycle but I never expected her to remember. She said a trip might clear my head. She was always right and that's how I got Thumper."

"Thumper! You named your motorcycle after a rabbit?"

"No, it didn't have anything to do with Bambi's friends. All single cylinder four strokes are called Thumpers. My Thumper got her name from the thumping she can give you. The first time I tried to kick start her was a painful thumping. I didn't know you were supposed to depress the compression release lever and kick it through a few times before you tried to start it. She backfired and launched me. I thought my leg was broken. At least Belle managed to ask if I was alright before she laughed her ass off. I eventually figured it out and now Thumper and I have been across the country three times. She vibrates like a jackhammer right up to her sweet spot but that bike will climb a building."

"What ever happened to Thumper? Is that how you broke your leg?"

"Yes, sir. She tossed me into a creek bed. Thumper's in the trailer waiting for another shot at me." Ty's gaze locked onto a passing farmhouse, "Don't these farmhouses remind you of a Norman Rockwell painting? The first time I came across the Midwest I remember thinking how picture perfect these peoples lives must be. Then you stop and talk to people in these little crossroad towns and you realize they don't see anything picturesque about it. To them it's always the same, everyday. That's why every conversation in the heartland starts with the weather. The weather is the only thing that changes out here."

Stan brought Ty back, "Why did you name Mom, Emma? Was it a legacy thing?"

"No, Belle named her after Emma Goldman, the political activist. Belle loved those strong women, especially the ones who stood up before it was socially acceptable. We almost named her Sojourner, after Sojourner Truth. She might have been a powerful woman but it would have been a tough name for a little girl."

"I've heard of Emma Goldman but I've never heard of Sojourner Truth."

"Don't feel alone. I taught history and I didn't know who they were. They should be in every text book. They were fearless, like Gandhi. Sojourner Truth was not only a woman, she was a black woman who stood up and spoke her mind when there were still slaves in half the country. Emma Goldman was a fireball. She fought for workers rights and she campaigned against World War One. It got her deported but what a proud name."

"Grandma sounds like she was pretty political. Mom is quite the opposite. Where did that disconnect come from?"

"Emma was only ten years old when Belle died. It was a bad time and I'm embarrassed to say I didn't do much to help your Mother find her way. We both withdrew a lot after Belle was gone. When my parental neurons started firing again, Emma was becoming a teenager. I've always felt like I left Emma in the dark, just like I felt Belle had done to me. I was supposed to make Emma feel safe and I know I didn't. She found her security with Big Stan and I have always respected him for that."

"Why didn't you ever remarry? It has been thirty six years."

Ty closed his eyes for a moment, "I have thought about it. I mean, I haven't been a Monk or anything. I've seen other women, I've dated." Ty grinned, "I've even gotten jiggy with some of them but I just couldn't do it. I've got this locket shot that always stopped me from committing."

"What the hell is that, Ty?"

"You know. You've seen those little pictures inside of lockets. That little faded, oval shaped snap shot. I've got a little locket shot of Belle burned into my mind. It's not like a full screen dream vision, just a little snap shop of Belle's smiling face. It's always been there. I see her every time I blink. I can only see one woman and that wouldn't be fair to another. The way I look at it. If I'm destined to love only one woman in my life, I'm good with that." Ty closed his eyes with a smile on his face. When he opened his eyes, he turned to Stan, "That's enough about us, tell me about Hannah."

Stan reflected before answering, "There's not a lot to say. I did love her and I probably still do but there is nothing I can do about it now. I wish I could be as philosophical about it as you are. I don't see her every time I close my eyes, but I can definitely picture her anytime I want." Stan took a page from Ty's playbook and changed the subject, "I'm going to stop for fuel, are you hungry?"

"Good idea, Stan."

Stan steered onto the off ramp trying to erase the picture in his minds eye but not succeeding. He had an ear to ear smile on his face as he pulled into the service station.

# Chapter (6)

The service station was typical of the thousands of service stations that sprung up around the interstate freeway system built in the middle of the last century. The overpass marked the bypass of the highway connecting to the small town that had been devastated by the placement of the freeway. The service business' clustered around the junction represented the boarded up business' that had been replaced in the town seen in the distance.

An elderly attendant, with an oil company logo above his shirt pocket, approached as Stan climbed out of Brutus.

"Hot enough for you? It's supposed to rain next week. What can I get you?"

Stan couldn't help but smile, "Fill her up please. Do you sell sandwiches here?"

"Sure thing, delivered this morning. Do you want regular or high test?"

"Regular is fine."

Stan stretched while he scanned the area. The only signs of life were the attendant and a couple of hitchhikers on the side of the on ramp. Stan went into the convenience mart. He selected two sandwiches, a bag of chips and some crackers, setting them on the counter.

The woman behind the counter smiled sweetly, "Scorcher, ain't it? If you want something cold to drink there is some homemade lemonade in the cooler. I made it myself." Without looking outside, she motioned at the attendant, "Lester loves my lemonade."

"Sounds good. I need a block of ice, also" She pointed to the back wall, "Ice is in the cooler next to the one with the lemonade." She began ringing up the purchases while Stan retrieved a gallon of lemonade and a block of ice.

"Where you folks headin?"

"We're going to Seattle. That's where I live. I'm moving my Grandfather out there."

"That's nice, all of our kids have moved to the city, too."

"I take it you've lived here for awhile?"

"All my life. I was headed to the big city when I got out of school, like everyone else but then I married Lester and life kind of closed in around us. It's quiet though. We used to own the filling station in town but now we just manage this one. At least we didn't have to move like a lot of folks did after the Interstate was built."

"There aren't many stations that still have attendants."

"The owner got both of us for the price of one but there ain't enough for both of us to do all the time, so Lester works the pumps like he used to do at our place. The owner thinks it gives the place a local touch. I think it keeps Lester out of my hair. That'll be thirty four twenty seven."

Stan paid the tab," Thank you. Have a nice day, ma'am."

"You fellas have a safe trip."

Ty had his back to the passenger window when Stan returned. He appeared to be talking to someone. Stan slid the side door open to find two backpacks on the floor and the two young hitchhikers from the on ramp sitting on the edge of the bed.

"Paul, Twyla, this is my grandson, Stan. They're hitching to a lake just up the road so I offered them a ride. They've been baking in the sun all afternoon."

Stan nodded, "Nice to meet you both." He put the ice and groceries in the ice chest, closed the door and walked around to the driver's side.

Ty continued as soon as Stan was seated, "Paul and Twyla are meeting their friends at the lake but Paul's truck broke down. I like people who don't let little things spoil their fun."

Stan looked over at Ty before he started the van. Stan narrowed his eyes and scrunched his forehead trying to convey to Ty his best 'I don't usually pick up hitchhikers look' but it was no more successful than his 'can we leave the bar look'.

Ty kept rolling, "I was just starting to tell these two why we were going to Arizona." Stan's head spun around to see a mischievous grin on Ty's face, "Stan here is an Engineer. He designed this composite raft we're going to test on the Colorado River. It's made out of this space age carbon fiber. I don't know everything that is in it but in the machine shop I can build a mold for anything Stan can dream up. You should see these things Paul, they're beautiful. We built three prototypes. They're already down in Page. I don't know if you have ever been to the Grand Canyon but it starts at the Glen Canyon Dam at Page, Arizona and goes all the way to Lake Mead. We're not going all the way. We're pulling out at Yucaipa. These things look like big kayaks with outriggers on either side so they are really stable. Stan's invention is the brilliant part. He calls them Smart Springs. The springs are what attach the outriggers to the kayaks. They look like a big radiator hose but they're made of carbon fiber with a spring wound through it. There are sensors all along the spring that are hooked up to a microprocessor. The wire is as thin as piano wire. What is the wire made of Stan, I always forget?"

Stan took a deep breath never taking his eyes off the road, "It's a metallurgical compound but mainly its titanium."

"That's right, these springs are trick, Paul. The sensors track the stress in the spring and the microprocessor, that's no bigger than a silver dollar, regulates the current in the spring. In a static position they're as strong as structural steel but if the sensor detects stress, the spring can reduce the rigidity anywhere in the spring. The end result is the springs are stronger than almost any bracket but they can also absorb the energy from a collision and move in any direction without compromising the structural integrity. Stan could explain how it all works but if you're anything like me you wouldn't understand a word of it. Engineers need other engineers to talk to. That's why Stan is so quiet. The other guys didn't want me on this trip but Stan talked them into it. He knew I wasn't going to let him have all the fun and leave me behind just because I'm old. Yes sir, you're going to be hearing a lot about Stan. When big engineering firms with million dollar R&D budgets get a load of Stan's ideas, he'll be famous. Someday my Grandson's name will be a household word."

Paul interrupted, "This is our exit coming up."

Stan steered down the off ramp and pulled onto the shoulder. Ty asked Paul, "Is the lake far from here?"

"No, not at all, we can hoof it from here."

Paul and Twyla got out and put on their backs packs. Paul stepped up to the passenger window, "Thanks for the ride." He leaned forward so he could see Stan, "It was a pleasure meeting you, sir. You make me want to go back to school."

Ty offered his hand to Paul, "Good idea, Paul. An education is the difference between a job interview on the top floor and one on the factory floor. Good luck."

Stan said nothing as he led Brutus back to the freeway. He, occasionally, snuck a peek at Ty who was giddily trying to avoid Stan's glances. Finally Stan couldn't contain himself any longer, "What in the hell was that?"

Ty burst out laughing, "Did you like that?"

"Where did all that shit come from? I thought you were all about the truth."

"Sometimes you need to challenge you imagination. It was harmless. The chance is nil we will ever see them again, but just think of the story they will be telling around the campfire tonight. They'll be talking about the young genius they met for years. It was an innocent, victimless story that added a small touch of excitement to their lives. We might even have inspired Paul to further his education, but the best part of the whole story was watching your face. Man, for a second there, I thought you were going to jump out of the van."

Stan shook his head, "Dad might be right about you. I noticed you didn't give them a chance to ask any questions, in fact I don't think you let them talk at all."

Ty shrugged, "It was a short ride and a long story."

"Well, do you have anymore stories? I could stand to be entertained for awhile so we can cover some miles. I know, what's the story behind that Wall Street sign? West Virginia is a long way from Manhattan."

"The sign is actually fitting. I might have the most diversified stock portfolio in the whole county. I have the minimum share blocks from dozens of multinational corporations. I'm a minimalist tycoon."

"Why would you even bother? You can't make any money with just a few shares."

"I have them just so I can get mission statements, growth prospectus' and profit and loss statements from all the corporations. I know that's where you're headed but I'm not a big fan of Wall Street. I can see the attraction for a young man, though. Wall Street is one of those epicenters where huge sums of money change hands second to second. I don't claim to understand everything about finance but I don't think that's necessary. I break it down to simple terms I can understand. The stock market, by itself, isn't all bad. The problem is they artificially inflate the value of the corporations being traded. Public ownership based on actual values could be a good thing for investors and corporations but the way Wall Street does it leaves everything grossly overvalued. That's exactly what happened with the crash in 1929. The financial world was riding high on all sorts of new financial schemes; margin sales, put options, commodity futures. At the same time the Federal Reserve had increased the money supply by seventy percent in the 1920's alone. Everything was grossly overvalued so a crash was inevitable. Crash is probably the wrong word because all that really happened in the markets was an adjustment back to reasonable values. The market is more out of whack now than it ever was in 1929. These bubble building genius' at the Fed have more than tripled the money supply in just the last few years. It's no longer a question of if it will happen, only when. I think these greedy morons have laid the groundwork for an epic global crash. I think the derivative side of the market is down right criminal. I mean all of it, too. The CDO's, security swaps, and every other way these assholes dream up to package debt for commissions and fees on things that have already been commissioned and fee'd to death. It's worse than a Vegas sports book."

"You can't be serious! You don't really believe speculation should be illegal? Do you realize how much money is in those markets and how many people make their living there?"

"People made money trading slaves, too, but that didn't make it right. Let me give you an example." Ty raised his hand to showcase the landscape before them, "There are cornfields in every direction. So let's pretend you're a corn farmer. The corn food chain starts with you and ends with the consumer. Along the way there are claims against the value of your corn; labor, transportation and distribution. All legitimate and necessary. Speculators are betting on different aspects in the process of your corn food chain. The problem is they don't get their money from each other, they extract it from the value or add it to the price of your corn. They don't add anything of value to the economy. They're vultures. They shouldn't exist."

"That is beyond an over simplification. In our economy, debt is a commodity like anything else. In a free market you are free to buy and sell whatever the market will bear. Caveat emptor, Ty."

"It looks like the buyer is becoming aware. The rest of the world is tired of buying all of our brightly colored bundles of debt. If the Far East equity funds stop buying, we're in deep shit. Our biggest export is debt. Shit, debt is over twenty percent of this country's gross domestic product. Manufacturing is less than ten percent of the GDP. We rebuilt after the Depression because we had the most powerful industrial base on the planet. If it crashes now, what do we rebuild with, debt? Don't get me wrong, Stan, I don't think Wall Street is the sole cause for the coming disaster. There's plenty of blame to go around. Corporate government has been gorging at the corruption trough for a long, long time."

"I had an Economics Professor who believed the Federal Reserve could head off most economic blips if they would be more proactive and less reactive. He thought the dotcom bubble and the housing bubble were both aberrations that didn't have to happen."

"Do you agree with him?"

"I don't know. I tried to get a better idea about the impact of the Fed by reading Greenspan's book but he seemed to be just patting himself on the back. I know during the recession of the early eighties, the Fed really jacked the interest rates which contracted the money supply but it pulled us out of the recession."

"I think the difference between then and now, is the dollar was strong around the world back then. Do you think you can push interest rates while the dollar is falling?"

"Good question. I don't think I have ever read about that happening with a good outcome. Maybe we should ask Dad. He's on the board of two reserve banks."

"You shouldn't have told me. I was starting to have fond thoughts about Big Stan, but Central Banks are high on my personal shit list."

"What's your beef with Central Banks? They're a pretty crucial part of the planet's economy."

"They are only crucial because we let them trick us into believing they are. The Federal Reserve Act was bullied and backdoored by a cabal of bankers. It was written by bankers."

Stan emphatically interrupted, "No it wasn't! Nelson Aldrich wrote it. He was a Senator not a banker. I remember it from a final exam."

"You should keep reading, Stan. Aldrich pushed it through Congress and he was present when it was written but the primary author was Paul Warburg. It was written at a secret meeting at J.P. Morgan's estate on Jekyll Island in Georgia. Paul Warburg was the head of the Federal Reserve Bank of New York after the act was forced through Congress. He was also the brother of Max Warburg, the head of Germany's Central Bank. Max Warburg was connected by marriage to the Rothchild dynasty who owned the Bank of England. Nelson Aldrich married into the Rockefeller family after he spearheaded the effort to steamroll the Federal Reserve Act through Congress. There are lots of great books about it. It's a great story. I'd suggest 'The Creature from Jekyll Island' by Edward Griffin. If you want another good story, try to find out who owns the private banks making up The Federal Reserve. I don't believe anyone has ever known all the names. It's not like there has ever been an audit of the Fed."

"The President should know. He picks the chairman of the board."

"Yes, he does, but he picks him from a list of five names provided to him by the bankers themselves, which is another great story."

"Okay, even if you're right, you can't complain about the results. They've been directing the economy for a hundred years and the last time I checked we were the most successful economic power in history."

"There's definitely been buckets full of money made. The problem is ninety five percent of the buckets belong to one percent of the people and the concentration of wealth is growing. The people don't share in the profits. How about another one of Ty's oversimplifications. Let's say you lobbied the government and legally or illegally you convinced them to replace the Federal Reserve with Stan's Bank. Dollars are declared useless and are replaced with a new currency, 'the Stan'. The country hasn't been on a gold standard for seventy years so you don't have to put up any of your assets to back your Stan notes. All you have to do is print Stan notes and sell them to the government at face value plus interest on every note. Since the 'Stan' is now the official currency, all debts, public and private, must be paid in 'Stan' notes. So you have to print more 'Stan's' for the government to pay back the debt from the other 'Stan's' you have already sold them. If every 'Stan' note you print is sold to the government plus interest, the result is a ponzi scheme. If the countries' debt to Stan's bank were ever paid off, it would wipe out the currency but it would be impossible to accomplish anyway. Pyramids go up. Almost every currency on the planet is issued by a Central Bank and few, if any, are backed by anything of value. It's a fatal flaw benefiting only bankers. Every government has the power to issue their own currency so there is no logical reason a private bank should be given that power. Abraham Lincoln and John F. Kennedy both wanted the government to issue the country's currency. Maybe you noticed other similarities they share. Woodrow Wilson wrote in his memoirs something to the effect that he had unwittingly sold his country to a cabal of financial interests. Even FDR wrote that if the truth be known, the country's monetary system had been controlled by a select group since the time of Andrew Jackson."

"Now you're drifting away from simplification to conspiracy theory."

"Conspiracy is another one of those hijacked words, like patriotism. People use conspiracy to silence and discredit anyone who doesn't agree with the official story. History is a never ending story of conspiracy."

A loud blast echoed inside the van. It sounded like a gunshot. Ty nearly jumped from his seat. Stan firmly gripped the steering wheel and calmly stated, "Blew a tire." Stan correctly refrained from applying the brakes allowing Brutus to decelerate to a stop on the expansive shoulder of the interstate.

When the van stopped, Ty looked to Stan, "Man, I'm glad you were driving. That scared the hell out of me."

Stan replied, "You do have a spare, don't you?"

"Yeah, it's in the trailer. Don't worry we don't have to sleep on the side of the freeway."

Ty pulled the jack, lug wrench and the spare from the trailer and they set about jacking up the rear of the van to remove the blown right rear tire. Ty shook his head in disgust when he inspected the blown tire Stan removed, "It blew out right through the sidewall. Bummer, this tire can't have more than five thousand miles on it. Must be a conspiracy."

Stan began mounting the spare which had well beyond five thousand miles on it. Their attention momentarily was diverted by the sound of a car pulling up and stopping behind them. It was a Kansas State Trooper with flashers and rooftop emergency lights flashing. They returned their attention to the spare while the trooper remained in his vehicle checking the registration plates from his on board computer. The trooper casually got out of his cruiser. His eyes, through his mirrored sunglasses, remained on the pair while he slowly and deliberately put his trooper's hat on his head. He slowly made his way to the side of the van where they were working. He stopped ten feet short of them and stood silently for a moment, waiting for the two to turn and acknowledge his presence, which was formidable. The trooper was six foot four and a well fed, two hundred and eighty plus pounds.

When he was convinced they were not going to turn around to be intimidated, he spoke, "You fellas' having troubles?"

Stan was busy tightening lug nuts and answered without looking up, "No sir, just a flat tire. We're almost finished."

"Where are you boys headed?"

Ty glanced at the trooper quickly before he started to lower the van off the jack.

Stan stood and stepped forward, "Seattle. I'm from Seattle."

The trooper leaned back indicating to Stan he was looking at the license plate on Brutus, "Plate says West Virginia."

Stan began to give the trooper an explanation, "I'm helping my..."

Ty interrupted, "Why does that matter officer? Is there something wrong?"

The trooper removed his sunglasses so Ty could see the big man was looking directly at him, "Nothing wrong. I just like to know who's going through my state."

Ty was grinning as he returned the jack to the trailer.

Stan quickly recognized Ty's tone and body language. Stan took another step forward to head off the chance of a confrontation. Ty had spotted either an automaton or a moron but this one had a badge and a gun, "I'm helping my Grandfather move to Seattle. That's all, Officer."

The trooper replaced his sunglasses, quickly glancing at Stan before returning his attention to Ty, "Tell you what. Since I'm here, why don't I check your license and registration?"

Stan took out his wallet and held out his driver's license. He turned to Ty, "Where do you keep your registration?"

"I'll get it." Ty turned his back to them and limped to the passenger's door. He wasn't two steps away when he said under his breath, but quite audibly, "Papers please."

Stan was instantly horrified. He had clearly heard Ty's remark and so had the trooper.

The trooper closely watched Ty retrieve the registration papers. The trooper took the paper from Ty. Without looking up from the form he added, "I'll need your identification, too."

"I don't have a license, I'm not driving."

The trooper slowly raised his head to look directly at Ty, "What do you mean, you don't have identification?"

Ty's patented grin appeared, "Don't need it. I know who I am. I could identify myself anywhere."

The trooper snapped, "I can't!" He looked down at the papers again before he nodded at the van, "What's in the car? Anything I should know about?" He watched Ty for his reaction to the question.

Ty kept grinning. Stan stepped forward, "Just my Grandfather's things. That's it."

The trooper looked back and forth between the anxious Stan and the grinning Ty, "So you wouldn't mind if I take a look then?"

Stan nodded his head vigorously affirmative, "No prob…"

Ty interrupted, "Actually, I would mind."

Wide eyed, Stan's head spun, "What! Why do you care?"

The trooper added, "Exactly! If you have nothing to hide, what's the problem?"

Ty replied, "The problem is we haven't done anything wrong unless flat tires are illegal in Kansas."

"If I want to look in the car, I can get a warrant and look whether you like it or not." He paused to let that sink in, "What's it gonna be?"

Stan looked frantically at Ty, who was still smiling. 'How did he do that?'

Ty replied, "That's a great idea. Let's make it official."

The trooper removed his sunglasses again so Ty could see his distain, "Why do you have to make this harder than it has to be? You got a burr under your saddle or are you hiding something? If you make me get a warrant, I promise you, I'll tear this car apart. You understand me?"

Ty nodded, "Perfectly. You seem to think we're criminals, so I'd like to have in writing what the probable cause was that led you to that conclusion. I still have that right, don't I? That's not one of the Bill of Rights that was repealed is it?"

"I see, you're one of those smart ass, by the book, Constitution people. Well smart ass, you're about to waste your day exercising your rights, but you're wasting my time, too, and that is going to piss me off!"

"Sorry about that, but you're absolutely right. I dig the Constitution and I have all the time in the world to celebrate it."

Another trooper's car pulled up, lights flashing, and parked behind the first. Trooper one went to meet trooper two at his vehicle. The two conferred for a few minutes, with trooper one repeatedly pointing at Stan and Ty.

Softly Stan said to Ty, "What the hell are you doing? You're just pissing him off. Just let him look in the van and let's get out of here."

A sudden realization came to Stan. His eyes widened, "There's nothing in there, right?"

60

Ty chuckled, "Not a thing. That's not the point. Until this is officially a police state, we're still innocent until proven guilty. So fuck him!"

The two troopers headed toward Stan and Ty. Trooper two went directly to Ty, "I understand you want to be difficult. For your information, the closest Judge is in Salina, three hours from here. You sure you want to waste a day just to prove a point?"

Ty continued grinning, "It's a lot less trouble than the men who gave us these rights went through. It would be a shame to dishonor their memory by not exercising the rights they fought and died for. So whatever you want to do is fine with me."

The two troopers retreated to the cruisers for another conference.

Stan whispered, "You're going to get us locked up. You're the hardest headed man I have ever met."

Ty's grin grew, "Patriotism is hard work."

The troopers spoke for another few minutes before returning. Trooper one summoned his harshest tone,"You two are lucky I don't have the time to sit here and baby sit your asses. You're free to go this time but if I see you again, believe me, I'll take the time to bust your chops. You, old man, the next time a representative of the government asks for your ID, you better have it, understand?"

"Is that any representative or just you law enforcement guys?"

The trooper roared, "Get out of here!" Both men returned to their cars. Trooper one glared at Stan and Ty as he slowly pulled away, purposely not turning off his emergency lights until he was well beyond them.

Stan was red faced and relieved as he drove Brutus back onto the interstate. Stan stewed in his anger for a long time before he looked over at Ty who was innocently watching the farmlands roll by.

"Did you enjoy yourself? You almost got us arrested!"

Ty didn't bother turning away from the passing landscape," I didn't almost get us anything. Stand up for yourself sometime, Stan. You might like it."

# Chapter (7)

The sun continued it's descent in the western sky directly in front of them. The closer the sun inched toward the horizon, the hotter the interior of the van became. The outside temperature was a mere ninety five degrees but inside Brutus, it was well above a hundred.

Stan picked up a towel from the dash and wiped the sweat from his face, "I think we should stop in the next town and get a room. I really need a shower."

"Sounds good to me but we had better be careful. The next town is Salina and we're wanted men."

"You know, I've had more confrontations in two days with you, than I have had in the rest of my life. You should take it easy on me. Remember I grew up on Mercer Island, not in the Projects. Honestly though, I'm sorry I got angry, but you have to realize, I wasn't even alive when you were raging against the machine. Don't forget, I'm in training to be part of the machine."

"Don't ever apologize for how you feel."

They drove past six small buildings in two rows of three. At a glance they appeared to be chicken coops or possibly abandoned. Closer inspection revealed cars parked behind the buildings, people sitting on porches and other tell tale signs of habitation.

Ty pointed at the shacks," There's the labor pool for your twenty first century machine. I've read estimates there could be thirty million illegal immigrants in the country but that's probably not far off. Those people in those shacks are the lucky ones, they have a roof over their heads." He huffed, "Doesn't it sound absurd to you to hear someone called an illegal immigrant? I mean, think about it. The idea of being an illegal alien means a person is attempting to exist on a certain spot of the planet without official authorization. The rulers can restrict lots of rights, but no one should be able to restrict a person's right to exist."

"The government is obligated to protect its own citizens first. Illegals take jobs and services that belong to the citizens. I think anyone who wants to live here should have to go through the legal steps to be here."

"That sounds more like a press release than an opinion. These people are here because they think they can make enough money to survive, nothing more. If there was no work for them, they wouldn't be here. There wasn't a problem with illegal immigration during the Great Depression. Corporate America is totally dependant on illegals because they can pay them squat. We don't have an illegal immigration problem, we have an illegal employer problem."

"You can't just blame everything on corporations. People have to shoulder some of the blame."

"Why? If these companies didn't hire illegals, do you really think they would keep coming? Do you really believe there are tens of millions people in Mexico, El Salvador, Honduras, Guatemala and everywhere else sitting around saying to themselves, 'I think I would like my family to starve to death in Kansas. I hear it's nice this time of year'."

"Maybe there is some truth to that but you can't deny the effects of the illegals. They might bankrupt California by overwhelming the social programs. Either way the tax payers pick up the tab so if it comes down to a choice. I think tax dollars should benefit Americans. Doesn't that make sense?"

"I think you nailed it. It's the system itself that pits one group of people against another, while the corporate world gets a free pass. Maybe it's not the people who need to change."

Ty pointed at an upcoming billboard, "Hey, there's a Denny's at the next exit. Doesn't a grand slam breakfast sound good?"

"Hell Ty, how can you go from starving people to breakfast in a heartbeat?"

"I can't save them all. All I know how to do is bitch about it. You have Big Stan's credit card. You could buy them all breakfast. We should stop, though, there's no telling how many Denny's restaurants are around."

Stan joined Ty in having a Grand Slam breakfast for dinner. After they had eaten, Rosita the young waitress, directed them to a nearby Motel 6. Ty took the first shower as soon as they got to their room. He was stretched out on one of the two double beds, wearing only his purple and gold boxers when Stan came out of the shower. Stan turned up the air conditioner before stretching out on the other bed. He was tired from baking in the afternoon sun.

Ty's eyes were closed so Stan asked softly, "Are you asleep?"

"Not yet."

"I was thinking about what we were talking about earlier. I know you think there is something sinister behind institutions but you don't buy into those extreme conspiracy theories, do you? You know, stuff like The New World Order and the 9/11 Truthers."

"Conspiracies are like legends and fables. They are almost always based on something factual. I've read a lot about 9/11, starting with the Commission's report. The way I see it, 9/11 was the largest mass murder of U.S. citizens in American history. It was immediately followed by the worst murder investigation ever conducted. Nobody should be satisfied with that. As far as The New World Order, the world gets re-ordered every few centuries and it's always by conspiracy."

Stan let Ty's words float in his mind as he drifted off to sleep. Ty sure had his own way of seeing things.

They had fallen asleep with the air conditioner on high leaving it freezing in the room when Stan woke up. He ran to turn off the unit. Ty was buried under the blankets. Stan dressed as fast as he could, "Time to get up, Ty. Wake up."

Ty didn't stir. Stan went into the bathroom. When he came out, Ty was still hidden under the covers, "Come on old man. We need to get going." Stan walked over to Ty and pulled back the covers. The sight took Stan's breath away! Ty was extremely pale, almost gray. He was totally still. At first glance Stan couldn't tell if Ty was breathing. Stan put his fingers on Ty's neck. There was a faint pulse. Stan's voice was frantic, "Wake up Ty! Wake up!"

Ty's eyes lazily opened, "Get my pills. They're in the glove box."

Stan looked into Ty's eyes for an instant and then sprinted to the van. Stan was back into the room quickly. Ty hadn't moved. He sat up and took the tiny pill from Stan, putting it under his tongue. Ty laid his head back onto the pillow.

Stan's eyes were locked onto Ty's face trying to pry any hint of Ty's condition from his expression, "Are you okay? Do you need an ambulance? What can I do?"

Ty held up his hand, "No ambulance, just give me a few minutes." He closed his eyes.

Stan quietly stood with his eyes trained on Ty's face. The silence lasted an eerie eternity. Slowly the color began to return to Ty's face.

Ty opened his eyes and flashed a weak smile, "I'm sorry I scared you. I'm okay. These nitro pills bring me right back. Really, I'm alright."

Stan relaxed slightly," You scared the shit out of me. I've never woken up next to a corpse before. Are you sure you don't need a doctor?"

Ty patted Stan's arm, "Seriously, I'm fine. I had one serious episode about six years ago but I'm doing good. I have a great story about that first heart episode. The hospital called it a myo cardio infarction. You know, I was plugged up. When I got home I started reading everything about the affliction I could get my hands on. I especially wanted to know what medications they were liable to give me. When I went to my first appointment with the Cardiologist I was expecting him to send me for some other tests about liver function, because a lot of these heart drugs are tough on the liver. The doctor listened to my heart and gave me two prescriptions. One for the nitro tablets and one for Zocor or one of those main stream pharmaceuticals. I asked him why he wasn't testing my liver and he told me it wasn't necessary. That was contrary to everything I had read, so I gave him the Zocor prescription and told him I wouldn't take it. You should have seen this guy. He got totally indignant and scolded me like I was a five year old. He told me if I ignored his advice, he would not be responsible for the outcome. That was the last time I ever saw him. At least I can say I didn't add to his incentive check from the pharmaceutical company."

"Don't you think that was a little irresponsible?"

"He was the one who was irresponsible. He put his profit ahead of my health. He could have been the poster boy for the whole healthcare industry. Profit before people is wrong no matter what industry it's in."Ty sat up and swung his legs off the bed, "I'm feeling better. Why don't we go?"

Stan kept his eye on Ty while he was dressing. The weather report the clerk at the service station gave to Stan didn't even register. Stan was concerned about Ty's condition. The open road is not the place to be when you have a serious medical problem.

Stan couldn't stop himself from peeking, continually, at Ty as they headed for the freeway, "Are you sure you're alright. If you drop in the middle of nowhere I'll have to strap you to the roof rack."

The Ty smile appeared, "I think I have a few good years left in me. Well a few years anyway."

Salina began to surrender its concrete and asphalt to the checkered farmlands surrounding the city in every direction. They rode quietly through the country side for a long while.

Ty spoke first, "Just look out across these plains. Can you imagine what it must have looked like a hundred and fifty or two hundred years ago? Instead of wheat and corn it would have been switch grass and buffalo. I read that at the beginning of the nineteenth century there were over a hundred million buffalo on the Great Plains. At the start of the twentieth century there was less than five thousand. That is piss-poor resource management."

"There aren't many signs of those days left."

"Yeah, the whole time is sort of lost to the winds. If you think about it, the Indians didn't get treated much differently than the buffalo. It was confinement or death for both of them. How do you think the story would read if they had successfully defended their land? The rich, white European history we teach in school sure doesn't tell their story."

"A lot of progress comes through conflict. We live in the most successful country there ever was so sometimes the ends do justify the means."

Ty gave Stan a stern look, "Thanks, Machiavelli. I don't think you will find any Native Americans who would call it justice. They were treated to a nearly complete genocide and you know what's really wild. To this very day there has never been an official apology. Not one single 'sorry', 'excuse me', 'my bad', nothing! Do you think since text books call the tragedy of Indian removal simply westward expansion, that a hundred and fifty years from now history books will call Hiroshima and Nagasaki urban renewal projects?"

Stan scoffed, "You spend way too much time thinking about the negatives of society and not enough about the benefits. Primitive cultures would never have brought about the Industrial Revolution and all the advantages coming from it. Try a little optimism sometime, you might like it."

"I have to admire your idealism. You're probably right, I am too cynical but in my simple mind the entire Capitalist industry is an invention by and an endeavor for the benefit of people. Since it is an activity by people and for people that should be the yardstick we use to judge its success. Ever increasing profit is the wrong criteria to assess success or failure of the system. Sorrowfully, the fact is over half the people on Earth live in abject poverty and the number is growing by the day. By any definition, an enterprise that fails the majority of the people it is supposed to benefit is a total failure. It definitely can't be called civilized."

"Boy, aren't you a little ray of sunshine. If this isn't civilization, what is it? And if Capitalism is a failure, what do you suggest? There is no shortage of critics pointing out flaws in the system but you're all suspiciously short on alternatives."

Ty sighed, "I'll have to give you that point. I know I don't have a clue. I know the system is fundamentally flawed but you're absolutely right, how do you stop and redirect it? If the music stops we seem to be four or five billion chairs short of having a place for everyone to sit. I will defend my characterization of civilization, though. In six thousand years of written civilization there has been only twenty six years when there wasn't a war being waged somewhere on the planet. Most times there was more than one war raging. There is nothing civilized about war. In sixty centuries the only thing that has changed about the primitive tactics of warfare are the weapons. Explain to me how in World War One, nine soldiers were killed for every civilian who died. In Iraq that has been totally reversed. There are ten civilians dying for every soldier. That isn't progress. We aren't becoming more civilized, we're just becoming more efficient killers. On top of that the general population is totally detached from the killing. If mankind survives, future history texts will remember the twentieth century as the most ruthless and lethal since the Inquisition."

Stan allowed Ty's remarks to settle before he replied, "Just when I start to think you may be out of touch, you say something that hits home. I know I never think about the human cost of progress. I don't know how to process it and I wouldn't have a clue what to do about it."

"That's what Belle did. She put a human face on all the events of the day. Teaching history got harder when I started investigating the human dramas behind historical events. I started questioning the supposed facts I was offering to my unsuspecting students. I wasn't terribly upset when I quit my job because I had already realized history had been rewritten. The story we know is a selective story written by the victors. Nations don't apologize for the atrocities they commit.

They simply don't acknowledge the events ever happened. It comes down to the oldest struggle in human existence. In the battle of good versus evil, nations are no different than an individual. If a person hasn't resolved that battle within himself before engaging in conflict, the villain could be either of the combatants."

"Okay then, I need to know something. If you don't believe in institutions, industrialization, capitalism or even history, how in the hell do you keep that silly smile on your face?"

Ty laughed, "People, man! People just like you. There are a lot more good people in the world than there are bad people. Always has been. We just didn't get the keys to the armory."

"Is that what you wrote about?"

"Most of the stuff I wrote did nothing but keep the wood stove burning. I published a few things but that was along time ago. I've always read more than I wrote. I still think about writing again. You never know when you might need a good fire."

"What kind of books do you read, all that left wing radical stuff?"

"Some of it for sure but if that's all you read then you're not any better than the right wing guys. You need as much of the stories as you can get if you want to form a balanced opinion. I've always liked how one book can lead to another. I'd read a book about string theory and end up reading a science fiction book about time travel. Once I read a book about the Boer Wars and that fueled my reading for a couple of years. That's what got me into Cecil Rhodes, The Round Tables and the Central Banks. There are hundreds of good books about the robber barons in America at the start of the Industrial Revolution. I used to love all those international spy thrillers, you know 007 against the evil genius. Once I figured out the characters and events in the thrillers are usually based on actual people and events, I just found the conspiratorial books better. That touch of realism makes the stories scary as hell. I do love the stories. What kind of stuff do you read?"

"During school I don't read much that isn't tied to a class but when I read for fun it's usually high adventure stories. When I was a kid I loved Treasure Island, Kidnapped, Billy Budd and all those pirate adventures. The Three Musketeers might be my favorite adventure. When I was a sophomore I had this poly-sci professor who had us read, Noam Chomsky, John Done and Chalmers Johnson but that's about the extent of my reading from the left side of the aisle except for a biography of Che Guevara."

"What did you think of those books?"

"Sorry to say, I didn't give them a lot of thought. I read them like a school assignment. I'm a true genetic Wainwright because I really liked the books on economics. Milton Friedman, Greenspan, Hayak, even Adam Smith. I got into it."

"I take it you're a free marketeer?"

"Pretty much. Keynesian economics had it's time but now we're into unrestricted deregulation. Milton Friedman died with a smile on his face but poor Hayak didn't live long enough to see his theories in practice."

"Since you're going to be a Wall Street whiz kid, I'd like your take on something. Why do you think ninety percent of the directors of The CIA are Wall Street bankers?"

"That's always made perfect sense to me. Remember I grew up on stories of Rothchild and the profitability of intelligence information so it seems like a logical choice to me. Why do you ask? You think there's something sinister going on?"

"Yeah, I'd call it sinister. It's no secret the CIA has funded and participated in overthrowing over fifty governments since they were formed in 1947. They maintain operations in almost every country on Earth. That isn't cheap and it isn't even remotely covered by the administrative budget they get from the taxpayers. I think they fund themselves the same way the British financed their empire, with drug money. It may be a nasty little secret but it's an undeniable fact that colonial expansion for over two centuries was funded by illegal drug money from the golden triangle. There's this ex-LA cop, Michael Ruppert, who claims the CIA is responsible for over ninety percent of the cocaine and heroin on the streets of the country. I was pretty skeptical about his claims until I read about Roberto Hernandez. He was president of Mexico's second largest bank, Banamex. He was under indictment in Mexico for his drug activity and money laundering. He lived near Cancun at a place the locals called 'Cocaine Alley'. In 2001 CitiBank bought Banamex. All charges were dropped against Hernandez and he was given a seat on the board of directors of CitiBank where he sat beside John Deutch, the ex-director of The CIA, and Robert Rubin, the former Treasury Secretary. If those two didn't know who Hernandez was they are delusional or inept. That was one of those connect the dots moments for me."

"Maybe there are some connections but don't you think you're making some giant leaps from dot to dot? You don't really believe The CIA is dealing drugs?"

"Not directly maybe, but they facilitate the process. Their interest is that the money flows through Wall Street. Doesn't it seem a little bizarre the inner cities are over run with cocaine and heroin which both require huge grow operations and intricate distribution systems while in the suburbs the drug abusers are simply cooking methamphetamine. I've got another one for you. You're an economist so you know how important cash flow is to business. Remember in 2001, heroin supplies worldwide were down ninety percent because the Taliban had eradicated the poppy fields in Afghanistan in 2000. Before 9/11 the Dow Jones was in free fall from the loss of cash flow. We invaded Afghanistan and the U.S. Military quickly gained control of all the land, sea and air routes into and out of the country. By 2003 the world wide opium and heroin trade had increased seven hundred percent. That doesn't seem like a coincidence to me." Ty pointed to a road sign, "Colorado, my boy. Soon we'll be in the Rocky Mountains. We need a new subject for a new state. What do you think?"

"Sure. You're well read, maybe a little sentimental for reality, but I have a question. Since you think the world is so sinister, what advice would you offer me?"

"That's easy, I wouldn't."

"Why not? I thought we were friends. You have opinions about everything, why not for me?"

"Because we are friends and you are exactly right, that's all I have are opinions. I'm not qualified to give advice. Life choices are virtually unlimited but they're all personal. The trick is to make sure the choices you make are your own. There's no doubt in my mind you'll find your own way without anybody's help, especially mine. You're right about me, I have a mountain of opinions but I don't have shit for solutions. I spent my life as an observer. The world isn't going to be any better because I was here. I'm a coward. Most people don't take the time to see what's going on around them. I took the time to educate myself about the condition of the world but I didn't do anything that made any significant difference. My generation is not leaving a better world than we inherited. I should be asking you for advice."

They drove in silence for a long while. Stan had expected a lengthy speech peppered with sage advice from one of life's warriors. He hadn't expected to be blown off. Having lived seventy plus years should have led to some profound conclusions about life's journey, not simply 'We blew it, you're next'.

Ty broke the silence, "What are you afraid of? What are your fears?"

Stan pondered the question before answering, "I guess I'm afraid of failure and since Hannah, I'm afraid I might end up alone. I want to have the same sparkle in my eyes you do when you talk about Grandma."

"You already do. As far as failure, there's only one way to never fail and that's never to try anything. I'm always searching for my next failure. Like Thomas Edison said' I didn't fail, I just discovered two thousand ways not to build a light bulb.'"

After they crossed into Wyoming, Stan pulled off the freeway to get fuel. When he returned from paying for the gas, Ty was nowhere to be seen. Stan pulled away from the fuel pumps and parked in front of an old auto repair garage next door to the service station. There was an antique red winged Pegasus sign in the front window but the business, aside from being nostalgic, appeared to be closed. Stan waited patiently for awhile but eventually he tired of waiting and got out to find Ty. Stan was headed for the convenience store when he heard Ty's voice from behind the garage. He rounded the corner of the building to find Ty engaged in conversation with a man easily as old as Ty. The man was standing in front of a thirty year old Ford pickup sitting on jack stands. He was wearing gray overalls and continuously wiped the grease from his hands as he spoke to Ty. They both turned when Stan appeared.

"This is the Grandson I was telling you about. Stan, this is Harold."

Harold nodded, "Nice to meet you, Stan. Ty says I outta be nice to you 'cause we're all gonna to be working for you someday."

"You've probably noticed Ty is a little prone to exaggeration." Stan didn't say anything more in case Ty was telling stories again. Stan didn't want to interrupt Ty while he was blowing smoke up someone's ass.

Ty replied, "I just enhance for effect. Harold offered to help us out, Stan. It occurred to me we no longer have a spare. Harold is going to Cheyenne tomorrow and he said he'd pick up a tire for us."

"Couldn't we pick up a tire ourselves and save Harold the trouble?"

"No trouble Stan. I go into town a couple times a week to get parts. I need a tie rod for this truck here and the Grand Prix over there needs a fuel pump."

Stan looked around at the numerous cars scattered about. He had assumed they were abandoned, junk cars, "I didn't know the garage was still open."

Harold shook his head, "Yes, I'm still workin. I still wrench for a few people but mainly I just fix these old cars nobody wants. I sell them in Cheyenne or sometimes in Denver. It keeps me busy and buys a few groceries."

"You must have been around here for awhile."

"My Father opened the garage after the big war. I just ended up sticking around. It used to be a goin' concern when we sold gas too but that was before the big boys hit town." He pointed at the service station, "You can't compete with them, but that's okay. I don't want to work that hard anymore, anyhow. Rockefeller can have the money, he probably needs it worse than I do."

Ty interrupted, "Besides, Harold tells me there is a great lake just down the road. We could camp out for the night. It'd be great."

Stan noted Ty's enthusiastic expression and again decided there was little chance of changing Ty's mind, "Why not. We aren't setting any land speed records anyway. What the hell, I haven't camped since I was a kid."

Ty turned to Harold, "I told you he was smart. I'll get the tire. Where do you want it Harold?"

Harold nonchalantly nodded at the garage, "Lean er' up against the wall. I'll have it back tomorrow afternoon."

Stan pulled his wallet out of his pocket. Harold held up his hand," We can settle up when I get back. You give me money up front, I might be tempted to run off."

Stan slipped his wallet back into his pocket, "Thanks, Harold."

Ty returned with the blown out tire, leaning it up against the back of the building. He walked up to Harold and held out an envelope, "This is for you. You can put this to better use than I can."

Harold accepted the envelope from Ty. He got a puzzled expression on his face when he removed the paper from the envelope, "What's this, Ty?"

"It's a stock certificate. You are now the proud owner of five shares of the Exxon-Mobile Corporation. Now you can tell your neighbors to back off because you're an owner."

Harold held out the stock certificate, "I can't take this. It's gotta' be worth a fair amount."

Ty held up his hands, "Don't hurt my feelings, Harold. I'm never going to do anything with it. I have lots of them from all sorts of corporations just so I can keep an eye on these crooks. Honestly, it doesn't mean anything to me. I insist."

Harold scanned the stock certificate again. A smile slowly grew on his face, "It would be fun to wave it in front of that asshole manager. Thanks, Ty. Thanks a lot."

Ty moved on, "Is there a store at the lake?"

"Yeah. They got a little store and a bait shop. Nice camp sites too. Mel and Ruby have had the place for a lot of years. Nice people, good fishin' up there."

Ty shook Harold's hand. Stan came forward to shake his hand also. Ty said," Thanks, Harold. I guess we'll see you tomorrow. Can we bring you back anything?"

"If you catch more trout than you can eat, I would sure fry 'em up."

"You got it."

Stan and Ty returned to Brutus and headed towards the lake. When they were on the road Stan said, "You know that stock you gave away was worth at least a few hundred. Is that your plan, to give away everything you have?"

Ty chuckled, "Hell yes. I figure if I can drop dead with just the clothes on my back and a penny in my pocket, I have perfect timing. Harold will enjoy the stock more than anyone I can think of. When I die, I don't think my life will be measured by the pile of stuff I leave behind. You leave with what you brought. Possession is a temporary illusion."

"So you're leaving nothing but a legacy?"

"I don't plan to leave that either. Legacy always seemed arrogant to me. A legacy is like building a monument to your own existence because you think your life is too important for anyone to forget. If anyone remembers me, I hope it puts a smile on their face and they say simply,' I liked him'. That's a good legacy."

# Chapter (8)

The store/bait shop was a small building that fit perfectly in the panoramic scene where it was located. There were peeks of the lake through the forest of pine trees behind the store. The hand painted wooden sign resting on the roof was simple, direct and all inclusive; Camping, bait, tackle, groceries.

They were greeted inside by a sixty something year old woman in denim jeans and a red flannel shirt, "You must be Ty and Stan. Harold called to make sure we kept a lake front campsite for you."

Ty held out his hand, "You must be Ruby. It's a pleasure."

"You fella's gonna fish?"

"I hope so. Harold said you have some nice trout in this lake."

"Sure do. The lake was stocked last year so the fishin's been good." Ruby took two fishing rods from the back wall and two tackle boxes from the floor below the rack. From a chest she pulled out a plain white cardboard container of worms and added it to the other gear. "There's a jar of salmon eggs in the tackle box if they won't hit the worms." She held out a registration card to Stan, "You're gonna need a license but Ty should be okay."

Ty replied, "I don't hide my age very well, do I? Ruby, do you have something we can throw on the fire for dinner?"

"There's some rib eyes and potato salad in the cooler."

Ty retrieved two steaks, a container of potato salad and a six pack of beer and put them on the counter.

Ruby began ringing up the rentals and their purchases, "You'll be in campsite three. Mel should have plenty of firewood there. You guys are lucky. You got here in time to catch the sunset on the lake. That's what sold us on this place."

Ty asked, "Are you and Mel refugees from the city?"

Ruby nodded slowly as she rang up their purchases, "Yeah, we've been here for almost twenty years now. I used to work for Ma Bell in Denver. Mel had a nice little hardware store in old town. The telephones all got automated and everyone started shopping at Home Depot so the city didn't have much use for us. I'm glad we moved out here. You meet a lot of nice folks." She turned to Stan, "That'll be seventy seven forty five altogether. I didn't charge you a deposit on the gear. You all look pretty honest. You'll want to get on the water early for the best fishin'. Our boats are all rented but you'll do just as good off the dock."

Stan smiled as he paid the tab, "Thanks for everything, Ruby."

Ruby returned the smile, "If you catch enough come on back for some corn meal and eggs. That'll make a good mountain breakfast."

They collected their supplies and made the short drive to the campsite. The picnic table and the fire pit were no more than fifty feet away from the water's edge. The lake was totally still. There wasn't a single ripple on the surface of the lake transforming it into nature's perfect mirror. The towering pine trees across the lake disappeared into the shore only to magically reappear in perfect symmetry on the mirrored surface. The sun hung just above the tree tops on its westward trek.

"Stan, if you want to get the fire started, I'll get the eating tools of destruction. I think I even have some barbeque sauce." Ty brought a box out of the trailer and set up the table for dinner. He covered the steaks liberally with barbeque sauce and threw them on the grate over the fire before joining Stan at the picnic table. Ty opened two beers, handing one to Stan. He tapped Stan's bottle with his own, "It doesn't get a whole lot better than this, Stan. You aren't going to kickback and enjoy many sunsets like this on Wall Street."

Stan was hypnotized by the colors reflecting off the lake from the fading sun. The brilliant blues and greens were ever so slowly surrendering to the reds, oranges and pinks of the setting sun. Stan finally found his voice, "This is incredible. Good idea, Ty."

Ty got up to turn the steaks, "If you like sunsets on the water, you should get yourself a little sailboat. Man, you live in the Pacific Northwest. When it isn't raining, you've got some of the most beautiful sunsets anywhere. Belle and I went everywhere in that little boat we had. If you ever get the chance, you should check out a place called Princess Louisa Inlet. You go up this fjord thirty miles into the mountains. There are six thousand foot granite walls on both sides of the boat and the water is a thousand feet deep under your keel. Princess Louisa is a fjord at the end of Jervis Inlet. Its five miles long and half a mile wide. At the end of the inlet is Chatterbox Falls. The glacier fed waterfall is a hundred feet high. It was raining when we were there and from where we anchored, we counted twenty nine waterfalls cascading from the granite cliffs. There's a long dock you can tie up to, but Belle read you could anchor in front of the falls, so that's what we did. It's kind of strange because you have to stick the nose of your boat over the sand bar at the base of the falls to drop your anchor. You pull back on your anchor and the out flow from the falls keeps you dancing back and forth directly in front of the falls. Its wild, your anchor is in five feet of water while there is a hundred and fifty feet under your keel. It has got to be one of the most beautiful places on Earth. The only problem with anchoring in front of the falls is you have the urge to pee all night long."

When the steaks were done they opened another beer and silently ate dinner while watching the last rays of sun light slowly drift into the darkness. While cleaning up after dinner, Ty asked," Have you ever slept outside, Stan?"

"No. The only camping I've ever done was at a summer camp but we slept in cabins."

"It's warm and dry so let's do it. You can add it to your list of life's simple pleasures."

"Why not?" Stan got the sleeping bags and pillows from the van while Ty laid out a tarp to put the bedding on. They settled into their sleeping bags and quietly enjoyed the show as the stars revealed themselves in the darkness.

There was a long silence before Ty finally spoke, "Promise me every once and awhile you'll take a break from your hectic life and get out into nature. Everyone needs a place to get away so they can stay centered. Mother Nature can wrap around you and remind you you're just a little speck in a huge picture. We all need to remember there is something bigger than ourselves."

"Good idea but that sounds suspiciously like advice."

"No, just a hope for you. The world you're heading for can crush people who forget there is something beyond that world. It's going to take real strength for you to make it there. You'll have to be focused and driven like your Dad if you're going to make it."

"Whoa! If I didn't know any better I'd swear you were complimenting my Dad."

"I am. I don't agree with Stanton about much but I respect him for what he is. He believes in what he does, even if I think it's a corrupt, ruthless business. He gave Emma what she needed so, for that, I will always be grateful."

"Do you think Dad has ever had second thoughts about what he does?"

"Wow. That's hard to say. Stanton was born into money just like you. He embraced the life with everything he had. I'm sure Stanton has made decisions that challenged his morals but all powerful men have to find a way to justify their actions because their decisions can tragically affect people's lives. Stanton is the only one who knows if he has any regrets. He's been in this world his entire life so he probably doesn't think about other lifestyle choices anymore. The choices he made early in his life may have been for his Father but they're his now."

"I think about that a lot. I know I feel resentment towards him, especially when he's pushing me hard. My whole life is out of my Dad's playbook. I don't make any major decisions for myself. Sometimes it's hard to know if it's my life or his. His shadow makes it hard to see."

"Everybody questions themselves. The problem is there isn't a playbook for life. You can't skip to the back of the book for answers, besides there is no right or wrong. There's only choice. If you try to find answers about yourself outside of yourself, you're looking in the wrong place. As far as resenting Big Stan, it sounds pretty normal to me. I'm sure Emma resents me. You just have to make the best decisions you can with the information you have at the time."

"But sometimes I'm afraid I do everything just for Dad. I don't want to resent him. I know he only wants the best for me, but I think he believes what's best for me is to be just like him. I couldn't honestly say if Dad is happy or if he ever was."

"Sounds like you're talking about Hannah."

Stan sighed, "I guess I am."

"Look man, nobody can judge Stanton's happiness but Stanton. He can try to direct yours but you're going to be the final judge. I disagree with what Stanton does in his business life because I could never do it. Stanton makes decisions that can have serious consequences on people's lives. Stanton has to justify himself to himself. Bad people can do bad things but so can good people. Soldiers have to do horrible things and the only way they can justify it to themselves is to believe they are doing it for the right reasons. Abraham Lincoln is remembered as a great man even though he ran the country like a ruthless dictator. In his eyes he was doing what he did for the most righteous of reasons, he was trying to hold the country together. I guess what I'm trying to say is, I think if you do anything for what you believe are the right reasons, that's all you can do. Even if it turns out badly. Great men are the ones who aren't afraid to make the tough decisions because it's almost always worse to not make one."

"Do you have a place you go to stay centered?"

"There's this footbridge over the creek behind the house in West Virginia. It goes over the creek to the hill where Belle was born. Did I tell you Belle was born there? That's why I moved to West Virginia. She grew up on the hill across the valley from where I lived. I've been to that bridge a thousand times. That's where I scattered Belle's ashes. It was hard to leave," Ty's voice trailed off.

Stan sat quietly allowing Ty his time with Belle. When Stan finally spoke he asked, "You said nature lets us know there is something bigger than us, do you mean God?"

"God is as good a label as any. I'll leave that to the theologians. What I do know is the only physical difference between a live human being and a corpse is that spark of life. Call it a soul, spirit, conscious energy, or whatever you want, but everyone who has ever lived is connected exactly the same way to whatever we are connected to. People can label it, write stories about it, and fight wars over different versions of it but in the end nobody knows anymore than you do. It doesn't matter how many roads you build or what names you put on the road signs, if all the roads lead to the same destination."

"So you're not religious at all?"

"Religions are institutions built to protect ideas. They exist by professing to know the answer to a question they couldn't possibly know. Doesn't it sound absurd to you that any person can be self appointed as gatekeeper, denying others access to an afterlife? More people have died in the name of religion than for any other reason. I can't find the righteousness in that. What about you? Are you a believer?"

"I don't know. I've been to church but I really don't know what to believe."

Ty pulled his sleeping bag up around his neck as he rolled over, "You'll figure it out. Get some sleep. See if you can conjure up a trout god, so we can have some breakfast."

# Chapter (9)

Stan awoke with a start, sitting up quickly. It took a few moments for Stan to realize he was in a sleeping bag, on the ground, in a campground in Wyoming.

Ty noticed the movement and turned away from the fire he was tending, "Good morning. I was wondering if I should call an ambulance. Coffee's on."

Stan dressed quickly before rolling up his sleeping bag and the tarp.

Ty poured two cups of coffee at the picnic table, "How'd you sleep?"

"Great! I don't remember anything but a visit from the trout gods, so I will definitely catch breakfast."

"Oooh, The gauntlet has been thrown. You're on."

They finished their coffee, grabbed the fishing rods and headed down the shoreline towards the dock. When Stan got out in front a few steps, Ty called out, "Not too fast. Remember, I only have a leg and a half."

Stan scoffed as he turned to wait, "It's too soon to play the gimp card. I haven't out fished you yet."

Ty stopped suddenly, picking up a small stone, "Whoa, Stan! Check this out."

Ty was rolling the stone over in his hand, inspecting it closely. Stan leaned in to get a closer look. "What is it?"

Ty squinted, intensely examining the small stone, "It's a sex stone."

"What in the world is a sex stone?"

Ty held the stone out for Stan to see. Suddenly he turned and threw the stone into the lake. Ty couldn't suppress the chuckle, "It's a fucking rock!"

Stan shook his head and turned away, "You're a sick man."

Once they were on the dock, Ty gave Stan a crash course on baiting a hook, casting and reeling. The trout god gave Stan the first bite. Stan leaped up hooping and hollering, like he had hit the game winning home run in the World Series. Ty was tickled at Stan's emotional outburst. It was impossible not to be infected by his enthusiasm. Ty quickly followed Stan by landing a respectable trout of his own. This was Stan's day, though. He landed the other two fish they needed to complete breakfast, the last one ending with an end zone victory dance.

Ty reeled in his line, "I'll clean and cook if you get the corn meal and eggs."

Stan helped Ty take the gear and their catch back to the campsite before walking through the nearly full campground to the store.

Stan proudly sat the cornmeal and eggs on the counter, "We caught breakfast."

Ruby rang up the items, "Good for you, Stan."

"We're going back after breakfast. We told Harold we would bring him back some fish."

"Don't bother, Stan. Some fellas left this morning and they were way over their limit so you can take some of them to Harold if you want."

"That would be great. Thanks, Ruby. I noticed on my walk down here that some of these campsites look pretty permanent."

"A lot of people work the ski resorts in the winter and hang around here in the summer. There isn't a lot of work around here. It used to be a lot of retired RV'ers but we're seeing more and more gypsies nowadays. Getting' tough out there."

Stan brought the cooking supplies back to Ty who had the fire stoked and the skillet hot. Stan poured a cup of coffee and settled back to watch Ty bread the freshly cleaned trout and toss them into the skillet.

"You look like you've cooked before."

"You bet your ass I've cooked before. I've been a fry cook. I've worked at a dairy. I've worked on the Census. I filled in at the Post Office. One winter I sold conch shells and postcards in the Florida Keys. I've done all sorts of things but mainly I've just hung out. Thumper and I have been on just about every dirt road in the Appalachians. All in all it's been a life well wasted."

Ty finished cooking, setting the plates on the picnic table. Stan dug in,"This is great Ty, good job. "He motioned over his shoulder as he ate, "Ruby told me a lot of these people live here after ski season. I guess there isn't much work around here."

"That doesn't surprise me. We're trying to replace forty million industrial jobs with minimum wage service jobs. That's what three decades of free trade agreements have done to this country. It's hard to imagine what it's going to look like when all the middle class living wage jobs have been exported. I guess we'll all just service each other when we don't make anything anymore."

Stan washed the dishes after they finished eating. They stopped briefly to return the fishing gear, pick up Harold's trout and say their goodbyes to Ruby. After the short drive back to the garage, Ty retrieved the fish from the ice chest while Stan went next door to use the restroom.

Stan was back at the van when a white Lincoln Town car screeched to a stop beside the garage. Stan couldn't see who got out of the car but there was no mistaking the booming voice of whoever it was as the man began addressing Harold who was behind the garage with Ty.

"God dam it, Harold! How many times do I have to tell you to clean up this junkyard? My lawyer said any car that isn't registered and insured has to be in a fenced area. I'll bet none of these junkers are either. And why don't you paint this dump! It looks like shit. And being next door to you, it makes my place look like shit, too."

"Sorry Jeremy, but these cars aren't junk. I'm fixing all of them."

Jeremy boomed, "My friends call me Jeremy, its Mr. Adams to you."

Stan appeared swiftly from around the corner, walking confidently toward Jeremy. Harold and Ty were both startled by Stan's sudden appearance, especially since he was wearing a button down shirt and a tie.

Stan stopped in front of Jeremy holding out his hand, not to shake hands but to present him with a business card, "Are you Jeremy Adams? The clerk at the store said I could find you here."

Jeremy looked down his nose at the shorter Stan as he accepted his business card, "Who wants to know? "

Stan looked, unblinking, into Jeremy's eyes, "My name is Stanton Wainwright II. I represent Fidelity Financial Services, Acquisitions and Development. We have recently acquired a securitized CDO package that includes your properties. You are the same Jeremy Adams who appears on the franchise agreements, are you not?"

Ty turned so only Harold could see him. He held his finger to his lips to indicate that Harold should remain silent.

Jeremy was quickly glancing back and forth between Stan and the business card. His voice dropped noticeably in volume, "You're kind of young for this aren't you?"

Stan didn't miss a beat,"The CEO and majority stockholder is Stanton Wainwright the First which opens doors for people with the same name. I don't have your file with me. How many franchises do you operate?"

Jeremy's voice started to betray his confidence, "I, I have three. I'd like to get more."

"We might very well be able to assist you with your expansion plans." Stan leaned closer to Jeremy, "Before we go any further I will need to have your assurance that anything I say to you will be held in the strictest of confidence. If I can have your word, I believe we can be quite beneficial to each other."

Jeremy nodded vigorously, "You have my word."

Ty looked at the ground to hide his smile. Harold looked shell shocked.

Jeremy pointed to them, "What about them?"

Stan continued, "This concerns Mr. Jackson also. This is the situation, Mr. Adams."

Jeremy interrupted, "You can call me Jeremy, Mr. Wainwright."

Stan didn't crack a smile, "Possibly when I'm sure we're friends. As I was saying, the Sioux tribe is negotiating a land swap which will enable them to build a casino resort. Our people in the State Capital assure us we can direct that project to this location. To accommodate the scope of this project will require an expanded overpass, access ramps and frontage roads. The bond proposals to finance the improvements are with the budget committee as we speak. We have been assured their approval in the next legislative session. Initially, two hundred forty acres will be allocated to get construction started. When completed, the resort will have an eighty thousand square foot casino, eight hundred suites, a golf course, strip mall and one of the largest auto and truck centers in the country. The fuel concession will comprise your stake in this project because the road improvements will displace your current location. The extreme secrecy is required because of the unique profit potential. The market capitalization is projected to exceed thirty to one from the onset. That is incredible pop which is why we are doing the securitization of the entire project ourselves. That is also why we need your property as well as Mr. Jackson's. If word of this project becomes public, investors and speculators will over run the process. If everyone plays his part, the profits will remain between us. The planning commission will quietly issue a building permit when the bonds are approved. At that time your property will be deeded to the tribe. Mr. Jackson, at that time, will become our new best friend. His original deed contains an open ended option for the adjoining three hundred acres. Controlling all the properties means we control the competitive forces and all future expansion. Do you have any questions?"

Jeremy was much too busy counting his new found fortune to formulate a question, "No, sir. It sounds incredible."

"It will be incredible as long as everyone stays on message. Government officials can always be trusted to respond to the proper incentives which leaves tribal leaders and ourselves. That is why I am here in person. We don't want agreement documents lying around for someone to stumble upon until the legislation and permits are in place. That is why your discretion is necessary, Mr. Adams."

Jeremy crossed his heart like a school yard pledge, "I swear I won't say a word."

"In addition, if you are contacted in regards to this project by anyone but myself or my staff you are to contact me immediately." Stan took the business card back from Jeremy, "In fact, let me give you my private number." He wrote a number on the card and handed it to Jeremy, "I'm serious, you contact me before you talk to your wife, or even before you go to the toilet. If a competitor discovers this project through you, your financing will become due and payable and you will not be able to secure alternate financing anywhere. I can assure you that you do not want to battle our legal department. When the permits are in hand we will meet with your attorney to draft the agreements. Do you have any questions?"

"No, Sir."

Stan shook Jeremy's hand, "Barring any unforeseen complications we should be business partners within two years. Now if you will excuse me, I need to speak to Mr. Jackson."

Jeremy began backpedaling towards his car, "Thank you. You can count on me, Mr. Wainwright."

Stan turned his back to Jeremy and slowly walked toward Harold. Stan said nothing until Jeremy's car started and began to drive away. Harold still looked shell shocked. Stan smiled broadly, "I hope that wasn't out of line Harold, but I bet that keeps him off your back for awhile. The best part is when it doesn't happen, you can blame it on him because he'll tell everyone he knows."

Ty limped over and slapped Stan on the back, "That was beautiful, Stan! Where did that come from?"

Stan shrugged, "I don't know. I heard him screaming out here and it just came to me."

Harold was still confused, "Is any of it true?"

Stan shrugged again, "Not that I know of."

Ty slapped Stan on the back again, "Where in the hell did you get a tie?"

Stan grinned and held up his tie, "I'm a Wainwright. Don't leave home without one."

The reality started sinking in to Harold and chuckles began escaping in spontaneous short bursts. Stan and Ty said their goodbyes to Harold and got back on the road.

They hadn't traveled a mile before Stan turned to Ty, "Let's stop in Cheyenne, get a room and have a nice dinner."

Ty just grinned, "Whatever you say, Mr. Wainwright."

Upon arrival in Cheyenne, Stan rented a suite. They quickly showered before getting a seat at the steak and seafood restaurant adjoining the hotel. Stan instructed the waiter to not allow them to see the bottom of the wine bottle.

Ty started the conversation, "You look like you're feeling pretty good about yourself but I'm sorry to inform you there aren't any Sioux around here. Bullshit must agree with you but I imagine that's a prerequisite in the world of finance."

"It's definitely part of the skill set. It was fun watching that asshole shrink right in front of me. When I heard him pounce on Harold it pissed me off. Harold is harmless."

"You better be careful, Stan. Defending the meek can be habit forming. Your inner bulldog is liable to leave a trail of weeping business associates."

"I can see why you struggle with things when you can see the faces. There are some really nice people around. Maybe business can find a way to be less abusive."

Ty held up his wine glass, "I'll drink to that but I think we both know that isn't reality. In the corporate world there can only be one winner and that's profit. The government that's supposed to protect us is totally subservient to the financial world. No politician can rise to power without corporate money and approval. Mussolini would have loved our system. He said Fascism should be called Corporatism because it's the perfect blending of business and government."

"You've got to be kidding! You don't think we live in a Fascist state? Next you'll be telling me stories about Nazi conspiracies."

"Why? Do you think the Nazi's just went away?"

"Yes, I do. Besides some racist skinheads and some hundred year old men in South America, the Nazi threat is an historical footnote."

"The first NASA facility was in Huntsville, Alabama. Do you know who the director was? Werner Von Brahn, the head of the Nazi V-2 rocket program. After World War II the OSS, the precursor to the CIA, brought 1600 Nazi scientists to America. The Nazi's were way ahead of us on rocket technology. Our space program was built by those Nazi scientists. I'll grant you, most scientists are more concerned with science than politics. Bankers and industrialists are no different. Money holds supreme importance, far beyond feelings of patriotism."

The waiter served dinner and brought another bottle of wine. Stan poured a glass, "You don't think there are Nazi sympathizers in our government?"

"You're getting hung up on labels, Stan. Nazi was just another way to describe government. To an International Banker or an Industrialist, Nazism, Democracy, Socialism and Communism are all different names for an evolutionary experiment to discover the most efficient way to control and profit from the public. The citizens of Earth have two purposes in the experiment, to fund it and to die in their wars. Don't ever forget that war is the most profitable activity on Earth. Both sides borrow incredible amounts of money to wage war. Hitler's two largest financiers were tied to IG Farben in Europe and Brown Brothers Harriman through the Union Bank in the America. The U.S government actually seized the Union Bank in 1943 under the Trading with the Enemies Act. George W's Grandfather, Prescott Bush, was president of the Union Bank and a director of Brown Brothers Harriman. He was a piece of shit but he wasn't alone. Ford and General Motors were large stakeholders in Opel and Kaiser, the corporations that built the Nazi war machine. You know how the Nazi's exterminated the Jews in such an efficient manner? IBM set up the punch card system the Nazis used for record keeping. What do you think that number on Holocaust survivor's arms was all about? The IBM machines and the billing invoices are still displayed in Museums. The one that really boggled my mind was what Standard Oil did with a chemical additive DuPont had patented. Tetra ethyl lead was the additive making aviation fuel possible. Standard Oil of New Jersey was the only oil company that had it. Through front companies in Spain and the Far East these profiteers supplied the fuel that made the air wars of World War Two possible. Profiteers are only patriots when there are subsidies or contracts to be had."

Stan finished his meal and leaned back in his chair, "I hope dinner is easier to digest than the shit that comes out of you." He picked up his wine glass, "Maybe I am a little naive. I never did pay a lot of attention to history. It was always just memorizing names, dates and places."

"It's just as well because the history they teach is bullshit. I know the history I taught was. Text books tell a selective story of supposedly great men and their struggle for power, glory and possession. Actual history is billions of personal stories of survival that seldom get written down."

"Ty, your inner optimist is no match for your inner cynic."

"You're right. I can't get past the human price for things. That's especially true about war. Anyone who says war is a civilized way to settle differences is clinically insane."

"You talk a lot about wars but not about wars in our own time. Why don't you talk about Iraq?"

"Iraq is a tough one. What do you think about it?"

"Well I think it was mismanaged and poorly executed. The premise was pretty shaky but I can see the geopolitical implications. I don't know if it was a mistake or not but the reality is, we're there. Do you think we should just leave?"

Ty poured more wine, "I know if someone tells you you're digging a hole in the wrong place, the first thing you should do is stop digging. I'll tell you why it's hard to talk about Iraq. It scares the hell out of me because I think I understand why that administration full of abstract war enthusiasts did what they did. Besides Z-Big Brezinski's geopolitics, the reality is peak oil. Some experts say we have already passed the Hibbert Peak and others say it's in the very near future. Either way, peak oil is a reality. The other reality is every economy on the planet is hopelessly dependent on oil. Agriculture, transportation, manufacturing, high tech, plastics and everything else involved in commerce requires oil. The military is not retooling with alternative energy weapons. There are no solar or wind powered weapons in our future. The military can not operate without oil and it is most certainly a declining resource. It's no accident no new refineries have been built in forty years. I'm afraid Iraq is the beginning of the resource wars because the structure of the corporate world does not allow for changes in direction. If America is going to be the lone surviving superpower, oil is an absolute necessity. You've read Chomsky about American exceptionalism. If you agree we deserve to rule the world then these intellectual morons did what they honestly believed they had to do. They secured a foothold, by whatever means, in the middle of the largest remaining oil reserves on the planet. There is no doubt in my mind we will fight for the last drop of oil, and to the death. You won't hear about it in the corporate media but the U.S. has built four enormous, permanent military bases in Iraq. All told, there are seven hundred and thirty seven military bases and installations spread out in a hundred and fifty two countries. The United States is the largest and possibly the most oppressive empire in history. If you believe we're entitled you can justify it. If you don't, all you can do are body counts. Know this Stan, all empires end badly."

"But sometimes you do think extraordinary methods are necessary?"

"I said I understood, I never said I agreed. I think the people who manipulated us into war are insane. These men believed they were smarter than everyone, even their own military leadership. I don't believe in war but I know if you wage war you call on soldiers. You don't rely on chicken hawk draft dodgers to develop war plans. Rumsfeld, Bush, Cheney, Wolfowitz, Bolton; every fucking one of them thought they knew a better way to fight a war. Iraq was supposed to be the first stepping stone across the Middle East and then across the planet until everyone bowed to their genius. The British occupied Iraq in the 1920's but they deployed over one million troops to secure the country. These genius' are still hailing their success in the face of failure. If they were in therapy, they'd all be committed. When a leader publicly states that America doesn't do body counts, humanity is gone." Ty poured some more wine and another bottle magically appeared, "Sorry man. I get lost in angry rants when I think about those fuckers. If we had actually elected these assholes I'd really be humiliated."

Stan held up his glass, "No problem. You have some powerful ideas. I don't agree with everything you say but I don't agree with everything my Dad says either. Maybe I can find some philosophical middle ground. What do you think?"

"I think you've had too much wine because you're delusional. Capitalism and poor people will end only with the death or total subjugation of one or the other. Corruption and survival are mutually exclusive. If you want to live somewhere in between it's because you're trying to please everyone. I say, please yourself and fuck us all."

The waiter returned to the table, "Can I get you anything else?"

Stan shook his head and poured more wine, "Just the check."

The waiter lowered his voice, "Can I ask you to please lower your voices. Some people have taken offense."

Ty turned in his seat to the couple at the table next to them, "I apologize, Madam. My Grandson is a terrible influence on me. I'm at that impressionable age, you know, between puberty and senility."

The woman didn't look in Ty's direction. The man seated next to her nodded before quickly adverting his eyes. Ty stood and inadvertently stumbled backwards, bumping into the woman's chair, "Again, I apologize. There seems to be a shit load of gravity in here."

Stan came around the table and attempted to grab Ty's arm. Ty pulled away and headed for the exit. Stan stopped to pay the check before joining Ty in the lobby. They laughed all the way back to their suite.

Once back in their room, Ty opened the mini bar, "You want a drink, Wainwright?"

"Maybe one more. You're not setting a very good example for me."

"Set your own example, young Stanton. You're waiting for someone to show you the way and none of us know any fucking more than you do. You want to find the way? Figure it out because no matter where you go, there you are."

"You're turning into a mean drunk. Chill out old man"

"Great advice. You identified the problem and offered a profound solution. Brilliant!"

"You sound like you're looking for an argument. I like listening to your stories. I'm not asking you to write a fucking script for me."

"Hey, listen to you. You can swear. Don't get pissed at me because you let everyone else make your decisions so nothing is your fault. You can't be a scared little boy forever just because you were bullied by an overbearing father. Daddy's expectations can't be that tough. You've got a lot of heart, now you need to grow some balls." Ty lowered his head so Stan couldn't see his eyes filling with tears, "I can't help you. I can't help anyone. There's only been two people who needed me and I failed both of them. I'm a fucking coward." He looked up, "And so are you!"

"You're just drunk and feeling sorry for yourself. You didn't fail anyone."

"What the fuck do you know? Did you know that Belle's Mother killed herself to get away from her Father? Yeah, she left a defenseless little girl with that abusive piece of shit. You may think I'm peace loving but I would of killed that mother fucker if I'd ever met him. Belle spent her whole life trying to fix other people's pain because she couldn't stop her own. She lived in pain and she died in pain. All I did was watch."

The tears were flowing down his face. Stan sat down on the bed opposite of Ty. Softly Stan said,"You were always there. What else could you have done?"

Ty looked at Stan through his red, tear filled eyes, "Don't you dare feel sorry for me." His eyes softened slightly before he spoke again, "I used to lie in bed and watch her sleep. She was so beautiful. She'd lay there like a peaceful angel. There were times she would cry in her sleep and I couldn't help her." Ty stiffened. His eyes hardened, "And I can't help you! You're all alone on this fucking ride!"

Stan felt the tears rising within him. He was tempted to grab hold of Ty and hug him, "She didn't need you to fix her, she just needed you there."

Ty's expression was turning to rage, "How the fuck do you know what she wanted, you don't even know what you want!"

Stan stood up, "I'm just trying to help, Ty!"

"Well stop! You can't help! Fuck you! Fuck everyone!" Ty turned away.

Stan didn't respond. He stormed out onto the balcony, slamming the sliding door behind him. He was mumbling as he looked at the view without seeing it, "Fucking miserable old coot. I should get on a plane and leave his sorry ass. I don't have to put up with this shit!" Stan stayed out on the balcony looking out into space for a long time. When he finally went back inside, Ty was passed out in the exact spot Stan had left him. Stan watched silently for a few minutes before he removed Ty's shoes, swung his legs onto the bed and covered him up. He then undressed and climbed beneath the covers on the other bed. He listened closely for Ty's even breathing before he drifted off to sleep.

# Chapter (10)

The morning sun was blazing in through the sliding glass door Stan had left open. Stan quickly got up to close the drapes, protecting his morning eyes from the brightness. Ty was still sleeping in the same position Stan had left him. Stan washed up and got dressed before taking the hotel phone out onto the balcony.

Much to his surprise, when he dialed his home phone, his Mother picked up on the second ring, "Wainwrights."

"Hi, Mom. I'm surprised I caught you."

"Stan! I'm so glad you called. I've been worried about you. Are you okay?"

"I'm fine, Mom. We aren't moving very fast. The van shakes your guts out if you go more than fifty five. We're in Wyoming now so we will probably be home in a couple of days."

"How is Daddy? Is he okay?"

"He's fine. He's quite a character. I really have enjoyed getting to know him, most of the time. He can be a little ornery at times."

"That's an understatement, but you are getting along well?"

"Actually, very well. He had too much wine last night and he got a little cantankerous. He's still sleeping it off."

"When Daddy drinks he gets terribly emotional thinking of Momma."

"Boy, you're not kidding. He got emotional and then he got angry. If he hadn't passed out, we would have gotten into it."

"I'm sorry you had to see that, Stan. He blames himself for Momma's death. She had so much cancer in her body but Daddy thought he should have saved her. There wasn't anything he could have done. There was nothing anyone could have done. Momma was the love of his life. Daddy truly believes if he would have loved her more, she wouldn't have died. Don't take it personally, Stan, it's not about you."

"I know. He thinks he abandoned you, too. He carries a lot of regret around."

"Daddy never abandoned me. Not for an instant. He was afraid to love anyone as much as he loved Momma. No one wants to feel that kind of pain again. He's a good man, Stan."

"Yes, he is. He's also the best story teller I've ever met. Sometimes I feel like I'm in a lecture hall and I should be taking notes. He sure knows a lot about a lot."

Emma chuckled, "His friends used to call him a compendium of useless information. I'm happy you're getting along so well. You haven't encountered any problems?"

"Not really. We lost a day with a flat tire but we camped out and I caught some rainbow trout for breakfast. That was cool."

"Well Stan, I'm glad you are enjoying your trip. I guess I'll see you soon."

"Yeah, it shouldn't take too long if this old van can pull this trailer over the mountains. She runs good but she's not a real power house."

"I can't believe it still runs. Why are you pulling a trailer? I told Daddy to ship his things."

"The motorcycle is in the trailer."

"The motorcycle! I hoped he had finally totaled that death machine. He won't accept he is getting too old to be falling off of that antique. Did he get his house taken care of?"

Stan smiled broadly, "I can definitely say the house is taken care of. In fact the people were going to move in right after we left."

"That's good. Well, Stan you be careful and remember to call your Mother. You know how I worry. I'll see you soon. I love you and so does your Father."

Stan rolled his eyes. Big Stan had probably forgotten Stan was even gone, "I love you, too. I'll see you soon."

Stan hung up the phone and went back inside. Ty was sitting on the edge of the bed with his head in his hands. He looked sheepishly up at Stan, "I, I'm sorry, Stan. I sometimes…"

Stan pointed at Ty and bellowed, "Not another word, old man!"

Ty sat bolt upright. His wide eyed expression was reminiscent of Harold's shell shocked look. Stan held his glaring look for as long as he could before the laughter escaped, "That's the first time I've seen you speechless. Forget it, Ty. We had too much wine last night. That's all. Now get your ass ready. I'm calling room service for breakfast so we will have enough energy to push Brutus over the Rockies."

Ty's solemn gaze lingered for a moment before he added, "Thanks, Stan."

They ate breakfast, checked out and hit the road. When they reached the outskirts of town Ty pointed to the western landscape, "Say hello to the mountains."

"So do you think Brutus is up to this?"

"No problem, just drop a gear. She'll heat up a little but she'll pull all day long at thirty five, forty." Ty looked around at the housing tracts on the outskirts of town, "Have you ever thought about the people living in the suburbs of the cities? There are millions of different stories playing out everyday but in the end they're all about the same thing. Survival. Survival in the burbs may be more upscale than Bombay but its still just survival. In the Third world people die over food and water. While in the industrialized world people kill themselves because their Lexus was repossessed. Survival levels aren't decided so much on economics as they are by geography. Americans don't live better than people in Ethiopia because we are all smarter than every Ethiopian. We live better because we were born here and not there."

"So Ty, do you think it's realistic to think everyone can share in the prosperity?"

"Not the economic bounty but we most certainly have the resources to feed everyone. That's the humanitarian disconnect between globalization and poverty. I don't believe basic human services and resources should be tied to profit. No one should die because there is no profit in their living. The right of existence should belong to everyone. I have one for you, Stan. Would you prefer to live somewhere like Darfur, surrounded by poverty and starvation never knowing there is another way to live, or somewhere like the occupied territories where poverty and starvation are also a reality but they have to look daily through the fences at an industrial world they are not allowed to share?"

"That's like asking which leg I would prefer to lose. The Israeli-Palestinian conflict is one of those things you can find volumes of material to support either side. Like you say, both sides have the right to exist."

Ty added sarcastically, "And God is on both sides, right?"

"So you think it boils down to religious differences?"

"Hell no. Government and religious institutions both flaunt God so they can pretend to be on the moral high ground. There is absolutely nothing moral about what people do to each other in the name of God. Have you ever wondered if God truly is an all powerful being with complete and divine control over humankind and God knowingly allowed the pain, suffering, death and destruction that has been man kind's history to persist? Would that make God a benevolent being or a sadist?"

"Whoa, big guy! You're going to get us struck down by a bolt of lightning."

Ty closely watched Stan's face to gauge his reaction. Stan downshifted to navigate a turn in the road. After the turn he pulled quickly to the shoulder.

Ty asked, "What's wrong?"

"Nothing, I thought we could give these two a ride."

Ty leaned forward so he could see out the passenger side mirror. There were two young women hustling toward the van with backpacks in hand. He leaned out the window and asked, "You need a ride?"

The shorter of the two leaned in so she could see the driver and the interior of the van, "Sure could. How far are you guys going?"

Stan smiled, "We're going to Seattle. How about you?"

The woman grinned, "We're going to Reno but we could use a ride to Salt Lake City."

Ty reached back and opened the side door, "Climb in, throw your stuff anywhere."

The two women tossed their backpacks on the floor and took a seat on the bed.

Ty turned sideways in his seat, "I'm Ty and this is my Grandson Stan."

The short woman replied, "I'm Georgia and this is Marcie."

"It's a pleasure to meet you. Stan came to move me from West Virginia to Seattle so my daughter can keep an eye on me. I'm getting old and helpless so I can't be trusted. What about you two? Are you from Reno?"

Georgia shook her head, "No, never been there. I've got some work lined up for a couple of months and then me and Marcie are going to Monterey. We're going to crew on a research ship for six months in the South Pacific. It should be a real trip. Marcie will get college credits for working in the lab."

Ty whistled, "Wow! That sounds like one hell of an adventure."

Georgia's eyes never stopped scanning Stan, Ty and the inside of the van, "So what's your story?"

Ty grinned, "You mean are we dangerous? I'm harmless but you should keep an eye on Stan. He's going to Harvard Business in the fall and someday we'll all be working for him. What are you studying, Marcie?"

Marcie shot a quick glance at Georgia, "I haven't decided. I've been in JC for two years."

Georgia cut in, "You'll have to excuse Marcie. She's shy and being on the road has her a little spooked. It doesn't matter; I talk enough for both of us."

Ty grinned, "So do I. We should get along just fine. How long have you two been on the road?"

"We left Daytona Beach about a week ago. We stopped to see Marcie's sister in Birmingham for a day or so."

Stan joined in, "Aren't you nervous out here alone?"

"We're not alone. We've got each other. Most of the people that pick you up are pretty cool. A guy in Missouri gave us an air mattress for our tent. There's a few dickheads. One guy dropped us off in the middle of nowhere in back Bayou, Louisiana. That was the worst so far. I've been on the road before but this is the first time for Marcie."

Ty asked, "The guy didn't try to hurt you did he?"

"No, but he had me pretty jacked. He was an old letch who thought he could get laid. I told him I'd stick him in the neck if he tried anything. I've never done anything like that but I swear I would have if he had tried anything."

"Did you turn him in?" Ty asked.

Georgia shrugged, "What was I gonna tell a cop? Some horny guy picked us up and said 'hump or dump.' Maybe if he'd tried something. Then I could of told them to look for a guy with a hard on and a knife in his neck."

Ty chuckled, "You're right, that would be a lousy way to lose a knife." Georgia let out a boisterous laugh. Even Marcie managed to squeeze out a snicker.

Ty continued, "I spent a couple of seasons in Florida. Are you both natives of Florida?"

Georgia was at total ease sharing her story, "Marcie is. I'm from Michigan. I ran off when I was sixteen. I went to Chicago for a couple of years but it's too cold if you don't always have a place to stay, so I headed for Florida. I tried Miami for awhile but there's too many coke heads and gangsters. That's when I moved to Daytona and met Marcie. We've been together for almost a year now."

Ty nodded, "Oh, you're a couple. I didn't catch that."

Georgia's eyes narrowed, "Is that a problem?"

"Are you kidding? I agree with both of you. I've never understood why any woman would want to have anything to do with men. I mean, the overwhelming majority of us are hormonal morons. You're in the right place, though, because I have some great man bashing jokes. Do you know what you call a woman who works like a man? "

Georgia asked slyly, "No what?"

"A lazy bitch!"

Georgia's laugh filled the van.

Stan shook his head, "No more jokes, Ty, or I'll have to jump out of the van so Georgia won't stick me."

Ty went on with his inquiry, "I take it you didn't care much for Daytona Beach if you're headed west?"

"It wasn't too bad except during race weeks, then it was a zoo. When Marcie 'came out' to her parents they threw her out. I was workin' this minimum wage shit job. We couldn't live on that so I started dancing again. That's how we got enough to pay for our deposits on the ship. The guy that owned the club I was working at hooked me up with a gig at a club in Reno. I should be able to make enough to get us through."

Ty nodded at Marcie, "Are you a dancer, too?"

Marcie shyly shook her head, "No, I could never get up on a stage, besides no one would ever pay to see me dance."

Georgia held up her hand, "Stop. Anyone can make a drunk drool. It's sure not something I want to do for long but you can make a lot of money pretty fast. Hopefully, Reno will be the last place I ever have to dance. After we get Marcie through school, then she can hold me up while I learn to do something else." Georgia looked directly at Ty, "I bet you don't hang out at strip clubs. I read people pretty good and you look like one of those true blue to the grave kind of guys to me."

"You nailed me. I didn't have a choice. My wife was a heart stopper like you. Besides I live by a strict code. I only disappoint one woman at a time."

"Sorry, man. I didn't mean anything."

"Don't apologize. My wife died in '72. After her I could never find anyone to fill her side of the bed. Ask Stan, Belle is one of my favorite subjects."

"That's cool. You must have really loved her."

Ty smiled widely, "Still do and that is the only thing I know for sure. What about you? What made you run away from Michigan? Not that you need a reason to leave Michigan."

"I grew up in Flint. The whole towns dying. With all the plants closing more than half the people are out of work. My Mom got laid off when I was a baby then my Dad got laid off a little while later. My Mom got strung out and my Dad threw her out. After that he just sat around and drank a lot. He was getting pretty bad and I knew I was gonna get hurt sooner or later, so I split. There's nothing left there for me."

Ty frowned at Georgia, "Don't tell me sad stories. I'll feel guilty every time I tell someone about the gorgeous, exotic dancer I met on the road."

Georgia replied, "It's not sad, it's just life."

Ty asked, "Would you two like to join us for dinner before we drop off the mountain? Stan's Dad is loaded and Stan has his credit card. He loves to use it."

Stan turned and smiled, "It's true."

The women looked at each other and nodded. Georgia answered, "Sounds good to me. We might as well get something out of Stan before he becomes the boss."

Stan stopped at a large log cabin restaurant that was probably a winter hot spot. Judging by the number of cars in the parking lot, the restaurant did a respectable off season business. After the foursome was seated, Stan told them to order whatever they wanted. The four ate and talked like they were long lost friends at a reunion. After dinner, they ordered dessert and coffee and the reunion went on. The restaurant wasn't at full capacity so there was no pressure to vacate their table to waiting patrons.

It was shy Marcie who first looked outside, "Whoa. The suns going down already."

Stan looked at his watch, "It is getting late. We should probably get going."

They were barely back on the road before Marcie spoke up, "You'd think with all that coffee I'd be wide awake, but I'm beat. Would it be alright if I laid down until we get to Salt Lake City?"

Ty waved her off, "You don't need to ask. Make yourself comfortable. We'll be in Salt Lake City in a few hours."

Marcie stretched out and was quickly sound asleep. When Georgia was content Marcie was sleeping, she moved forward and sat cross legged on the floor between Stan and Ty, "Marcie hasn't had a good nights sleep since we left."

Ty spoke quietly, "Looks like you're taking good care of her."

Georgia shrugged, "I'm trying. That asshole in Louisiana really shook her up."

Ty replied, "Although you don't show it I'll bet your heart was pumping."

"No shit. I've been on my own for a long time and I've had to stand up before but I never stabbed anyone. One of my Dad's drunk friends came into my room one night. I grabbed a bat and knocked his snot a block. He was lucky I was only twelve or I might of killed his ass. That dickhead in Louisiana was a fat old salesman type but he was a lot bigger than me. If he had tried to hurt Marcie, I guarantee you he would never have forgot me."

Ty reached back and patted Georgia's shoulder, "Marcie is in good hands. You two stay devoted to each other, you'll do well. I'm glad to hear you want to make a living with your clothes on. There's nothing wrong with dancing but it usually takes place in a rough world."

"Sure does. Most of the girls get into it for the fast money but then they get caught up in the party life. There's a lot of drinking and drugs so a lot of them end up alcoholics or strung out. Some of them even end up hookin'. Most of them think some rich sugar daddy is going to come to rescue them and take them away. I knew this one chick that was doin' it right. She went to college and was bankin' all her cash. She was buyin' an office building downtown. She was pretty cool. The guys that work there are alright. They look after the girls pretty good. It's kind of funny. If the men that go to the strip clubs knew how many of the girls don't even like men, it would blow their minds. It doesn't matter to me. As soon as the blood drains out of a guys head, the money falls out of his wallet. That's all I care about."

Ty snickered, "You're a heartless woman, preying on defenseless men. If you were more philosophical about men you'd see it's all quite logical."

Georgia wrinkled her forehead, "What does logic have to do with men stuffing money in a G-string?"

"They can't help it. None of us can. Look at it this way. Have you ever seen something in nature that just blew you away? Like for me it was the first time I saw the Grand Canyon at sunset. It was beyond words. There are shades and colors they haven't even named yet. It's beyond description. You have to see it to appreciate it. The people working there don't even notice the sunsets after awhile. It's not special to them because they see it every day. The point is people gauge beauty by their emotional response when they see it. There is absolutely nothing in nature that brings about a more intense emotional response to visually oriented men than the sight of the female body. A woman is the only thing in nature a man will never tire of seeing because the female body is, hands down, the most beautiful of nature's creations. Some men may be pigs, but some are just worshipping at the alter."

Georgia tilted her head, "Man, that's beautiful. You really are a romantic."

"Maybe, but I had to defend the penis side of the species. You're probably right though, most men are dickheads."

Georgia smiled, "If there were more guys out there like you maybe I wouldn't have switched teams."

She reached into her shirt pocket and produced a hand rolled cigarette, "Would you guys mind if I smoked a joint?"

Stan turned quickly to look at Georgia and then at Ty. Ty sat forward in his seat, "No problem but why don't we switch seats so you can blow the smoke out the window? If we get Stan busted his parents might ship me off to a high security nursing home."

They switched seats. Ty pulled the ice chest over to sit on, "If I sat like you were, I'd be stuck in that position permanently."

Georgia lit the joint and took a deep lung full. She held it out to Stan, "You want some?"

Stan shook his head, "No thanks, I've only smoked a couple of times. It would only put me to sleep."

Georgia held it out to Ty, "How about you, Ty? You look like one of those old hippie dudes."

Ty declined, "I'm like Stan. I'm a lightweight. I used to smoke a lot but I'm one of those people who zones out and doesn't get anything done."

Georgia took another hit, "This couple that gave us a ride in Arkansas gave me a handful of joints. They only took us fifty miles but the whole way they were smoking it up. They never said anything but I'll bet they were growers. I was blitzed when they let us off. They were cool. I like pot. I won't spend money on it but it's sure better than drinkin. Alcohol makes me stupid, it makes everyone stupid. I like getting stoned before I go on stage. It mellows me out so I can get that 'Do Me' look on my face for the tips."

Ty said, "You don't have to justify yourself to me. There isn't a death certificate anywhere on the planet that says 'Death by Marijuana' unless a bale of it fell on someone. You can't say the same thing about tobacco. It's pretty ironic, something that will definitely kill you is legal while something that won't hurt you, in fact can be medicinal, is illegal. Whenever I hear of them busting a growing operation I can't help but think if there was any common sense they'd be busting an illegal tobacco growing operation."

Georgia hit the joint again, "Right on, man. Why is it illegal anyway?"

Ty answered, "It started as another racist policy. Marijuana became a schedule one narcotic in the 1930's because black musicians and the black culture was using it. It was just another way to step on a minority. Race and drug enforcement have always been tied together. That ridiculous powder law they passed in the eighties is as racist as it gets. Selling rock cocaine will get you sentenced to ten to twenty years more in prison than selling powder cocaine. It's the same thing but in the inner cities, it's sold in rock. That's why the prisons are almost sixty percent black even though less than twenty percent of the population is black. It's bullshit. Especially since it all comes from the same place."

Georgia butted the joint on the outside mirror and slipped the roach into her pocket, "You're right man. I knew these two dancers in Daytona that got popped in some little shit hole out in the Glades. The public defender separated their cases before they went to trial. The blonde bimbo got thirty days suspended and time served. The black chick got a year and a day, so she went to the penitentiary in Tallahassee. That was fucked."

She pointed ahead, "I can see the lights of the big city. We plan on getting through there as quick as we can. I've talked to girls that worked there. They say it's pretty uptight on the outside but underneath they're just as twisted as anywhere else."

Stan pulled into a service station for fuel.

Georgia looked back at Marcie, "Boy she's really out cold."

Back on the road Georgia said to Stan, "You can let us out when you need to turn off."

Stan replied, "There really isn't anything we need to see in Idaho so I'll tell you what. If you guys will keep me awake, we could drive straight through to Reno. That's another place I've never seen."

Georgia was floored. She looked at Stan, at smiling Ty and back to Stan, "Are you for real. That's hell and gone out of your way."

Ty chimed in, "Stan's driving. It's sure okay with me."

Georgia slapped Stan's leg, "Stan man! That would be awesome."

They dropped into the city and followed the freeway through town. They were on the western outskirts of town when Ty said to Georgia, "If you'll keep Stan awake, I'll get some sleep and relieve you in awhile."

Georgia replied, "No sweat. I'm not tired at all. I'll talk poor Stan's ear off."

Ty pointed at Marcie, "If I lay down back there, she won't wake up and kick my ass, will she?"

Georgia slapped Ty on the arm, "Don't worry, I'll protect you big guy. Catch some Z's. We'll be right here."

Ty carefully climbed onto the bed, as close to the wall as he could so he wouldn't disturb Marcie.

Georgia looked to Stan, "You sure you're up to this?"

Stan smiled, "No problem."

Georgia settled back in the seat, "Man, it's still hotter than hell. I think your air conditioner is broke."

"Ty calls it a TWD-60 air conditioner. Two windows down and sixty miles an hour. The problem is the van tries to self destruct at anything past fifty five."

Georgia put her feet on the dash, "This is so cool of you. I wasn't looking forward to sleeping in the desert. There's too many poisonous creepy crawlies out there." She paused, "Stan, tell me if I put you off. I've been told I shock some people but I don't see any reason to hide shit or to soft soap it. It is what it is. I know I've never hurt anyone that didn't deserve it. I've always just did what I had to do. I'm not ashamed of nothing'."

"You might be one of the more balanced people I've ever met, Georgia. How do you hang onto it? It sounds like your childhood was pretty tough."

"Everybody's childhood is tough. They're all just different. You might have been raised with all sorts of money but I'll bet you're dragging around all kinds of baggage. I went with this guy in Miami for awhile. His family had big bucks but he was all fucked up. He lied to his parents about everything he did in his life. He sure never told them he was going out with me. They would have shit. He was a nice enough guy, he just didn't have a clue about how to live his own life. When I broke it off he screamed like a wild man. He kept yelling about how I wasn't ever gonna find anyone that could give me everything he could. Money was all the guy knew. He figured if he gave me a new necklace, it was okay for me to hide in the closet if someone in his family came by." She looked over at Stan, "You seem to have come through your childhood pretty much intact. How'd you swing that?"

"I'm not sure I have. I'm twenty one years old and my whole life is right out of my Dad's script. I know I've had opportunities most people will never have. When I hear your life story I feel petty even thinking I've got problems. I'm another sniveling rich kid who resents the expectations."

"I'm not buying that shit at all, Stan. You think money is the answer, too. Just because you got money your problems aren't real. Your pressure is real, it's just different. Listen man, if one guy gets his old Chevy stolen in Michigan and another gets his Ferrari stolen in Beverly Hills, it still hurts. One guy's pain just costs more."

"Well, just the same I'd rather hear about you. My story is pretty typical. You mentioned dating a guy in Miami, so you haven't always been into women?"

"No. In fact Marcie is only the second woman I've ever been with. I'm probably more bi than gay. Some people say they've always known, but not me. Marcie always knew. I think that's why she's so shy. She's been pushing it down for a long time. I never even thought about it until I met this one chick. We were really good friends, which is something I've never had with a guy. The physical stuff just kind of happened but that wasn't what it was about anyway. It was cool to wrap up the emotional and physical stuff in one person. With guys it was always wrapped up in the sex. Marcie needs me. I like that."

"Have you ever been in love with a guy?"

"I don't think so. I'm not sure about love, anyway. The way I feel about Marcie is probably as close as I've been. It sure feels right. With guys it's always been about sex first, so maybe I never gave it enough time. When I was fourteen I had this huge crush on this guy down the street. He was seventeen and I thought he was a rock star. He took my virginity and then he avoided me like the plague. I was floored. Finally, I went to his house to beg him to tell me what I did wrong. He was real friendly and he took me up to his room. His buddy was there and they both started sweet talkin' me. Can you believe that shit? Here I am this lovesick puppy and these two assholes are trying to get me to do them both. I started crying and tried to leave. His buddy blocked the door so I fucking hammered him. If my brother had been around those guys would have been dog meat."

"Where was your brother?"

"He enlisted in the Army in high school. He was in Afghanistan when that shit came down. He was my hero growin' up. Man, if it hadn't been for him I don't think I would of made it, especially after Mom left."

"Where is he now?"

"He lives in a group home in Virginia. He got hurt pretty bad and it really messed with his head. He's all zoned out on morphine now. I went to see him but it seems like he's not even in there anymore. He got a raw deal and it took him out." Georgia paused, "What about you, Stan? You got any dysfunctional brothers and sisters?"

"No, I'm an only child."

Georgia frowned, "Bummer. So all the shit came down on you. I feel sorry for you. That's a lot of pressure for one kid."

Stan turned to see if Georgia was being sarcastic. He couldn't begin to envision someone who had lived tragedy like Georgia feeling pity for someone who had grown up fabulously wealthy.

There was no hint of sarcasm as Georgia calmly asked, "Is there a love story in your life? Is there a future Mrs. Stan out there?"

"I'm afraid not. A couple of years ago there was a girl, Hannah. My Dad hated her and it finally got between us. I don't even know where she is now. Maybe you'll run into her in Monterey. She was going to be a Marine Biologist."

"It won't do you any good for me to run into her. Tell you what. I'll give you a call if I see her. You look like you're not sure if you did the right thing. You think you still love her?"

"Maybe, I don't know. I still think about her a lot."

"Well, it's only a mistake if you don't do anything about it. Life's too short. You should look her up. You need to be sure about it, like Ty back there. It sure isn't up in the air if he was in love."

"No doubt. It's been over thirty years and he's still head over heels. The other night he got a little drunk and started thinking about Grandma. He got pretty emotional. All the same, I'd sure like to feel that way about someone some day."

"You'll find it Stan man. You're like Ty, you're all heart. Who else would go a thousand miles out of their way for two people they just met."

"It's not that far out of the way. Besides I'm not in that much of a hurry to get home."

"Man, it's still hotter than hell." Georgia unbuttoned her shirt and hung it on the back of the seat. Her white sleeveless undershirt was form fitting, showcasing her ample assets even in the dimness of the dashboard lights. It was difficult for Stan to stop himself from sneaking a peek, let alone from staring.

Georgia grinned when she noticed Stan sneaking a glance, "You don't mind do you?"

Stan turned purposely and with great restraint, managed to look only at Georgia's eyes, "No problem."

Georgia chuckled, "Good discipline, Stan. Most guys don't even know I have a face, but that's what makes them money makers. I always thought big tits were a curse. I started developing at thirteen. Must be the Polish blood. I went out with this guy in Chicago. He was this big macho dude, but when we were alone he was zeroed in on me. I think he had mommy issues. When I broke it off he went nuts. He beat the shit out of me, broke my jaw and some ribs. You should have seen me, both my eyes were almost swollen shut. I looked like 'The Fly'. Man, I thought he was going to kill me. I guess I just attract dickheads. That's why I've always been careful to stay away from the guys in the clubs. Most of them are just frustrated married guys but there are some real freaks out there, too. You have to keep tellin' yourself you're only there for the money. One time I was giving this preppy jock type guy a lap dance and he kept grabbing me. I kept pushin' his hands away and tellin' him he wasn't allowed to touch me but he wouldn't stop. Finally I got pissed and I clocked him. Knocked his ass right off the chair. The bouncers roughed him up real good before they threw him out. They took all his money and gave it to me. You didn't have to mess around with the bouncers to get them to take care of you but a lot of the girls did anyway." She paused, "We keep slipping into my sordid history. Tell me about you. Tell me about Hannah."

"There's not much to say about me. I'm the good son. I've done everything I was supposed to. I went to a private prep school. I just graduated from the University of Washington and in the fall I'm going to Harvard. I'll most likely end up being an investment banker like my Dad and his Dad. I'm the poster boy for legacy and entitlement. I'm not much of a rebel so all I had to do was the work and then it was easy. Pretty boring, huh?"

"I don't know about the boring part but you tell your story like you're reading a grocery list. Did you like your childhood? You haven't even mentioned your Mom."

"My childhood was alright. I guess I'm kind of like my Mom. We're both a little scared of my Dad. He's an intimidating guy and he dominates everyone around him. As long as I stay on message he mostly ignores me except for when he's lecturing about my future. Mom's life is all about social events. They're more like business partners than a married couple. They were probably in love at one time but I don't know if they still are."

Georgia grinned and shook her head, "You poor fuck. You don't know the shit you're carrying around is really baggage. At least the stuff in my life was right in my face. You either deal with it or it kicks your ass. Everything in your life is hidden in the shadows. I'd rather see it comin'. I'll bet Hannah was poor like me. That's why your Dad didn't like her."

"You're right. I never brought Hannah home. I did everything I could to keep her a secret but he found out anyway. Dad has spies everywhere. I never got away with anything."

"Did you meet Hannah in college?"

"Yeah. Hannah was working her way through school. She was the first one in her family to go to college. She knew exactly what she wanted and she wanted everything. It was infectious. She made me feel like I was completely alive. Hannah has been the exciting chapter in my life so far. You would have liked her, almost everyone did." Stan stopped for a reflective moment, "The day she walked away I thought I was going to die. I thought my heart was going to simply stop beating. At the time I almost wished it would." Stan snapped back to the present, shyly glancing at Georgia, "Sorry, I usually don't talk much about her."

"Don't apologize for having feelings. It's people without them that are fuckin' everything up. You're a romantic like Ty. Hang on to that. That's pretty cool that Hannah was puttin' herself through school. Maybe I'll go back to school someday."

"If you did what do you think you would like to study?"

"I don't know. I would have to get a GED first. I quit school when I split from Flint. I wasn't goin' to school much anyway."

"What made you run away?"

"I just had enough, you know. The town was depressing enough but I was dealing with that okay. One night my Dad climbed into bed with me. He was always drunk but he had never tried anything like that before. I got the hell out of there. You should of seen it, man, its November and it's colder than hell. Here I am out in the alley, barefooted, in a damn T-shirt waitin' for my Dad to pass out. When he went down I grabbed some clothes, all the money I could find and split. I could handle being his maid but I wasn't goin' to be his whore. I've never been back. I call every once and awhile to see if he is still alive but I hang up as soon as he answers. There's nothing for me there anymore." Georgia reached for her shirt on the seat back and retrieved the roach from her pocket. She held it up, "Mind if I finish this?"

"Go for it."

Georgia lit the roach just as Ty stuck his head between the seats, "How're you two doing?"

Stan glanced at Ty, "Great. We're in Nevada now. One more fuel stop and we will be in Reno before you know it."

Marcie's voice broke in from the back, "Where are we? Did I hear you say Nevada?"

Georgia released a lung full of smoke, "Hey sleepy head. You were really out. Yeah, we're in Nevada."

Marcie was really confused, "I thought you guys were going to Seattle?"

Stan replied, "We are as soon as we drop you off in Reno."

Marcie was now stunned and confused, "Wow! I can't believe you would do that."

Stan smiled, "That's what friends are for."

Ty beamed, "I told you he was something." Ty leaned forward so that Georgia could tell he was looking at her, "I want to know how Stan kept his eyes on the road. You're quite a distraction, woman."

Georgia laughed, "You would've been proud of him, Ty. Stan was the perfect gentleman. He did sneak a couple of peeks but he might as well see them before they become BLT's."

Stan purposely looked as he asked, "What are BLT's?"

"Belt length tits."

Stan laughed, Ty roared. Georgia went on, "I always felt sorry for the older dancers that were stacked. It don't matter how hard you exercise, eventually gravity wins and if you got big tits they head south. The older women that keep dancing end up working in some real dives."

Ty added, "I'm sorry I'm not the gentleman Stan is, but you're pretty spectacular lady."

Georgia took a final hit before letting the tiny roach go in the wind, "If you hang around Reno you can catch my farewell tour."

Ty whistled, "I don't think so. I've got a weak heart and the sight of you might take me out."

Stan took an exit on the outskirts of Elko to get fuel. Ty turned around to Marcie, "Do you think you could drive this old heap? We could let these two get some sleep."

Marcie nodded, "Sure. I've never driven a column shift before but I'm sure I can do it."

After they got fuel, Marcie and Ty took the front seats. Stan and Georgia climbed into the back. Marcie killed the engine twice before they got rolling toward the freeway. Georgia stretched out and closed her eyes. Stan laid down trying to suppress the urge to sneak one more look at Georgia before closing his eyes.

With her eyes closed Georgia said, "Night, Stan."

"Goodnight, Georgia. Thanks for keeping me company."

Ty had little success getting Marcie to open up. She was beyond shy. Marcie was terrified at the idea someone might see into her thoughts. Ty realized the quality quickly and entertained Marcie with frivolous, silly stories. He still managed to pull an occasional giggle past her shy defenses.

It was the lack of motion that woke Stan. Georgia was still sleeping. It was daylight. Ty turned around, "Feel better?"

Stan yawned, "Yeah, I feel good. Where are we?"

Ty made a sweeping motion with his hand, "Beautiful downtown Reno. Can you believe it? We found another Denny's. Why don't you wake up Georgia and we'll have some breakfast?"

Stan reached gingerly and shook Georgia, "Wake up. We're here. Let's go eat breakfast."

Georgia rolled over rubbing her eyes, "That sounds good." She slowly sat up and swung her feet to the floor. She smiled at Stan, "Do you think your Dad will buy us one more meal?"

Ty interrupted, "Hell woman, if he ever saw you he'd buy you a car. Let's go eat."

The foursome went inside and just like the previous evening, they lost all track of time. Stan picked up the check when the waitress began looking anxious about their tying up the table.

Ty stood up, "Sorry Stan, but you're going to have to get the tip, too. I'm going to the bank across the street. I hate being penniless. I'll meet you at the van in a couple of minutes." Ty pointed at Georgia and Marcie, "Don't you two take off before I have a chance to say goodbye. Do you hear me?"

Stan and the two women were standing next to the van with their packs leaned up next to the door when Ty came limping back from the bank.

Marcie pointed down the street, "Showgirls is two blocks that way. We saw it when we drove through town."

Georgia looked at Stan, "This must be the place. Really Stan, I can't thank you enough for the ride. You have been a lifesaver."

Stan shook her off, "It was an absolute pleasure." He reached into his pocket for a business card. He wrote his phone number on the back and handed it to Georgia, "If you ever need anything, call me." He smiled broadly, "Even if you don't need anything."

Georgia took the card and put it in her back pocket, "We'll keep in touch. If I run into Hannah I'll give you a buzz." She turned and gave Ty a hug, "You take care of yourself, big guy."

Ty lingered with his gaze, "See you again, brown eyes."

Georgia smiled, "You're too much." She turned to face Stan, "Take care of this guy, Ty." She took a step towards Stan, then stopped just in front of him. Georgia burst into a huge smile as she pulled her shirt up to her neck before she grabbed Stan and hugged him tight. When she released Stan, she stepped back and deliberately pulled her shirt down slowly so the stunned and speechless Stan could take it in. She looked directly into his eyes, "Take care of yourself, Stan man. Don't repeat your mistakes."

Stan returned the smile,"I promise."

Georgia and **Marcie** put on their backpacks, Marcie added a meek goodbye before they walked away towards Showgirls. Neither of the women looked back but Stan didn't take his eyes off them until they were a block away.

Stan finally looked at Ty who was intently watching him, "You ready to roll, old man?"

Ty nodded, "Sure. She's really something, isn't she?"

Stan looked after the women one more time before heading for the driver's side, "She sure is."

# Chapter (11)

They drove north to hook back up with the freeway. Ty was content to let Stan quietly reflect. Without a glance Stan said, "I don't think I've ever met anyone like Georgia. There's no lies, no judgment, no shame. Everything with her is right up front. She's so honest she had me talking about things I don't normally talk about. She was an experience." Stan flashed a quick smile, "And that was, hands down, the best hug I've ever had."

Ty burst out laughing, "I didn't think you would ever blink again."

Stan added, "I do hope she calls. I'd like to know they're okay."

Ty was still grinning, "You'd better be careful, Stan. You could turn into a people person. I told you, there are a whole lot more of the good people around. You're right about Georgia, she is a powerhouse. Most people who were dealt cards like hers would have folded. You don't learn life lessons like hers' in sociology class. We'd all be slaves by now if it weren't for people like Georgia. You can't lock up that kind of spirit. You surprised me when you stopped to pick them up. What made you stop?"

"I don't know. I just saw them and I was on the shoulder before I really thought about it."

"I'm proud of you, Stan. See what can happen when you hold your hand out to someone?"

Stan stopped to get fuel before they got onto the freeway. He began unfolding a road map when he returned to the van, "I figured we better find the best route since we're so far south from where we should be."

Ty shrugged, "We don't need a map. It's easy. We go north on 395 until we get to the Willamette Highway in Oregon. Then turn left. If we hit water we've gone too far."

Stan continued to study the map, "It looks like it might be quicker to cut across at Susanville and pick up I-5 at Mt. Shasta."

"Maybe, but wouldn't you prefer to stay off the freeway as long as we can? It's a lot more scenic the other way. We'll go right by Crater Lake. Have you ever seen Crater Lake?"

"No, I haven't."

"Cool. Besides I have a good friend in Klamath Falls who would probably put us up and we can take some showers. I can call him from Alturas."

Stan folded the map, "Your plan is better than no plan."

Stan pointed Brutus north at fifty five miles per hour. He was surprised by the 'Welcome to California' sign they passed not twenty miles north of Reno. He didn't realize Reno was a border town. The four lane freeway was reduced to a two lane highway just a few miles into California. The traffic was heavy in both directions and everybody was in a hurry. The oncoming southbound vehicles were full of hopeful gamblers racing to enjoy the slot machines and free buffets while the northbound travelers were fleeing the realization that high rise casinos are not built on the proceeds of winning gamblers. Stan methodically watched the rear view mirrors so he could be prepared to use the pullouts and passing lanes to allow the fleeing cars and trucks to pass the much slower Brutus.

Ty interrupted Stan's concentration, "You should cross the country a few times. Next time you should try the northern or southern route. The difference in the people you meet is mind boggling. There are places in the Deep South that are like foreign countries. Texas is a world of its own. You can literally find people in the South who don't accept the Confederacy lost the Civil War or even that it's actually over. Isn't that wild? There are real people who refuse to see the evil of slavery. Can you even get your head around what it must have felt like to be subjected to slavery? I used to try to imagine what someone like Dred Scott could have been thinking and feeling when the Supreme Court handed down the Dred Scott Decision. How could you possibly pacify yourself when the highest court in the land legally classifies you as three fifths of a man? Is that not one of the most insane things you've ever heard? I've got one for you, Stan. Quiery. Slaves gave their labor to their owners because they had no choice. Wage slaves choose to give their labor to the owners for worthless scraps of paper. Who's the fool?"

"I'm not going to try to justify slavery but don't you think there's a lot of blame to go around? America was not the first or only society to use slave labor."

"Stan, I can't accept the defense, 'They did it too' for anything. You still need a qualifier for your premise. History dramatically perverts the definition of slavery. A lot of cultures include indentured servitude as slavery but those people were simply paying off debts. They aren't much different than the wage slaves of today. Slaves didn't get a choice and they never paid off their debt. Everyday people, didn't own slaves. Only the rich and powerful felt the need to own other human beings."

Stan shook his head, "You have an uncanny ability to tie most anything in a neat little package and drop it on the rich, ruling class. Do you honestly believe there is an elite Capitalist ruling class conspiracy?"

There was no hesitation with Ty's response, "I might not characterize all elitists as conspirators but in answer to a Capitalist conspiracy my answer is a resounding yes! I don't believe everyone in business is clandestinely meeting to plot world control but there is no doubt Capitalism is the engine propelling a select few up the ponzi pyramid. The names and players may change but the game remains the same. For the past few centuries, Capitalism has been the vehicle for consolidating wealth. Think about it. Whenever a kingdom or an empire falls, there is no transfer of power and wealth to the people. Power vacuums are immediately filled. Since the beginning of written civilization there have been men and women who spent every minute of their entire lives either in power or in the pursuit of power. The best and the brightest of every generation, for six thousand years, have spent every second scheming and struggling for power. The game has never paused, not even for an instant. Kings, Queens and Emperors had their time. Conquerors had theirs. The Catholic Church was the dominant power for sixteen hundred years. The power game did not end with Capitalism. Capitalism is the evolutionary product of six thousand years of power struggles. Try to find a text book telling a story of the struggle for power ending because Capitalism perfected the human experience. It's merely the latest tool of control. Capitalism is about assigning a value to everything and everyone and controlling that value. .Everything in the world is valued in currency. In this country it's dollars. Dollars have an assigned value but no actual value. Why do you think the elite shelter trillions of dollars in endowment funds and tax exempt foundations? There is no profit to be made there but they have more dollars than they could possibly spend or invest. Yale's endowment is thirty billion dollars. Harvard's is twenty seven billion. Count the colleges and universities and do the math. The tax exempt think tanks and foundations number in the hundreds. The Rand Institute, Alpine Institute, Carnegie Foundation, Heritage Foundation, Council on Foreign Relations, The Tri Lateral Commission. The list goes on and on but there is no way to assess the wealth sheltered there. All these institutions are in a never ending search for the best and brightest to join in the quest of plotting the course for human kind. The overwhelming majority of public policies are rooted in policy papers from these omnipotent institutions. Nowadays not only do the ruling elite control the money, they control the message. Ninety five percent of the media on Earth is now owned by five mega corporations. Some media outfits are huge financial losers. The Washington Times loses seven hundred million dollars a year. It's no accident the majority of the population has no idea what is being done to them. The media reminds us daily of the virtue and need for our rulers. Did you know over half of all reported news is not news at all? They're press releases. In Washington D.C. there are hundreds, possibly thousands by now, of public relations firms. These firms can package, spin and sell whatever image they want to be known. Burston-Marsteller handled the media image for Dow Chemical after their plant in Bhopal, India killed seventy thousand people. That tragic disaster is still referred to as an accident and there has never been any restitution to the victim's families. Think tanks create policy and the media sells it. I've got another one for you and this one is really hard to think about because the implications are so horrendous. It was in 1974 or 75 after the oil crisis. Henry Kissinger presented to the Council on Foreign Relations a position about the natural resources of Africa. He stated that the biggest obstacle to utilizing the resources of the African continent were the people of Africa, there are simply too many of them. Kissinger said ideally the population should be reduced by half a billion people so they wouldn't use up their own resources. Now replay the past thirty five years with an adding machine. Count the deaths in Uganda, Ethiopia, Sudan, South Africa, Rwanda, Darfur, the Congo and on and on. Then add up the number of people who have died and are dying from treatable diseases. In addition, the largest Aids epidemic on the planet is in Africa but it is the most difficult place to get treatment. Religious blockades stop these poor people from even getting condoms to prevent further spreading of the virus. There are over a hundred million people who are going to die of Aids in Africa. Add up all the numbers and we are quite possibly watching, in real time, the largest genocide in human history. Don't think for a minute genocide can't be suppressed, ask an Armenian. The Armenian genocide killed over a million people and it has been denied for almost a hundred years. Don't get me wrong, Kissinger isn't personally responsible for Africa but no worry, he's got at least ten million deaths in South East Asia on his tab. People like him don't personally kill people. They simply direct policies and strategies making it inevitable."

Stan jumped in, "Whoa! Time out! Holy shit, Ty! It scares the hell out of me you even think that way. I know there are bad people in the world but I can't believe how cynical you are about them. You can't hang all the evil on Capitalism."

Ty looked solemnly at the floorboards, "Sorry, Stan. Like I said, I get angry when I think about helpless people in hopeless situations. You don't think this is only a third world problem do you? Grab your adding machine, step back and take a broad view of what happened in New Orleans after Hurricane Katrina. Before the hurricane there were six hundred thousand people in New Orleans. After Katrina, four hundred thousand residents, mostly poor African Americans were not allowed an opportunity to return. They actually bulldozed forty six hundred low income buildings that were never flooded. Those pictures didn't make the six o'clock news. The media and the pundits can spin it anyway they want, the numbers don't lie. Adding to the tragedy is the fact it happened in broad daylight in front of the world but the stories of the majority were never told."

"Don't you think there are any good people in business, Ty?"

"Sure, I think you're going to be one of them Stan. The world needs people like you. You have the opportunity to assume great power and authority but you have heart, logic and compassion. I think you could achieve great things but on the other hand it wouldn't break my heart to see you turn your back and just save yourself. Hell, I'll drive the getaway car."

"I appreciate your encouragement but I think I'll start small and maybe branch out later. Is that okay?"

"Good plan, Stan. Sorry I get a little dark sometimes. There are just so many things I can't wrap my head around. I can't find any spark of logic in things like terminator seeds or nuclear weapons. How about these uranium munitions they're poisoning Iraq with. It's completely insane. The people who made that decision should be stripped naked and dropped in down town Baghdad with a sign strapped to their backs saying 'Which way to the Virgins'. I think we should take politicians, immediately upon leaving office, and put them in prison for the same amount of time they served in office. Then we'd be even."

"It might be a little hard to retain good people with a policy like that."

"We can't find good people now, so who would notice."

Stan slowed down to twenty five as they entered Alturas. He surveyed the buildings as they drove down the main street, "Boy, there are sure a lot of boarded up buildings. It looks like a ghost town in the making."

"It's a snapshot of the new middle America."

Stan pulled into a service station. Ty got out of the van, "Stan, do you have a long distance card? I don't want to feed a pound of change into the phone."

Stan pulled out his wallet and handed a card to Ty, "Just dial the number on the back of the card. The prompt on the phone will ask for the authorization number on the other side of the card. Then just dial the area code and number, nothing to it."

Ty looked at the card, turning it over in his hand. He smiled at Stan, "No doubt about it. Technology has totally simplified life. You know the last phone I had I picked up and told the operator,' Berta, get me Wesley'." Ty turned and limped away shaking his head.

Stan parked next to the phone booth after fueling the van. Ty's conversation took quite awhile before he hung up and returned to the van, "We're all set. Sorry it took so long, but if you miss one digit your call ends up in some foreign country and I don't speak Mandarin."

"Very funny. Did you get good directions?"

"Yeah, it's before Klamath Falls. We're supposed to watch for his sign on the highway, 'Artifact Imports LLC'. He said we can't miss it. We're supposed to be hungry, too. He's making dinner."

"What does he import?"

"You'll have to ask him. I don't know. I met Darnell when he was a teacher, before he became a lawyer. We stay in contact but I haven't seen him in awhile. I've never been to this house."

They spotted the sign easily. Stan turned onto the dirt road leading to his house which could be seen a half a mile from the highway. Being still in the high desert of the Great Basin, the terrain was flat with nothing but sagebrush in every direction. The van and the trailer raised a billowing dust cloud forcing Stan to slow to a crawl. Stan was surprised at the size of the house. It was a two story wood structure, easily eighty feet across the front side. A porch appeared to wrap around the entire house. The front door swung open as they were getting out of the van. Stan was momentarily stunned. Marching towards them, smiling from ear to ear was the biggest Native American Stan had ever seen. The man was easily six foot six and had to weigh three hundred pounds. His long black hair was pulled back into a ponytail. He was wearing blue jeans, cowboy boots and a jacket made in an Indian blanket pattern. He was headed, quickly for a big man, directly at Ty.

Ty made no attempt to extend his hand for a shake. The big man swept Ty up into a bear hug and swung him around, "Man, it's good to see you!" He sat Ty down, "I'm surprised to see the van still running. I'm shocked to see you still going."

The big man turned to face Stan. He extended his hand, which was easily twice the size of Stan's. In a gentle voice he said, "You must be Stan. It's an absolute pleasure to meet you. I'm Darnell Yellow Feather."

Stan took Darnell's massive hand as he looked up into eyes as gentle as his voice, "The pleasure is all mine, sir."

Darnell released Stan's hand and added with a huge smile, "You call me sir and we won't be friends for very long. Come on in."

Stan and Ty stopped once inside. The house was one great room with a loft at either end of the house. The lofts were connected by a railed walkway across the back wall. The effect was one of wide open space.

Ty whistled, "Wow! This is pretty amazing Darnell. How long have you lived here?"

"I built it to entice my wife to live out here in the middle of nowhere with me."

Ty looked quickly at Darnell, "Are you married again?"

Darnell grinned and shook his head, "No. She liked the house but she didn't like me. I kept it just to spite her." He took off the Indian blanket jacket and hung it on the wall hook next to the front door, "I have to get out of this thing. I wore it just to give Stan the whole effect. If you guys want to hit the shower, help yourself. There's one upstairs and one downstairs but you don't want to run them both at the same time. The guy downstairs will get all the hot water."

Ty motioned to Stan, "You can take the first shower while Darnell and I catch up."

Stan took a long, leisurely shower. When he returned, Ty was sitting on a bar stool at the breakfast bar watching Darnell fix dinner. Stan sat on a stool next to Ty, "Sorry I took so long but that felt great."

Ty stood up, "I guess I'm up. I'll be back in a few."

Darnell asked, "Do you want a garbage bag to wrap your cast?"

Ty held up his hand, "No thanks. I'm hoping it will fall off."

Darnell looked at Stan, "It's pretty informal here. If you want something just help yourself. I haven't shopped in a few days but there should be something to drink in the fridge. If you dig deep enough you might even find a beer in there."

Darnell continued chopping veggies for the salad while Stan got an iced tea from the fridge. Darnell kept working as he spoke, "Ty tells me you're going to Harvard business in the fall. That's pretty impressive. Ty sounds like a proud Papa. He can't stop bragging about you."

Stan answered shyly, "My Dad had more to do with me getting into Harvard than I did."

"Don't downplay your accomplishments. Your Dad might open a few doors but if you walk out with the paper it's because you did the work. You only get a diploma in the mail if you're a Rockefeller or a Bush and their daddy's have to add a wing to the schools library."

Stan walked over to the book shelves lining the back wall, "I see you like the left wing stuff like Ty."

Darnell glanced at the shelf Stan was browsing, "Being a Native American naturally leads you to the seat of power. That's where the story started and that's where it still is. Have you ever read any of those books?"

"A few. For Poly Sci I read 'Blowback' by Chalmers Johnston and 'Nation in Crisis' by John Done. It looks like you have everything they've ever written."

"I probably do."

Stan looked at the next bookshelf containing law books, "Ty says you're a lawyer. Do you still maintain a practice?"

"I'm still licensed but I don't maintain a practice. There's a couple of people I handle legal matters for but that's it. It was actually Ty and Belle who talked me into going to law school. I was teaching at Evergreen with Ty when they convinced me to take advantage of all the grant money available to me. Personally, I think Belle wanted a lawyer for the army she was building to save the world."

"What kind of law did you practice?"

"Mostly contract law. I had this grand vision I would get my people the restitution they were promised in all the treaties. It didn't take long to pop that bubble."

"So you represented tribal interests?"

"I did for a few years but I got totally disillusioned. The government never met a treaty they couldn't break and, besides, my people didn't want to be helped."

"Fighting government always seems to be a frustrating job."

"No shit. I was like most people. I thought the law and the government for that matter, was about right and wrong. They are about one thing and one thing only, process. Government is so mired in process they're totally impotent. It's probably just as well because the people in government are completely beholden to the special interests funding them. We certainly get what they pay for. As far as the tribe is concerned, I'm sorry to say they're too many generations removed from the original struggles. There are still people concerned with the heritage but for the most part it's a welfare state and the majority of the people are content with that. You can't help someone who doesn't want help." Darnell opened the oven, "I think we're almost ready. Are you ready for an authentic ethnic meal?"

Stan nodded, "You bet. What are you making?"

Darnell removed the pan from the oven and innocently replied, "Lasagna."

Ty returned from his shower, "It smells great, Darnell. Do you need any help?"

Darnell motioned to the wine rack, "Why don't you open a bottle while I set everything out. We'll have to eat at the bar, my Ex got the table." He laid out the food and utensils, then moved a bar stool to the other side of the bar facing Stan and Ty, "Help yourself, there's plenty. If you don't see it, I probably don't have it."

They served themselves and dug in. Stan grunted, "Darnell, this is the best native lasagna I've ever had."

Ty's forehead wrinkled as he looked quizzically at Stan but he continued eating.

Stan's eyes bounced back and forth between Ty and Darnell while he ate. Darnell grinned at Stan, "You're trying to figure out our story, aren't you? It's probably not what you think. We weren't two crazy hippies who occupied buildings and dropped acid with Timothy Leary. All young man are crazy just in different ways. If you want crazy it would have to be when Ty and Belle went to Alaska. Nobody works long enough to get tenure just to quit as soon as they get it. That totally blew me away. Those two always danced to their own music." Darnell looked earnestly at Stan, "It's a shame you didn't get to meet Belle, she was really something. She wanted to save everyone but the only one she saved for sure was this old guy here." He smiled at Ty, "Except when she bought him that stupid motorcycle. Everyone who knew Ty figured he was going to die on that thing. Every time I saw him he was bandaged up or he had a cast on some part of his body. He hit everything in sight." Darnell paused. His eyes opened wide. He leaned back and pointed at Ty's cast, "Don't tell me?"

Ty hung his head and nodded slowly.

Darnell slapped his leg and burst out in laughter, "You are a diehard, man. Belle was the only one on the planet who believed you would survive that motorcycle." Darnell pushed his plate away, "When you're done, let's go out on the porch where it's a little cooler."

Ty held up the bottle of wine, "Do you want more?"

Darnell shook his head, "No thanks. Help yourself but go slow. You might be the only guy around who drinks worse than me and you're not even Indian."

Ty held the bottle out to Stan who also declined.

Darnell was watching Stan, "Looks like Stan has already seen a patented Ty alcohol meltdown. Did Ty tell you what we did one night while drinking at Bahama Mama's?"

Stan grinned at Ty, "No. I think he might have skipped that story."

Darnell went on, "Actually we were being good. All we were doing was having a few beers and shooting pool when this guy came up and put a quarter down to challenge the table. It wouldn't have been any big deal but this guy was obnoxious as hell. On top of that he was incredibly arrogant. We really did try to ignore his attitude but eventually the guy went off on Ty. He started bitching about pool etiquette and rules. Ty was cool. He looked at me and we both grabbed hold of the moron and not so gingerly escorted him to the door. I already had a few beers in me which woke up my inner Indian so I added a little momentum to the guy's exit. Anyway, the guy rolled across the parking lot and we went back inside to shoot pool. The bartender was frantic. He kept on saying, over and over, 'You can't do that.' Ty told the bartender the guy was an asshole and the bartender said, 'Maybe, but he's the owner.' That was the last time we went to Bahama Mama's."

Darnell picked up the empty plates, putting them in the sink, "Why don't you guys go outside while I clean up. I'll join you."

Stan and Ty seated themselves on the wooden rockers on the porch. The sun had just slipped behind the peaks of the Sierra Nevada Mountains. It was totally calm but there was a strange sound coming from every direction. Stan inquired, "What is that noise?"

"They're June Bugs. They live in the sagebrush. Don't worry they go silent after dark. Soon it will just be desert sounds, crickets and coyotes."

Darnell came onto the porch carrying a three foot long peace pipe. Stan pointed at it, "Is that one of your artifacts?"

Ty answered, "No, that one is real." He looked quizzically at Darnell, "Same one?"

Darnell smiled, "You bet your ass it's the same one. Are you up for it?"

Ty's gaze lingered on the pipe, "I don't know, man. It's been a long time."

Darnell looked at Stan, "It really is an authentic peace pipe. My Father gave it to me. I have no idea how many generations it goes back, but I'll bet I'm the first generation to smoke pot in it. The idea is still the same." Darnell lit the bowl and took a deep draw. He held it out to Ty who hesitated. Still holding the smoke in his lungs, Darnell said, "You better fucker, it took me an hour to clean this thing."

Ty took the pipe and looked at Stan, "My boy, you are about to hear the word spoken around the country in the sixties. 'Ere'." Ty lit the bowl and took a hit. He handed it Stan and said, "Ere."

Ty lost the smoke in his lungs as he and Darnell exploded into laughter. Stan shook his head as he took the pipe from Ty.

Stan took a small pull from the pipe and held it out to Darnell, "Ere."

The pipe made three more rounds before Darnell set it aside, "You guys good?"

They both nodded with an herbally enhanced grin.

Darnell asked, "So Ty, why are you going back to Washington?"

"Well, you know Emma. Even without a phone she was nagging me to move closer so she can keep an eye on me. She's a worrier, always was. That's alright, though. It gave me a chance to spend some time with Stan. I like that. What about you? What are you doing out here in the sticks? I figured you'd end up back at Pyramid Lake."

Darnell shrugged, "Moving back was always one of those 'some day' things I never got around to. When I went back after law school, they pissed me off so bad. I guess I'm still not over it. I'm kind of embarrassed about what I'm doing now. You saw the sign."

Ty looked confused, "Why? Are you doing something illegal or just stupid?"

"Nothing like that. I import native artifacts. They sell in gift shops on the reservations. I sell to the tribes under a contract with the Department of the Interior. Shit Ty! I sell authentic looking trinkets made in Indonesia. I'm exploiting my own people. Philosophically, I can't decide if I'm an opportunist or if I'm just ironic."

"Ask Stan, our resident economist. If the market wants artifacts it will get artifacts. Someone is going to cash in. It might as well be you. We all joined the game to some degree or another."

Darnell nodded, "I guess you're right. I was afraid you'd give me shit about it. Belle would have kicked my ass." Darnell looked to Stan, "She was viscous when she thought she was right. You should have heard her and Ty fight. If you didn't know them you'd swear they hated each other. She was ruthless when she thought Ty wasn't thinking for himself. She wouldn't accept anything but free thinking from Ty. She was right. You can't have freedom without imagination and there is no imagination without free will. We were all too idealistic back then. We'd get stoned and argue about shit but it was important shit: Vietnam, Nixon, oil, nukes, racism. It was great! That's how you solve things. People with different viewpoints sit down and talk about it. Yeah Stan, where you're from will give you a pretty unique perspective. Maybe you'll see things better."

Stan held up his hands, "Don't look to me for any answers. If either of you think I'm hiding something profound, you're both delusional."

Darnell grinned, "Not at all Stan, you're missing the point. There's no certainty, only possibility. The world needs more honest people from different perspectives. Imagine what these think tanks could accomplish if they brought together intelligent, honest people instead of filling the seats with people who all think alike. Your life is different than anyone else's so if you make up your mind about shit you'll have a unique perspective. Honest people from your side of the aisle are a rare thing."

Ty interrupted, "Careful, Stan. Don't forget he's a lawyer and they've been known to eat their young."

Darnell smiled, "Only truth, Professor."

Stan asked, "It sounds like you two are on the same page. Do you guys disagree about anything?"

Darnell laughed, "Are you kidding? We have had it out more than once. One time we really got into it. I don't mean a fist fight," He paused and smiled slyly at Ty, "Because I would have crushed you. Anyway, I got all jacked up when I was asked to consult with the legal team after the Wounded Knee episode. Man, I thought I was in on a world changing event. I was going to fight the fight of the righteous. I mean, how could we possibly lose with truth on our side. Ty didn't see it that way. He kept badgering me. Telling me I was approaching this thing with blinders on. He was relentless, telling me truth had nothing to do with reality. I remember Ty saying over and over not to forget what happened to the legal actions after The Ludlow Massacre."

Stan interrupted, "I'm not familiar with The Ludlow Massacre. What happened?"

Darnell replied, "Well, legally nothing. I think that was Ty's point. The Ludlow Massacre happened in Colorado in the thirties. There was a strike at one of Rockefeller's mines. Since it was during the Depression the state couldn't afford to pay the National Guardsmen to evict the strikers. Rockefeller paid the guardsman's salaries and that's where the story gets blurry. It depends on where you hear it, but up to fifty men, women and children were shot from the hilltops around the striker's camp. Not only did the survivors lose their legal battles, history doesn't even acknowledge it happened. That's why Ty was pounding on me about Wounded Knee. He knew I was setting myself up for a disappointment. He was right, too. I was like people blinded by love. I refused to see what was happening right in front of me. I felt like these 9/11 Truthers do today. They know they have profound evidence of something. All they have to do is hold it up for the world to see and justice will be served. They're finding out just like I did. The message can be blocked, altered and, ultimately, most people don't want to know the level of corruption in the country where they live. Ty was absolutely right but I was demoralized. Man, I thought I was in on the ground floor of one of those Pearl Harbor moments and it kicked my ass. You'd think a tragic event of that scale couldn't be covered up. Hell, ninety nine percent of American's question the conclusion that Lee Harvey Oswald used a magic bullet to assassinate John F. Kennedy, especially anyone who's seen the Zapruder Film, but it didn't change a thing. Nothing! Whoever the power seekers who killed him were; the Cubans, The Mafia, The Bankers or Marilyn Monroe's body guards, it doesn't matter because we will never know. An event like Wounded Knee wouldn't even be mentioned on the news today. History is what you can make people believe. The actual truth is known only to the perpetrators and the observers."

Darnell hit the pipe again and handed to Ty, "I agree with you about history, Darnell. Just like with Kennedy, in fifty to a hundred years all that's left is the official story and legend. Every event get's a documented official explanation surrounded by legends and myths. They're all great stories but that's all they are. I agree with Lenin about how to find out who is behind a story. See who benefits. I would love to know the story behind The Emperor Constantine, The Holy Roman Church and The Council at Nicaea. I'd really love to know why the Library at Alexandria was burned. That could be the single greatest intellectual loss in human history. Who benefited? Whoever wanted to change the story."

Ty handed the pipe to Stan who held on without lighting it. Darnell took it from Stan, "You know the stories I'd like to know are the stories that were never told. You know, like the guy who saw the gunman on the grassy knoll but got taken out. How about the sentry who knew who was really in Hitler's bunker but died in the blast. Oh, what about the laborers who were killed to ensure secrecy after they placed, whatever the treasure was, under King Solomon's temple. You know, the treasure The Knights Templar were looking for. There is definitely more to those stories we don't know and what we do know is suspect."

Ty joined in, "Some of my favorite stories are all the shit around the royal bloodlines. The Merovingian kings, The Knights Templar, The Priory of Sion and all the secret organizations evolving from those stories. All these secret societies are protecting something that can only be accepted on faith. They are great stories, though. There isn't any historical right or wrong, only consensus. If society accepts a story, it must be true." Ty took the pipe from Darnell, "Enough about power and politics. Why don't you tell Stan the story of mankind's destiny according to Darnell Yellow Feather?"

Stan smiled, "So you have it figured out? Ty tells me we are headed up a Capitalist pyramid to our fate. I'd love to hear your take."

Ty interrupted with a grin, "Now Stan, don't be bad mouthing my pyramid. Have you wondered what the future holds if I'm right," Ty slyly added, "And I am. If this ponzi scheme continues, at some point someone has to reach the top. That's the nature of pyramids. The man who claims the top will be the owner of the Earth and all the labor required to sustain her. That King or God will own everything because all the subjects have been convinced the worthless paper that has been assigned as the measure of Earth's value was real."

Darnell began, "Ty's right. The Capitalist system as it's practiced has a fundamental flaw at its inception and all else flows from that. My story is different in the fact that it revolves around an absolute truth. In fact it may be one of the few things I know for sure. Stan, you've studied biology so I'm sure you understand the process of entropy. Entropy is simply the energy burned to sustain life. From the cellular level to the cosmic level, life stores and consumes energy. From the moment we are conceived until the instant we die we are burning energy. If our entropic level drops below the point of sustainability, we die. It works exactly the same way at the planetary level as it does at the cellular level. Carl Sagan was perfectly correct when he stated we need to view the Earth as one living organism. For billions of years life has been burning stored energy. Plants take in sunlight and through photosynthesis they convert the sun's energy into stored energy. That is the balance of nature. Energy comes in to be stored and energy goes out, burned to enable life. The dinosaurs appear to have upset that balance. I don't know if the dinosaur's demise was cosmic or divine but it was certainly inevitable. Mankind's story is playing out right before our eyes in real time. The ancient sunlight Mother Nature has been storing for millions of years is being burned at an unbelievable and unsustainable rate. Since the Industrial Revolution began, man has been burning stored energy thousands of times faster than the Earth can replace it. There is no debate about that fact. It is an absolute truth. It doesn't matter if you are driving a car or running on foot. When you run out of fuel, you die. The Earth is no different; she merely exists on a larger scale. Life requires energy and what mankind is doing cannot be sustained. The only unwritten part of our story is the ending. Ty's capitalist world and my entropic world are chapters of the same story. Mankind's influence on the story is fatally flawed from its inception."

Stan was intently listening to Darnell's story. He reflected for a moment before responding, "Between the two of you the picture looks pretty bleak. With all your prophetic gloom how do you expect anyone to remain optimistic? You seem to be saying we're on a runaway train that can't be stopped."

Darnell flashed a smile at Ty, "That's the irony and the tragedy. The only thing required to stop the train is the will to do it. Evil of any kind has no power without the support of the people. Hitler would have been nothing but another crackpot screaming to himself on a street corner if no one would have listened to him. It's Achems Razor, the simplest explanation is probably correct. If you don't want something, don't accept it. The dilemma we face is idealism can't stop the forces of power. That was my failure and the failure of my entire generation. We didn't embrace the reality of the story we wanted to change, so we didn't change it."

Stan cut in, "So how do you change the story? You can't just call a time out so you can rewrite history. Like you say, without the witnesses you still wouldn't know what was true. It seems to me if you write a story based on fiction, it's always going to be a fairy tale."

Ty nodded, "What a great way to put it but it's not all fiction. History is blurbs of truth veiled in a cloak of myth. There is truth behind everything happening today because there are witnesses. To remain optimistic, all you have to do is go back to the oldest struggle of mankind, Good versus Evil. If you believe in the goodness of man, the only thing missing is truth and free will. It's been the evil side of man who has written the story so far."

Darnell added, "Myself, I'm waiting for the Great Awakening. When the people discover what the ancients knew, that our collective energy holds incredible power. I believe when the inherent power within us all is rediscovered, positive energy will result in positive action. That will awaken the masses to our true nature which has been suppressed for over six thousand years. That will take us to a tipping point which will unmask the unscrupulous people who have forced us into this horror story. My awakening is the inverse of Biblical Revelations. It's the beginning."

Stan smiled, "Finally, something I can live with. I'm too young to give up hope."

Darnell stood up, "Sorry man, Ty and I enable each other's rants." He picked up the pipe, "You guys let me bogart the pipe." He held it up, "It does makes me look authentic, doesn't it? It's a good thing because authenticity is my life, except when I'm ripping off tourists.

But you got to have a hobby." He stood up, "Well guys, I'm pretty blitzed so I think I'm going to hit it." He turned to Ty, "Once again my friend, we have solved absolutely nothing." He smiled at Stan, "You're going to be alright, Stan. You guys can sleep wherever you want. There's a bed upstairs, the couches fold out, sleep on the porch or on the ground. Whatever you want. I'll see you in the morning."

Stan and Ty thanked Darnell for his hospitality before he retired. Stan said to Ty, "I should be tired but I'm not. Being terrified by you two must have woke me up. I'm glad we stopped, Darnell is an interesting guy. He's passionate with a splash of angry. Do you think that's from his divorce?"

"I doubt it. Darnell's been married quite a few times. I'm sure the next ex-Mrs. Yellow Feather is right around the corner. That's perceptive of you to spot his burden. He may have been disappointed with his tribe and he's definitely skeptical of government but first and foremost he is a Native American. He is genetically connected to the land so the rape of the planet weighs heavy on him. Did you notice, although Darnell is well read about environmental and civic issues he didn't elaborate about nuclear issues? He gets angry when he talks about anything nuclear and I'll tell you what, Darnell scares the shit out of me when he gets angry."

"I understand being against nuclear weapons, but is he against nuclear power, too?"

"Anything nuclear. The whole industry is illogical. Hell Stan, the people are being lied to. Everybody knows the dangers of nuclear weapons but they are trying to convince us nuclear power is a logical alternative energy source. It's ridiculous."

"Why is it ridiculous? Nuclear power has a pretty good track record and we definitely need the power. With the exception of Three Mile Island and Chernobyl, nuclear power has been beneficial. Nuclear provides power for ships, submarines, space probes and lots of other things safely every day. The only down side is storing the waste. Don't you think there is a positive place for the nuclear industry?"

"Not even for a second. Look at it from your field, the financial sector. Nuclear power plants are now and will always be subsidized by the taxpayers because they are completely uninsurable precisely because of the danger. You can't build a nuclear power plant without a backup, conventional power source to ensure coolant for the reactors. Like you said, no one has a clue what to do with the waste and the spent rods. Hell man, that shit is going to be poisonous for millions of years. What's logical about adding to a mountain of waste that can kill you? I don't know if you're old enough to remember the Great Northeast Blackout. It was a huge power outage covering the Northeastern U.S. and Canada. It was big time news. The story that didn't get reported was there were sixteen nuclear power plants inside the grid that lost power. Those plants all had diesel powered backup plants to cool the reactors in case of power loss. Nine of those backup generators failed leaving the reactors without cooling water. If the power had not been restored in the last twelve hours of the blackout the cores would have melted down, China Syndrome. That scares the shit out of me but nothing like the weapons. They have detonated hundreds of atomic and nuclear bombs for tests, above and below ground. That radioactivity hasn't gone away. It never will regardless of what is reported. The depleted uranium they are using in Iraq and the rest of the Middle East guarantees radioactive dust will be blowing around for the next nine billion years, long after we're gone. It's insanity! Did you know Curtis Lemay, head of The Joint Chiefs of Staff in the Pentagon in the sixties, and Edward Teller, the nuclear physicist, actually tried to convince our leaders a nuclear war was winnable. Madman Lemay actually said if two of us survive and only one Soviet, then we win! Can you believe there are people thinking like that in positions of power? Even Eisenhower bought in. He may have warned us about the threat from the Military Industrial Complex in his farewell address but when he was elected there were a few hundred nuclear weapons. When he left office there were eighteen thousand. It's insane to build enough weapons to wipe yourself out hundreds of times. It's like spending every penny you have on ammunition so you can shoot yourself in the head. Leaders don't have the right to put everyone's fate at the discretion of their egos. I've got another story that blew me away when I read about it. When NASA sent up Cassini, the space probe, it was supposed to go around the sun and then fly back past Earth for a final slingshot into deep space. I don't remember the exact amount but there was something like forty pounds of plutonium on Cassini to power the probe and to transmit back to Earth for as long as possible. These geniuses' were going to bring the probe as close as possible to Earth to get the optimum slingshot effect. Trajectories are not an exact science. The variables for calculating trajectories are infinite. Luckily for us, saner minds prevailed and Cassini passed Earth at a more sensible distance. If they had miscalculated and Cassini had been drawn into our atmosphere, the probe would have burned up and the plutonium would have killed us all. That wasn't even offered up to the public for consideration. NASA's entire budget comes from the Pentagon so you can be assured every space launch has a military purpose. We have no idea what these heroes have flying around up there. They want space based weapons. Do you believe that? Star Wars my ass! You know once the Space Shuttle hit a paint chip during an orbit. At eighteen thousand miles an hour, the paint chip nearly breached the hull. If these morons blow up a satellite or anything else, the debris field will make space inaccessible for all time. As far as radioactivity goes we are stuck with what they have already introduced into the environment. I'll guarantee you every man in America has trace amounts of plutonium in their testicles from the testing already done. Those poor soldiers being exposed to the depleted uranium in Iraq should probably not even procreate. The birth defects in Southern Iraq are skyrocketing." Ty sat back in the rocker, "Sorry Stan, it seems like I am always ranting at you but that's one story you'd rather hear from me. Darnell would have scared the shit out of both of us."

"How in the hell could I be more scared. You two prophets of doom could stop me from ever sleeping again if I took everything you said to heart. I think I will take your little slice of sunshine and go to bed. I hope your cynicism doesn't cause me to jump off a bridge in my dreams. Tell you what Ty, I'll just shoot for being aware. Absolute terror doesn't suit me." Stan stood up and tapped Ty on the shoulder, "Goodnight Ty."

# Chapter (12)

Stan woke, once again, to the momentary confusion of waking in a strange bed in an unfamiliar place. He quickly realized he was in the loft bedroom in Darnell's house. Ty was sleeping soundly on the foldout couch when Stan descended the stairs.

Darnell was seated at a desk wedged in between the bookshelves. He looked up from the computer when he spotted Stan, "Morning Stan. There's coffee in the kitchen. I need to check my e-mail and sales orders. You can check your e-mail when I'm finished if you'd like."

"No thanks, I'm good."

Stan poured a cup of coffee and sat down at the bar. Darnell joined Stan at the bar after he finished his work at the computer, "Did you sleep okay?"

Stan held up his cup, "I slept great. Thanks again for putting us up."

"It was a pleasure, Stan. I hope Ty and I didn't overwhelm you with our witty insights. You must have felt like you were in a lecture hall. We have a tendency to ramble when we're together."

"I enjoy listening to you guys. Don't forget I grew up in a bubble so these ideas are all new to me. I was taught to be a patriotic conformist and not ask too many questions."

Darnell chuckled, "Patriot. I went to a tribal school but we still said the Pledge of Allegiance every day. By junior high school my inner rebel voice was waking up and the pledge started to feel out of place. I began feeling traitorous to my people when I declared my support for the government that had slaughtered my ancestors. The Pledge of Allegiance puts a Native American in an absurd position. Personally,

I think all loyalty oaths are stupid. Why do we have to declare our honor and respect for the leaders of institutions just for the privilege of existence. We all live on Planet Earth, so real patriots should all be environmentalists."

"Interesting idea. I guess I can see your dilemma. It's probably hard for all minorities, just in different ways."

"Yeah. In this country we've oppressed them all. We've hated Blacks, Irish, Chinese, Okies, Wetbacks, Communists and of course Indians. Lots of minorities got a shot at being society's doormat but the blacks always seem to get stuck on the bottom. They might be the only people who have been more oppressed than the Native Americans. They just killed us. You know what the Civil War did for the blacks? It gave them the choice of where they wanted to live while they were being discriminated against. I used to wonder what I would have done if I had lived in those times. Would I have been strong enough to stand up? It must have been unreal to see that unstoppable wave of humanity coming at you. There were some very proud tribal leaders who had to surrender their pride and their heritage so their people wouldn't vanish."

Ty joined them, "Darnell, are you dragging Stan right back into the netherworld? Be gentle, I still need him to drive."

Darnell pointed at Stan, "He started it! I think he might be a little masochistic."

Ty poured a cup of coffee and joined them at the bar, "We're not keeping you from work are we?"

"No, I do everything from here. I don't even see the crap I sell. It comes on a container to Seattle or Portland and then it goes to a distribution center in Reno. I forward the sales orders to Reno. If I didn't have to eat, I wouldn't have to leave the house. I run my practice and publishing company from home, also."

Stan asked, "You have a publishing company, too?"

"Yes, it takes less of my time than my law practice. I haven't put out anything in awhile but we still have some books in circulation."

Stan drained his coffee, "You know Ty, we should probably get going. Mom is already wondering if I'm lost or if you kidnapped me. We don't want Dad's secret police hunting us down."

Ty nodded in agreement, "You're right." He smiled widely, "Darnell, It's been awesome to see you again, my friend."

Darnell hugged them both, "I'll see you both again soon, right? You know you're welcome anytime."

Stan and Ty made a quick exit. They got their bags, said one more quick goodbye and made their way back to the highway.

Once on the road, Stan said, "I sure have met some interesting people this week." He flashed a quick grin at Ty, "Even you, old man."

"I knew you would like Darnell. He is as real as it gets. I've only met a handful of people in my life who are exactly who they appear to be. Darnell is one of them. Most people have a public face which doesn't remotely resemble their private persona. Darnell is real all the time."

"I hear you. I've seen Dad at the office and that guy isn't even close to the guy we see at home. Mom's as phony as a person can be around her Garden Club and Rotary Club friends. I shouldn't talk, I'm no better. We have an unspoken law. Whatever happens, no matter how bad, we pretend it didn't happen. We never mention it and we bury it deep enough so it never resurfaces. The outside world is supposed to see only the perfect family so everyone wants to be us. It's sick, none of us know who we really are."

Ty didn't respond. He left Stan to his self reflective thoughts. Stan pulled into the first service station they encountered in Klamath Falls. Ty went into the store while Stan paid for the gas. Back in the van, Ty peeled back the wrapper to a breakfast burrito for Stan, "Here you go, Stan. There's probably some real meat by products in there somewhere. The up side is the preservatives should slow down the decay rate of our corpses."

"I'll bet nothing we've been eating is on your dietary chart. That'll change once Mom gets a hold of you."

"Then I better junk out fast. You know, I just had a funny thought about corpses."

"Funny and corpses, now there's two words you don't normally hear in the same sentence."

"Think about it, Stan. Archeologists will find a skeleton, an arrowhead and a piece of pottery. From those few clues they attempt to reconstruct a vision of that civilization. Imagine what will happen thousands of years from now when future archeologists unearth a female from our time. Saline implants, silicone injections, shriveled ink stained skin and jewelry piercing every orifice. How would you like to reconstruct our society from those clues?"

"You're twisted, only you would look for the humorous side of the end of our civilization. You and Darnell should be wearing t-shirts saying 'The End is Near.'"

"We do tend to paint dark pictures. You have to admit I'm harmless but Darnell will, honestly, scare you when he gets wound up. I was glad to see he still smokes pot. He's too big and too angry not to have a way to chill out. We all have our triggers and we all need a release. Look at you. You stay composed through anything but you tighten up when you talk about your own life. Don't you think it's strange to remain passive while hearing about millions of horrible deaths but for your blood pressure to rise when you think about your own situation?"

Stan thought long before responding, "Maybe it is strange. I can't do anything to help the millions but I could help myself. That's probably why I'm resentful. I've never questioned being a spoiled little rich kid. I've gotten almost everything I've wanted just by going along with the program. I think I was embarrassed when you were terrorizing Freddie at the supermarket because I'm as much an automaton as he is. More so, because I get a bigger payoff. I've enjoyed seeing other people's lives but I can't turn that inquisitive eye on myself. Freddie was a free spirit compared to me."

Ty whistled, "Man, you're tough on yourself. Do you think someday you're going to uncover some kernel of truth or ignite some spark of self awareness that's going to remedy the ills of your perceived past? I don't think it works that way. You can either acknowledge your past or ignore it. Self examination is hard to do. I know I'm not very good at it. I don't know many people who are but you have to keep trying."

"I'm not looking for truth, Ty. I don't have a clue what I'm looking for. I've been on cruise control most of my life. The people we've met have been great but they don't exist in my world. In the boardrooms and classrooms these people are nothing but statistics. I don't know if this whole experience has been eye opening or just a curiosity. When we get home my life will still be the same."

"Man, you're as dark as I am. You're going to be whoever you decide to be. You're wrong about one thing, though. When we get to your house you're going to bear witness to a time honored ritual dance that's definitely going to be different. Big Stan and I have only been together in short bursts. We're headed into virgin territory."

"Do you think it will be entertaining or should I wear a black and white striped shirt and carry a whistle?"

"I really don't know what to expect. We always do alright for awhile. We'll have inane conversations about silly, safe subjects but at some point one of us will throw out the catalyst remark taking us to another level. It will sound harmless at the surface but just below it will be sarcastic and insulting. It's at that point both of us will implement our audio dysfunction scrambling devices."

"Hold it! What in the world is that?"

Ty chuckled, "You know what it is. It's an internal device empowering you to hear another person's meaning regardless of their words. When Big Stan asks, 'What have you been doing with yourself' I hear 'You're worthless and always have been'. When I ask Stanton to pass the potatoes, he hears 'You are robber baron scum'. It usually spirals into chaos from there and ends with Emma pleading for a ceasefire. I hope you have film in your camera."

"It could be fun to watch. At least it won't be the one sided discussions Dad and I normally have. He's always had the hammer on me. He could restrict, intimidate, or simply blackmail me. It will be interesting to see Dad deal with someone he doesn't control. How about you and Mom. Are you guys strained too?"

"Emma and I get along pretty good but it's superficial. I know we love each other but we're more like two neighbors talking over the back fence. There's a barrier between us. I've been at arms length in Emma's life ever since Stanton filled the emotional gap I left after Belle died. You want to know something funny? I have no clue what Emma has told Stanton about me or my past but I'd be willing to bet it's as little as possible. I don't think Emma is ashamed of me but I'm sure she would prefer to avoid the subject. The last thing Emma wants is for her and her society friends to pull the sticks out of their asses so they can compare bloodlines." Ty's head followed the passing road sign, "You missed the turn off for Crater Lake. You really should see it sometime. It's spectacular. I must have driven past it four or five times and every time Belle would say that very thing. Belle was driving late one night when we were headed this way. We were low on gas and she was supposed to stop at the next station. I woke up at a lookout above Crater Lake. It was an amazing sight at sunrise. Unfortunately, the sight of the gas gauge on empty brought me back to reality. I aggressively pressed her about her plan for getting fuel since there were no services at Crater Lake. Belle told me to chill out and enjoy the view, the return trip was mostly down hill. Besides, if she would have stopped for gas it would have woken me and I would never agree to go out of our way to see the lake. I questioned her logic and she suggested I do something I wasn't flexible enough to accomplish. When you're with the same woman for many years you come to recognize the times when you should press a point and the times when you should just sit back and enjoy the view."

"Were you coming this way to see Darnell?"

"Yeah, Darnell was living at Pyramid Lake back then. He worked for the tribe for a couple of years before he moved back to Washington."

"Darnell sounded bitter about that experience."

"He was extremely disappointed. He told me it was like trying to break up a fist fight and having both combatants turn on you. That whole period of time was enlightening for Darnell. He was involved with one case right after he got there that really opened his eyes. He was offered a high profile case immediately after he passed the bar exam. The son of a State Senator had gotten busted with a few pounds of pot. The press was all over it. Darnell didn't understand why they had chosen a rookie, untested attorney until they were assigned a courtroom. The judge was from the Paiute Tribe, like Darnell. The case ended up being fairly easy. The kid went to rehab and Darnell plea bargained for probation. Darnell figured having access to a State Senator was the perfect opportunity to press his personal agenda for the legalization of marijuana. Darnell said it was one of the most bizarre experiences of his life. The Senator met with Darnell four or five times and the Senator even arranged meetings with other Senators. Darnell said it was like talking to Stepford Children. Every meeting with the Senators began with the recitation of the Senator's resume'. They then professed their morality and compassion for others. That was followed by commending Darnell for his involvement before promising to take his request under consideration. They finished by assuring Darnell there was nothing they could do at this time. Darnell said every one of them were like form letters with faces. After all the meetings and correspondence, Darnell had absolutely no idea where any of them stood on the issue. Law makers rarely express opinions until they've been informed what their opinion should be. The Judge cleared it up for Darnell. The Judge said legalization would never be presented on the floor of the Legislature because, despite any logical arguments, it would be political suicide. The next political campaign would enable your opponent to label you soft on crime and name associate you with every criminal who ever lived. Even though they might actually vote for legalization no one would ever, personally, present the proposal on the floor of the Legislature."

"Are you an advocate?"

"No, and neither is Darnell anymore. He understands the road blocks. It was always more important to him than it was to me. Darnell is one of those people who get motivated when he's high. It just makes me lazy."

"So the drug culture wasn't a big part of your life?"

"Not really. I've always been a social smoker, like you. I smoked a lot with Belle when she was sick. She preferred it to the heavy narcotic pain killers the doctor gave her. I could never handle speed or cocaine. My mind is already going a thousand miles an hour and those speedy drugs would have blown the top of my head off. Big Stan would never believe that. I think he always believed I was tied up in the drug trade but he's a banker first so he'd never condemn any activity that creates cash flow."

"You're not going back to that CIA/Wall Street connection are you? I have to tell you I have a hard time believing that one. I'm not naïve enough to think illegal money isn't laundered but a direct connection is hard to get my mind around."

"I understand. I'm not insinuating they are drug lords. I'm simply saying they are facilitators. The volume of drugs in this country could not persist without their compliance. It's easy for the Wall Street guys to look the other way when they take the money. They didn't personally grow, refine, transport or distribute it, so justification is simple. If one of your buddies stops by your place with a six pack, a pizza and a video someone else had stolen, you probably are going to have a beer, a slice and watch the movie with a clear conscience."

"Thanks for clearing that up. I can safely work on Wall Street if I adhere to the five degrees of separation rules. That's good to know."

"You bet, Stan. You can have the Ty seal of approval for Wall Street but if you ever attempt to enter the world of politics, I'll come back from the dead to haunt you. If you develop an interest in politics I suggest you follow your Dad's example. Big Stan would never enter the political arena. He knows the real power is in owning politicians."

Stan steered Brutus around a sweeping turn putting them on Interstate 5 north. He settled her into the right lane at her customary fifty five, allowing the cars and trucks equal opportunity to spin Brutus' mirrors.

Stan settled in, "It's obvious you don't care for the political process. Do you vote?"

"I've voted on local issues but I haven't voted nationally for a long time. As long as they keep using electronic voting machines, I'll probably never vote again. Electronic voting pisses me off. How in the hell can you have an honest election if you can't check the votes? It's another one of those logic bombs I can't get beyond. The only way to check machine accuracy is with the source code in the software. The corporations, like Diebold and EDS, manufacturing the machines aren't legally obligated to share the source code with the states buying their machines. Once a person presses a touch screen their vote goes into a virtual black hole. Josef Stalin said it best. 'It doesn't matter who you vote for, it only matters who's counting the votes.' American voters will never again know. I don't know about you but hearing George Bush, James Baker, and Antonin Scalia say 'Trust me', just didn't do it for me. When the Supreme Court called the election in 2000, it was not only unprecedented it was completely unconstitutional. Bush was the only president ever elected by a five to four margin. It's another of those instances highlighting the fact there are powers behind the curtain pulling the levers here in Oz. Think about what we witnessed in that debacle. Al Gore is an elite, rich white man who had been groomed for the highest levels of government his entire life. His supporters spent obscene amounts of money attempting to get him elected to the highest office in the land only to have him accept the results of an election a high school civics student could see was unconstitutional. I honestly believe participants at the national level are so indebted to private interests they don't even remotely represent the people. When a Mafia crime family gets a new Godfather, it doesn't change the business in the least. The only difference between the two political parties are the corporations owning them. They should all be required to display the corporate logos of their owners when they campaign so we could vote on the corporations we want to write our public policies. I'm not saying there haven't been well meaning people in government, I'm just saying policy decisions are made for benefactor's first and people second, if at all. We've had Presidents who have been pressured to make horrifying decisions. The Pentagon pushed Truman into dropping atomic and hydrogen bombs on Hiroshima and Nagaski and to fire bomb civilian cities in Germany and Japan. Those decisions were geo political, not strategic, because both wars were widely accepted as being in their final days. Officials are still passing the buck for Southeast Asia. All of them; Nixon, Kissinger, Johnson and McNamara pointed fingers but that doesn't change the fact our country spent over a decade dropping bombs on Vietnam, Cambodia and Laos because it was a key game piece in the power hungry game of Worldwide Stratego. Tens of millions of people died and nothing changed. All presidents are pressured but some of them piss me off for what they didn't do, like Bill Clinton."

Stan laughed loudly, "You've got to be kidding. With all the subversive stuff you talk about, it's a sex scandal that tops your list. Say it ain't so, Ty."

"It ain't so. It is kind of ironic that Clinton will always be remembered for Monica and not for selling out American labor with NAFTA. I think it should be written into the Constitution all Presidents should orgasm daily just to keep their minds clear. I wish someone would have caught an intern with Bush's zipper in his or her mouth so we could have impeached him. Violating the law didn't seem to do it. Bill Clinton was in a position to do something great for everyone on Planet Earth but he ignored the opportunity. The Cold War had just ended leaving America as the lone superpower. It was the first time in fifty years nuclear disarmament would have made sense to everyone. Clinton could have made us all a little safer but he was afraid of the Pentagon. Instead of reducing the threat during a time of peace, he increased military spending. That's my gripe about Clinton. He could still have sold out the country while making us safer." Ty paused, "I kind of drifted off message again. What about you? Do you vote?"

"I'm registered but I haven't voted yet. Shocking as it might sound, I'm a registered Republican. At U-Dub I was in the Young Republicans. Dad thought it would look good on my resume for Harvard. Maybe I'll wait for an honest politician before I vote."

"That's an oxymoron, like Senate intelligence or Catholic priest abstinence."

"You really don't think there can be an honest politician, do you Ty?"

"The overwhelming majority of them are so highly compromised by the moneyed interests supporting their campaigns they are totally inept. Corruption is a relative term. Most politicians have a moral or ethical line they don't want to cross but there are some who don't believe there should be any lines. The system itself has been perverted to accommodate corruption. The difference between national and local politics is not one of ethics but of scale. I've got a true story for you. It happened at the local level but it's a microcosm of the system at any level. I had a good friend who's brother was found dead in his apartment. The police ruled it a suicide but no one will ever know for sure. He was a young guy with a good job so he had lots of nice toys, but no will. My buddy went to see the probate judge to see about securing ownership of his brother's classic truck and his motorcycle. The judge told him and a few of his friends to submit sealed bids to the court for the two vehicles. The judge said to make sure my buddie's bid was the highest and none of the bids were ridiculously low. The judge assured him there shouldn't be any other bids. The day they were to open the sealed bids arrived and lo and behold that very judge outbid my buddy by one dollar on both vehicles. It was obvious the process had been corrupted so my buddy was instructed to forward any complaints to the very same probate judge. Is it legally considered corruption if it can't be proven? There are stories like that one at every level of government." Ty snickered, "There was a county commissioner in Washington who bought a hundred and fifty acres for a dollar the day before he cast the deciding vote to approve construction of a golf course adjoining the property he had just bought. Unethical to be sure but it wasn't illegal. Remember when Dick Cheney had his private meetings with the corporate energy executives to write the countries energy policy. Not only wouldn't he release the documents he wouldn't even tell us who had attended the secret meetings. The watchdog groups and the Freedom of Information people appealed all the way to the Supreme Court. Justice Scalia spent the weekend with Cheney at a private sportsman's club, before casting the decisive vote. Scalia voted to protect Cheney's secrets even though it violated Federal Transparency laws. Cheney won, the people lost and the ethical line got a little blurrier."

Stan exited the freeway to get food and fuel. As soon as Brutus was settled in the slow lane on returning to the freeway, Stan asked, "Why don't we camp out for one more night. If we stop somewhere below Olympia we'll miss the morning gridlock."

"Sounds good, Stan. Are you trying to avoid the traffic or going home?"

"Maybe a little of both. It's funny, I love my Dad but I seem to spend an extraordinary amount of time trying to avoid him. I think Mom avoids him, too. I've been with my parents for twenty one years and I have no idea what kind of relationship they have. I see only their public face, unless I'm in trouble."

"Stranger than fiction, isn't it. I think power couples are the hardest to figure out because it's all an act. If you really want to take your mind to the horror dimension, try to imagine some of these power couples having sex. I can't picture George and Barbara or George and Laura or Kissinger and anyone without losing my appetite. Monica makes sense to anybody who has ever seen Bill and Hillary look at each other. They may have been in love at one time but now they simply look like corporate partners. I'll bet the impeachment hearings were the first time they had talked about sex in years."

"Don't you think a couple can have a healthy relationship without sex?"

"Sure you can but why would you want to if it wasn't neccessary? This is a physical dimension and physical relationships are right at the top of life's physical experiences. Love is an emotion you can't touch, you can only feel. If you meet someone you share your love with, you've discovered the ultimate human experience. If you connect your emotional gift with a physical experience you've hit the Homo Sapien jackpot. Love is a safe, warm, comfortable home where you share yourself. Sex is the exhilarating amusement park ride in the backyard. Lots of people are happy to stay in the house but some people will walk if the ride closes down."

"So love is enough?"

"Definitely. There's a very good possibility love is the answer to the age old question, 'Why are we here?' There are relationships that are strictly emotional and some which are merely physical. I think if you can find both, you're closer to finding that yin/yang, alpha/omega balance in life."

"You're not just a political satirist, now you're a philosopher."

"I'm no philosopher. I'm just an old man with an opinion on a broad range of subjects. Hell, the philosophy isn't even mine. That was Belle's analogy. She had another good one. 'A relationship is like a trek up Mt. Everest. When you reach the summit, you will be overwhelmed by the spiritual power it evokes from you. If you discover there is an alpine sled ride option for the descent. You'd be foolish not to experience the ride.'"

"Grandma sounds like a wise woman."

"Smarter than me. That's for sure. After she got sick, she started harping on me about being open to love after she was gone. It used to piss me off to hear her go on and on about it but I finally promised her I would. I lied through my teeth. I'm a selfish old son of a bitch and

I'd been up Mt. Everest so I couldn't see any reason to go looking for K-2. That's just the way it is."

Stan and Ty quietly watched Portland pass by. They stopped for dinner in Vancouver after crossing the Columbia River. Returning to the freeway in search of a campground, they found a sign for camping at Battle Ground and followed the signs to a KOA campground. The campsite was little more than a parking place and a picnic table but it was backed by an expansive meadow leading to an evergreen Washington forest. Stan visited the restroom. When he returned Ty was sitting at the picnic table dreamily staring at the landscape. Stan grabbed two beers from the ice chest and joined Ty at the table.

"Whatcha watching?"

"Just the world. It's nice to slow down and enjoy it. Life's too fast paced. Most people don't have the time to notice anything. Check out the blackbirds. When they take flight they look like a school of fish in the air. That perfect synchronization is awesome. Just think of the trust required from every bird to accomplish that maneuver. The natural world has an honest rhythm."

"Why do you think people can't cooperate to achieve that sort of unity? You'd think we are smarter than a flock of birds"

"I wish I knew. If you think about it, Stan, the blackbirds are an accurate analogy for society. We're all following along to some, as yet, undetermined destination. It doesn't matter who's in the lead for the blackbirds because they're all engaged in the same activity, survival. A long time ago some unscrupulous people figured out the human flock will follow anyone who appears to know where they are going. These people discovered total control could be accomplished by placing like minded people on the leading edge of the flock, the ruling class. The faces change but the general direction is always the same. Occasionally a dominant person will get out in front to direct the movements, but even when he falters the leaders still keep society's flock moving in a direction benefiting the leaders. As a civilization we will never find a natural rhythm until we can trust we're all going somewhere that benefits all."

They watched the blackbirds land and take flight numerous times. Stan finished his beer, "They have showers at the restrooms. I think I'll go take one. I'll be back in a bit."

Ty was still sitting at the table when he heard Stan, long before he saw him. Stan was moving fast and angrily mumbling as he stormed back to camp. Stan's face was crimson. There were veins protruding from his temples and forehead, "I got ripped off! They stole my fucking wallet! I don't believe it!"

Ty's voice remained calm, "Who ripped you off? Where?"

"In the shower! They took my pants right off the hook! They got everything! Cash, credit cards, my drivers license! Everything!"

Ty remained calm, "Looks like you got your pants back. Maybe they dropped your wallet, too. Where did you find your pants?"

Stan stepped back, trying to reign in his anger so he could think more clearly. His eyes partially cleared, "They were lying in the road."

"Let's go look around and see if we can find your wallet."

They headed for the shower with Stan grumbling in an attempt to continue stirring his anger. He pointed, "They were over there."

Ty started in that direction, "Whoever it was headed this way. Maybe they dumped your wallet after they rifled it. Check the bushes." Ty looked at the surrounding campsites, "Check the garbage cans."

Ty began scouring the bushes while Stan was checking garbage cans. The can at the second campsite he checked revealed his wallet, just as Ty had predicted. Stan retrieved his wallet, immediately opening it to check out what remained.

Stan turned holding up his wallet, and yelled to Ty, "They got the cash and the credit cards." He quickly opened the wallet again, "Shit! They took my fucking drivers license! What the hell do they want that for?"

Ty joined Stan, "Sorry Stan. Try not to get so upset. It's just stuff. Did you report it?"

Stan dejectedly shook his head, "No, I haven't. I'll go to the office and call the cops. I should call Mom so she can cancel the cards, too."

Ty was lying on the bed in the van when Stan returned, "Did you get it reported?"

"Hell no. The Sheriff won't even come out here to take a report. If I want to file a complaint I have to go to the station. I did call Mom and left a message about the credit cards." Stan closed the door and joined Ty on the bed, "Sorry I got so upset."

"No problem. There's always someone around to remind us we're not all good people. It really is just stuff. Try and get some sleep Stan."

# Chapter (13)

It was a fitful night for Stan. The first rays of sunlight woke him and there was no chance of getting back to sleep. He shook Ty awake and with little conversation they visited the restroom before hitting the road. Breakfast at the diner next to the freeway was another somber affair.

Ty said nothing when he left the tip but he couldn't resist as he rose to pay the check, "It's a good thing I hit the bank in Reno. I don't have any credit cards so we'd be doing dishes about now."

Stan's mood was too deeply rooted to allow a smile to escape. They were back on the freeway when Stan finally spoke. Sullenly he said, "I'm sorry I ranted like an idiot. I was already a little down because our trip is almost over. The wallet just put me over the top. I've honestly enjoyed this trip. It's been one of the few adventures in my life."

"I'm glad you've enjoyed it. It's been my great pleasure getting to know you. Seriously though, I don't know why you're depressed. You're going on to Europe, I'm the one headed to a nagging daughter and her overbearing husband who thinks I'm a delusional deadbeat. On top of that I'm bringing home their baby boy; penniless, pissed off, with two days growth of beard. You've got it easy."

Stan managed a grin, "Okay, I give up. As always, everyone has it tougher than the rich kid, but I've worked hard on this mood and I'm not going to let you cheapen it."

The conversation faded once more as they closed in on the Seattle metro area. The familiar landmarks were all leading Stan home. Ty was content trying to recognize different views from his past. In silence they started the decent onto the bridge across Lake Washington to Mercer Island.

Under his breath Stan whispered, "There's the finish line."

He took the exit he had taken hundreds of times. His mood darkened, realizing he was just a few blocks, through the exclusive neighborhoods, from the end of his adventure. The sound of a siren startled him and snapped him back to the present. He checked the rear view mirror to see if the police siren was directed at him before pulling over to the curb, "Shit! What a perfect finish."

Stan continued watching the mirror. He saw the patrolman slowly getting out of his cruiser. Reality struck Stan like a lightning bolt. His face turned instantly bright red, the veins in his temples immediately burst to the surface. Stan slammed the palm of his hand with a fury against the steering wheel, "Shit! I don't even have a driver's license! This is fucking great!"

Ty saw the instant rage and attempted to calm Stan, "Be cool, Stan. It's not a problem."

The officer was now at the driver's side window, warily assessing the two men in the old van, "Let's have your license and registration." He paused for a quick second, "What's your business on the island?"

Stan turned to face the officer with fire in his eyes. His voice was a low growl, "What did I do?"

The officer cautiously eyed the agitated young man before responding, "I didn't say you did anything, now did I? License and registration." He paused to add emphasis, "Please!"

Ty opened the glove box and handed the registration to Stan who relayed it to the officer. The officer took the form and added, "Your license, Sir!"

Stan's anger flooded his face with the remainder of his raging blood. His hand slammed the steering wheel again, "I don't have one! Some fucker stole it!"

The officer immediately took two steps back and dropped into a defensive stance with his hand on his service revolver. The officer's partner who had been standing quietly beside the passenger side of the cruiser saw his partner's retreat. He immediately drew his pistol.

The first officer barked at Stan, "Get out of the car! Now!"

Stan barked back as he viscously flung the door open, "I didn't do anything!"

The officer retreated a few more steps while he drew his gun and trained it on Stan, "Get on the ground!"

Stan glared wild eyed at the man, seemingly unphased by the gun pointed at him, "What for? I didn't fucking do anything!"

Ty saw the danger unfolding before him. He quickly opened the door to get to Stan. The second officer leveled his gun when the passenger's door flew open. He began shouting, "Show me your hands! Show me your hands!"

Ty raised his hands but he didn't hesitate. He hopped around the front of the van, "Don't shoot! Don't shoot! Stop Stan! Don't shoot!"

At the same time the first officer continued barking at the red faced, frozen Stan, "Get on the ground! Get on the ground!"

Ty was still shouting, "Don't shoot!" when he reached Stan. Ty grabbed hold of Stan, putting himself between Stan and the gun. Both of the patrolmen had their guns trained on Ty's back. Ty wrapped his arms around Stan and forcefully pushed him against the van. Ty looked directly into Stan's eyes, "Stop it Stan! Stop it now!"

Stan looked up into Ty's intense eyes. The cloud of rage quickly gave way to the reality of their situation. Ty saw the change. He released Stan and put his hands in the air. Ty slowly turned to face the guns, "Don't you dare shoot! His name is Stanton Wainwright. You do not want to shoot him! Check it out! Do you hear me?"

Both patrolmen relaxed slightly but they kept their aim. Ty went on, "Check his wallet, he has a student ID. Check him out. You don't want to make a mistake here."

The two policemen glanced at each other. The first holstered his gun but his partner held his aim. The first officer took a step forward barking at Stan, "Slowly take out your wallet!"

Stan took his wallet out of his pocket and held it out. The officer edged closer, never taking his eyes off of Stan. He snatched the wallet and quickly stepped back, "Both of you! Put your hands on the car!"

They complied while the officer retreated to the radio and computer in his cruiser. Another police cruiser squealed to a stop behind the first while Stan and Ty leaned, with hands high on the side of the van. Both occupants of the second patrol car exploded from the car with guns drawn. As they cautiously approached, one of them asked, "What's going on?"

The partner answered without taking his eyes and gun from the two suspects, "Don't know, Ben's checking them out. The driver is jacked up or something."

The three patrolmen covered Stan and Ty for an uncomfortable few minutes until Ben exited his cruiser, "That's who he is alright. I got a printout on him. He's got a KMA stamp."

The other three relaxed and slowly put their weapons away. Ben walked to Stan and Ty, "Turn around." He said as he held out Stan's wallet, "Why did you react that way? Are you alright? Do you understand why we reacted the way we did?"

Stan took his wallet and returned it to his pocket, "Why did you stop me to begin with?"

"It doesn't matter. When a police officer tells you to do something, you'd better do it. You could have been seriously hurt. I thought you were high on something. Do you understand?"

Stan took a deep breath, "I still don't know what I did wrong to cause you to stop me."

The officer looked intently at Stan, then Ty and back at Stan, "You didn't look like you belong here. Sorry for the misunderstanding." His gaze lingered for a few more seconds before he turned to return to his cruiser. The four cops exchanged some good humored banter before they got into their vehicles. Stan and Ty silently watched the two cruisers slowly drive away. The first cruiser was the last to pass. The officer in the passenger's seat casually waved as they drove by as if Stan had just purchased tickets to the policeman's ball.

Ty didn't see the wave. He was focused on Stan, "You almost got yourself shot, man. I don't know about you but that scared the shit out of me."

Stan looked sheepishly at the ground, "Sorry, Ty. I'm losing it. I was pissed already and this pushed me over the edge."

Ty put his hand on Stan's shoulder, "Come on Stan, let's sit down for a minute." Ty led Stan to the curb in front of Brutus. They sat down. Ty grinned, "Well, now you can say you've officially been profiled. You didn't seem to care much for it."

Stan couldn't manage a smile, "Well hell, I've lived here most of my life. I could probably get those assholes fired."

Ty snickered, "What for? You already got special treatment."

"What! You call that special treatment? And what the fuck is a KMA stamp anyway?"

"Yeah, I call it special treatment. You didn't get a ticket for driving without a license, did you? As far as a KMA stamp, I'm not really sure. I've read about KMA chips in reference to the RFID chips they want to implant everyone with. I think KMA stands for 'kiss my ass', it's like diplomatic immunity."

"I still don't get it."

"What's not to get? They stopped two unshaven men in a beater car with out of state plates. Then the driver blows up like he's on crack. We look exactly like someone who doesn't belong here. I'm sure they thought they were stopping a home burglary. That's their job." Ty leaned forward to make eye contact, "Don't stew about it. Think about what just happened. How you feel right now is how most minorities feel about authority all the time. What you just experienced is a daily occurrence to inner city minorities. How do you think you would feel knowing every cop, every store owner and most people you saw naturally assumed you were a murdering, drug dealer. You got a small taste of their entire existence. Wrap your head around that."

"I'm really not in the mood for a sociology lesson. I just want to feel like shit for awhile, okay?"

"No problem. You can feel however you want to. Personally, I've tried to imagine what it must feel like to live under a fulltime suspicion cloud, but I can't. It's like trying to understand how a woman feels about menstrual cramps. It can't be done. I watched the black comedian, Dick Gregory, when he was on the panel at the Black Caucus convention. He showed me a little spark of what the black experience was about. Comedy is truth. Ever notice how you laugh the hardest when you're saying, 'That is so true'. Anyway, Gregory started rolling with one truism after another about being black. Tavis Smiley and Cornell West were almost rolling on the floor. One of the things he said was particularly enlightening. Gregory said you could be a highly regarded, successful black politician, lawyer or businessman in Washington DC, but if you're going home to Virginia, late at night, in your new Mercedes and you see red flashing lights in your rear view mirror, you realize instantly you're just another black man in a white man's world."

The color was returning to Stan's face, "I get it. I know I overreacted but they still had no reason to stop us."

Ty shook his head, "There you go again with that right or wrong thing. It has more to do with perception than righteousness." Ty slapped Stan's shoulder, "I've changed my mind, I would like to offer you some advice. Would you take me somewhere tomorrow? I'd like to show you something."

Stan nodded, "Sure. It wouldn't happen to be in another state, would it?"

Ty grinned, "Good, your humor is coming back. No, it's close." Ty stood up, "What do you say we put a cap on your good humor and go to your house? The people across the street have been peeking through their curtains since we got here. They've probably called the cops again."

Stan stood up and they returned to the van. At the exact moment Stan turned the ignition key a police cruiser rounded the corner headed toward them. Stan muttered, "Nice call"

The final few blocks to Stan's house led them past one luxurious home after another. Stan turned into the circular driveway of the largest home they had seen thus far. Ty leaned forward to take in the full panoramic picture of the mansion.

"It looks like the White House. Are you sure there's room for me?"

Stan didn't look up, "I think we'll squeeze you in. Personally, I'd lobby for the apartment over the garage. I've been begging for it for years."

Stan led the way to the oversized double entry doors. Ty couldn't stop shaking his head at the massive scale of the house. He motioned at the double doors, "Quite an entry. Big Stan must have some huge friends."

Stan opened the door, muttering, "Dad doesn't have friends. He has associates and employees."

The door opened to a marble foyer which was four times the size of Ty's cabin in West Virginia. Hallways led right and left while directly in front of them was a dramatic staircase leading to the upper floors. Stan pressed a button on the intercom next to the door, "Mom, are you home? We're here."

The response was quick. Margaret, the head maid, answered, "Your Mother is in the atrium, sir. Are you hungry? Can I serve you lunch?"

Stan pressed the button, "No, thank you, Margaret." He turned to Ty, "This way."

Ty followed Stan down the hallway to the left. They passed through the formal dining room to the rear of the house where Emma sat at a small table in the glass atrium overlooking a swimming pool and the manicured grounds behind the mansion. Emma rose with a reserved smile on her face. She wore a pale blue silk robe although her perfect hair and makeup belied the idea she had recently woken.

Emma gently hugged Stan and whispered in his ear, "I'm so glad you're home." She turned her eyes to Ty. Her eyes lingered for a second before they shared a sparkle, "I'm so happy you're here, Daddy."

Ty stepped forward to hug Emma. After releasing her, he stepped back to survey his daughter at arms length, "It's great to see you, Em. I forgot how beautiful you are. You don't age at all." He grinned, "You're not doing that 'We can rebuild you better Cher thing' are you?"

Emma smirked," Don't be silly." She motioned at the table, "Have a seat. Would you like some lunch?"

Stan shook his head, "No thanks, Mom. I'm going to take a shower. I have to go to the Department of Licensing. Why don't you two catch up."

Ty sat down after Stan left. Margaret magically appeared to take Ty's request for an iced tea. Ty surveyed the park like view through the atrium windows, "It looks like Stanton is taking good care of you. You two have done a great thing with Stan. He's an impressive young man. You should be proud."

"We are proud. He's a lot like his Father."

Ty chuckled, "Maybe not as much as you think."

"Daddy, you haven't been bashing Stanton to Stan, have you? I wanted you to get to know him. I didn't want you to confuse him."

"Not to worry, Emma. That's what's so impressive about Stan. He has his own mind. Besides I don't bad mouth Stanton, I just spar with him. Stanton defends vigorously because he is a true believer. You can't ask for more than that. The only opinion that truly matters is yours. Are you happy?"

Emma smiled and patted Ty's hand, "I have everything I could ever want. Stanton denies me nothing."

Ty returned the smile. He couldn't let the remark fade, "Yes, I can see you have nice things, Emma."

"That's not what I meant. I'm quite happy with my life. I have a very active social life. Even though Stanton is extremely busy, we manage to entertain frequently. We get on very well."

"You know what you want. That's all that matters."

Ty and Emma were quietly seated, looking out of the windows when Stan returned, "I feel human again."

Emma replied, "You look much better. You looked like a wild man with that beard."

Ty interrupted, "Stan how would you like to show me to the garage apartment so I can get cleaned up, too." He looked to Emma, "Stan says that would be the best place for me."

Emma shook her head, "Why? There's more than enough room in the main house. We have four guest suites. You can't even reach the staff from the apartment. There's no intercom."

Ty held up his hands, "That's fine. I don't need too big of a dose of reality too quickly. If it becomes a problem, I can move later."

Stan rose, "He'll be fine, Mom. You know I would have moved up there a long time ago if you would have let me."

Ty followed Stan through the dining room and the kitchen to a side door leading to the garage. When they were outside Stan asked, "So is everything cool with you two?"

"Yes, everything is fine. Emma and I are like two old friends who run into each other after many years. You know how it goes. We happily greet each other and quickly realize our past is the only thing we have in common. We cautiously avoid anything potentially contentious. I only asked one personal question and Emma quickly pointed out she has nice stuff. We pretty much left it there."

Stan started up the outside stairway behind the garage. He stopped halfway, noticing Ty struggling with the stairs because of his cast, "Sorry about the stairs, but there are stairs no matter where you stay in this house. At least out here you'll have some privacy."

"Why did they build an apartment out here anyway?"

"Dad was going to get a limo so he could work during his commute, but he changed his mind. This was for the chauffeur. He decided he couldn't trust anyone to be around his work."

Stan opened the door and turned on the lights, "Everything you need. Even a kitchenette. I'll get your bags before I go to get my license."

Stan returned with Ty's bag. He quickly turned to leave, "If I don't see you before, I'll see you at dinner. Seven o'clock sharp. Main dining room. It's not formal but you might want to wear a shoe."

# Chapter (14)

Ty entered the main house through the side door into the kitchen. Margaret and another woman were busily preparing dinner. Ty nodded to them, "Good evening, ladies."

Margaret looked up and quickly averted her eyes, "Good evening, sir." She went immediately back to work. Ty continued into the dining room. There were place settings for four so he was confident he was in the right room. He opened a bottle of wine and poured a glass. He sat down at the head of the table which could accommodate twenty plus people. Ty was quietly sitting in Stanton's chair when Stan appeared.

Ty held up his wine glass, "I was hoping I was in the right place. Is there a kiosk with a map somewhere if I get lost?"

Stan sat down in his customary seat to the left of Stanton's, "If you get lost just pull up to an intercom and ask for help."

Ty stood quickly when Emma entered the room. She was wearing an elegant lime green floor length gown, tastefully accented with a single strand of pearls. Ty tried to remember if her hair was different than it was when he had seen her hours earlier, "You look ravishing dear."

A booming voice came from the opposite entry, "How about me?" All three heads turned to see Stanton standing confidently in the doorway.

Ty started toward Stanton with his hand out, "Nice to see you, Stanton."

They were shaking hands when Stan exclaimed, "You're wearing shoes! Where's the cast?"

Ty smiled widely, turning all the way around, "Not bad, huh? I soaked it off in the bathtub. It was supposed to come off soon anyway."

Ty poured wine for everyone after they took their seats.

Stanton looked appraisingly at Stan, "I assume all went well? You seem to be in one piece."

Stan nodded, "Everything went fine. It was a great trip. I enjoyed it."

Stanton's eyes went back and forth between Stan and Ty before settling on Stan, "Why did you need a new driver's license?"

Stan flashed a quick grin at Ty, "Someone stole my wallet in a campground shower. You must have gotten my message."

Stanton calmly added, "No, I didn't. We monitor those things. There have been many people who have attempted to assume our identities. It's a safeguard, like monitoring police activity. It appears Mercer Island's finest didn't believe Ty's jalopy was consistent with our neighborhood. I saw it out front. I can see how they could make that mistake."

Stan shook his head, "You're amazing Dad, nothing gets by you."

"Nothing passes involving business or family. There is security in information." Stanton turned his attention to Ty, "How have you been? You haven't exposed my son to any delinquent behavior have you?"

Ty shrugged, "No, I've been good and yes, I've been just fine Stanton. Still the same, just older."

Stanton retorted, "That was my fear."

Emma interrupted, "Don't you two start snipping at one another. Let's have a nice dinner. You can insult each other after I leave."

Stanton continued, "No offense intended. I do need some clarification about a matter concerning you two. My assistant received a phone call yesterday mentioning both of you and I wanted to hear from you before I had it investigated. The caller identified himself only as Harold. He said to thank Stan and Ty and someone named Jeremy wants to paint his garage. What in the world does that mean?"

Stan and Ty exploded with laughter. Stan turned to his Father, "It doesn't mean anything, Dad. Harold is a guy we met in Wyoming. We helped him with a small problem, that's all. I floated one of your business cards. That's how he got the number. It's really nothing."

Stanton warily eyed them both, "It sounds quite humorous. Maybe you can fill me in on the joke sometime." He turned his attention to Ty, "So Ty, were you able to get your business affairs in order before you left?"

Ty nodded, "You bet. Everything is as it should be."

Stanton continued, "Did you ship some items? You couldn't possibly have brought a life time of possessions in that old van."

"Quite the contrary. I brought everything I cared to bring. I left some things with people who could use them."

Stanton pounced, "Like your house! You quit claim deeded your house to a complete stranger. That is insane even by your standards."

"They weren't strangers and they needed it, I didn't. It made me feel better than a cashiers check would have. Supply and demand Stanton, I had it and they needed it. Why would you care anyway?"

Stanton sneered, "Being liberal minded and charitable is fine but giving away your most valuable asset defies logic."

Ty grinned, "I don't think you've cornered the market on logic, Stanton. There are things that can't be valued on a Dunn and Bradstreet report. Don't worry, you don't need to bankroll me. I can support myself."

Stanton looked disgustedly at Ty, "I don't care about that. Emma wants you here. I'm simply trying to understand your thought process because from my perspective, giving away your home is beyond illogic. It is a completely irresponsible act."

"It was my decision, I made it, and I'm happy with it but if you have this logic thing nailed down, I have lots of questions."

"If you're searching for free financial advice, I'm afraid you're beyond help."

"No, my finances are just fine. I just thought you could use your superior insight to explain some things that never made any sense to me."

"I don't believe any of us will be around long enough to find the logic in your life but what else do you need to know?"

Ty kept grinning, "I've always wondered about Phoenix. It always seemed like an illogical city to me."

Stanton frowned, "What in the hell are you talking about? Every time I talk to you, your mind wanders off in some bizarre direction. But seeing how this is your first night with us, I'll bite. What is so illogical about Phoenix?"

Ty continued, "The fact it even exists doesn't make sense. I have this mental picture of the first settlers stopping in the middle of the desert, looking around and saying to themselves 'It's a hundred and twenty degrees in the shade and there's water barely a hundred miles away. Let's build.'"

Stanton's face couldn't mask his contempt, "Maybe it will come to you in a flashback."

He turned his attention to Stan, "Have you been exposed to this high level intellectual thinking across the whole country?"

Ty interrupted, "Sorry Stanton, I'm just trying to keep the mood light. You're still wound pretty tight."

Stanton quickly stood up, "I'll leave you merry pranksters to your fun. I have work to do."

Emma stood, excusing herself and followed Stanton from the dining room leaving Stan and Ty alone at the table.

Stan shook his head, "That was more civil than I expected."

"Don't worry, it'll get better. Your Dad is afraid I've infected you with a liberal virus. He's just trying to protect you." He stood up, "I think I'll retire too. Will you get me up early tomorrow?"

"Sure, see you in the morning."

# Chapter (15)

Ty was waiting and ready when Stan knocked on the door at seven thirty. They piled into Stan's six year old Acura. Stan turned to Ty, "Where to big guy?"

"Snoqualmie Falls. Have you ever been there?"

"Yeah, a few times. What did I miss?"

"I'll have to show you."

The rush hour traffic was its normal slow procession. Progress was slow with commuters flocking to the city centers. The traffic thinned out considerably when they turned onto Highway Two, opposite the worker's vehicles hurrying to their places of employment.

They were nearing the falls when Ty pointed, "Park on this side near the observation deck."

Stan parked in the near empty lot. They made the short walk to the observation deck. The viewing platform was directly across the canyon from the towering hundred foot water fall. The deck had a hand rail to keep the tourists from plunging to their deaths into the raging river below. The volume of water cascading down the cliff was impressive even though it was midsummer. Mist from the falls filled the air while the tremendous power of the falls sent shockwaves, noticeably vibrating the deck below their feet.

Stan and Ty stood at the rail admiring nature's handiwork for a few minutes before Ty finally spoke, "I wanted to tell you of a native legend about this spot. The legends say young lovers have gravitated to this very spot for thousands of years although they didn't have a deck to enjoy the view. The problems encountered by young love in ancient tradition are that most unions were either prearranged or were indentured servitude agreements so many love connections were 'never to be'. Scores of love struck men and women cast themselves into the torrent, professing their devotion to an unattainable love. The legends say their voices cry out from the falls to their lost loves. It's said if you close your eyes, calm your spirit, and clear your mind, you can still hear their cries." Ty looked earnestly at Stan, "It might sound silly but I was hoping you would give it a try."

Stan's eyes narrowed with skepticism, "It does sound a little out there. It's not a joke, right? You didn't bring me all the way up here just to make fun of me?"

Ty put his hand on Stan's shoulder, "No joke, Stan. It's only a joke if we're both laughing. I'm dead serious. Just try it. Relax and open your mind to it. It can't hurt."

Stan stepped to the rail. He leaned his hips against the metal rail and closed his eyes. He could feel the mist on his face. The deck vibrated beneath his feet. The roar of the falls was the only sound. He tried to relax to the uncertainty.

After an excruciating length of time, possibly five minutes, Stan cracked his eyelids for a quick peek. He asked in a whisper, "How long does it take?"

Ty answered softly, "However long it takes."

Stan tried even harder to relax, though, it became doubly hard when a group of sightseers joined them on the deck. The sound of their voices and their footsteps diverted Stan's attention from the voices in the falls. It was another distorted length of time before Stan opened his eyes and turned to Ty who was standing silently beside him, "I don't think I can do it. I don't hear anything. Do you?"

Ty opened his eyes, "No, not a thing." He motioned at a bench, "Let's go over there and sit for a minute." They sat down and Ty continued, "Maybe you didn't hear anything but what were you thinking?"

Stan pondered the question before replying, "I was trying to focus on the falls but I couldn't shut everything else out. When I heard people's voices on the deck, I couldn't concentrate at all."

Ty nodded, "I hear you. I don't know about you but when I heard the people I couldn't stop thinking anyone of them could push me or simply grab my legs and flip me over the rail to my death."

Stan nodded vigorously, "For sure. I couldn't stop thinking about it. I felt helpless and completely vulnerable."

Ty's patented grin appeared, "Isn't that something. I mean, seriously think about that. You've lived here your whole life and of the millions of people who visit this spot, have you ever heard of someone being pushed, let alone by a stranger. This is a lesson about indoctrination and control. We are all programmed with fear. Fear causes us to view the world in an unrealistic light. The fear isn't real, Stan. It's manufactured. Odds are you could stand at that rail forever and no one would ever push you but your fear of it happening is absolutely real. Shark attacks make the news because they're rare events but millions of people shun the water because of the threat of sharks. There hasn't been a documented case of a wolf attack on a human in a hundred years but man still hunted them to near extinction out of fear. Fear as a social control mechanism has been used forever. The sociological term for it is 'Hegelian Dialectic'; event/solution/ synthesis. The Patriot Act was a Hegelian reaction to a fear inspiring event. Fear empowers evil people while it silences sane voices. What I'm trying to say, Stan, is most fear is an illusion and it can be totally debilitating. Use your own judgment, Stan, and make up your own mind. That, my friend, is the extent of my advice for you."

Stan looked into Ty's eyes for an extended time before offering his hand, "Thanks."

Ty slapped his hand away and hugged Stan.

Stan stood up, "Tell me the truth, Ty. Do you hear the voices?"

Ty looked at the falls, "Hell no. If I ever got that relaxed, the only sound you would hear is my scream after I fell over the rail."

The following days made Stan feel like a kid again. Working side by side with Ty tearing down Thumper is what growing up male is all about. Young men and a fascination with machinery. There were no shop classes at prep school so this particular right of passage had evaded Stan. Ty, always the teacher, allowed Stan to immerse himself in the project. Ty answered every question, he explained every component. Stan was in heaven. It wasn't a lack of desire which had precluded Stan from owning motorcycles and go karts in his youth. Stan once attended a motocross race when he was fourteen years old, followed by years of dreaming and scheming to acquire a dirt bike of his own. There were motorcycle magazines stashed in his desk and brochures of motocross bikes taped on the walls of his closet. Stan couldn't reconcile he lived a privileged life but he couldn't have the things he wanted. 'It's too dangerous' is not an acceptable excuse to a teenage boy. Teenagers are invincible. To a hormonally powered teenage male, stunts are an inspiration not a deterrent. Stan was frustrated because he had the desire and the means. What he didn't have was his parents' approval. His Father's disapproval seemed strange. Hadn't he been a teenager once? Why didn't he understand? Stan convinced himself to force a confrontation, man on man. He had been bullied by his Father for his entire life. Stan was sixteen years old and the time had come to stand up and be counted. He spent days mentally rehearsing undeniably logical reasons for motorcycle ownership. Stan summoned all of his courage and stormed the castle door to his Father's study. Logic and benefit were lost before he finished his first sentence. The confrontation ended like all before. They were all progressive events; starting slowly, fading quickly and falling apart rapidly. That particular day ended with Stan's sheepish retreat to the sound of his Father's bellowing response, "Get that fucking motorcycle out of your head! It's not going to happen! It's trailer trash shit! You have things to do that can't be accomplished from a wheelchair. I didn't invest in your future to see you throw it away on a boyhood fantasy. If it's pain you want, I'll kick your ass. Get it out of your head and get out of here, I have work to do."

That was the last time the word motorcycle was spoken in the house until Thumper arrived. Thumper was now a sea of disassembled parts spread out on the garage floor. Stan and Ty sat on stools surveying their handiwork.

Ty said, "If you get a pen and paper, we can make a list of the parts we need. What would you think about taking a trip to Portland? There used to be a place called Hub Cycle, they specialized in British bikes. It was a great place to browse. The walls were lined with restored Triumphs, BSAs, Nortons, Vincents, AJS's, Ariels, almost anything you could think of. A friend of mine had a John Player Norton. Hub Cycle had the only other one I ever saw outside of a magazine, hanging from the ceiling. I hope they're still there."

"We can go tomorrow if you'd like. I'm anxious to hear her run."

"Good, because I don't think my ankle will be strong enough to kick start her so you'll have to do it. Do you think your Mother would want to go with us? I never see her except at dinner. Where does she hide all day?"

Stan chuckled, "You can ask but I seriously doubt she will come. I can't remember the last time Mom went anywhere with me. She has luncheon friends, shopping friends, and country club friends. If she isn't at a social function or entertaining, she's usually in her room in the Queen's Wing. I talk more to her on the intercom than I do in person. Dad stays at the office suite a lot so I only see him a few times a week. Yes sir, we are one tight family unit. We're only close when there are witnesses. If you want to ask her, I'd call her on the intercom. If you ask her at dinner, Dad will answer for her and he should be home tonight. He very rarely misses three in a row."

Ty moved to the intercom and pressed the page button, "Emma! Emma! Are you out there? Talk to me woman."

Ty waited patiently. It took a minute before Emma replied, "Yes Daddy, what do you need?"

"I just wanted to talk to you. Can we meet somewhere?"

There was a noticeable pause, "I'll meet you in the atrium in a few minutes. Is that alright?"

"See you there Em, over and out." Ty shook his head as he turned away from the intercom, "That is one of the most impersonal contraptions I've ever seen and I thought phones were bad."

He left Stan seated, contentedly staring at the ocean of Thumper parts. Ty stopped for an iced tea on his way to the atrium where he waited almost forty minutes for Emma to arrive. She appeared, seemingly dressed for an exclusive cocktail party. Ty caught a faint scent of alcohol as Emma leaned to kiss his cheek.

"Hello Daddy, what can I do for you?"

"I just wanted to talk to you. I only see you at dinner. Stan and I are going to Portland for some bike parts and I thought you might like to go with us."

"That's really sweet, but I can't. I have so many details to attend to. We are hosting the museum fundraiser this year, but thank you for asking."

"When's the fundraiser?"

"It's not until September but there is so much to do before then."

"Wow, you're down to the wire. Only two months to go."

"Don't be sarcastic. These events are important to me. Stanton's business associations are pivotal to my charity work. I take it quite seriously."

Ty thought better of challenging, "I don't mean any disrespect Emma. It's strange for me to see you as a socialite. I missed the transformation from the daughter of a drop out professor to the Queen of the Seattle social scene. Your life is so ordered, everything has its place. I'm lucky if my socks match."

Emma's voice lowered, "Stan seems to enjoy spending time with you. Have you told him about your health issues?"

"He knows about my heart problems but I haven't told him about the cancer. You're right, I should tell him. Honestly, I don't feel differently yet, so I don't think much about it."

"I wish you would try the available treatments. Watching Momma deteriorate was horrible. I don't want to see you suffer needlessly."

"Emma, I've thought about it for over thirty years. I've replayed what Belle went through a thousand times. Not only do I understand why she refused the chemo and radiation, I agree completely. You need to remember her strength and stop focusing on her pain. Your Mother was one of the smartest people I've ever known and I'll guarantee you she made her decisions based on sound thinking. Introducing enough chemicals and radiation in the hope of killing the cancer without killing the patient is totally illogical to me. It reminds me of medieval bloodletting and I won't do either."

"But Daddy, medical care has advanced by leaps and bounds in the decades since Momma died. It doesn't have to be like that anymore."

"I'll agree the technology and training has advanced but the healthcare industry is farther off base now than they ever have been. Cancer is no longer simply a disease, it's a multi billion dollar industry. With profit as the primary driving force in healthcare there is no incentive to eliminate sickness. Profit comes from treatment not cures. The healthcare industry lives in the corporate world and corporate profits can only be increased by higher fees or increasing illness. I don't trust them. It's that simple. But I will talk to Stan."

Emma rose, "You are still the most hard headed man I have ever known. Don't ask me to watch the end. Now if you'll excuse me I have to dress for dinner. Stanton called earlier and he will be home this evening. I will see you at dinner."

Ty watched Emma retreat to the Queens Wing. He was stunned she felt the need to change from one designer outfit to another just to eat in the next room. 'High society is labor intensive.'

# Chapter (16)

Stanton, Emma and Ty were seated when Stan arrived for dinner. Stan took his seat and poured himself a glass of wine.

Stanton asked, "When do you plan to leave for Europe?"

Stan took a leisurely sip from his wine glass before answering, "I don't think I want to go. I thought I would hang around here with Ty. We want to get the motorcycle running and we've talked about chartering a sailboat."

Stanton frowned, "You would prefer wasting your summer here instead of touring Europe? I feel a little slighted. This trip was a graduation gift."

Stan recognized his Father's tone. Stanton had, obviously, consumed a few cocktails before dinner. That always called for tact, "I really appreciate it, Dad. I just think I might enjoy myself more at home. I hope that isn't a problem?"

Stanton looked warily at Stan and then at Ty, "No problem, Stan. I should probably be more concerned you would rather spend your time with Ty than your friends. Ty's bleeding heart could splash all over you. You have worked too hard to have any of his nonsense interfere with your future."

Ty snickered, "You don't give your son enough credit, Stanton. You should talk to him some time. He has a mind of his own. I would be honored to spend my time with Stan."

Stanton's alcohol induced scowl was deeply embedded on his face. His eyes were ablaze with contempt, "I don't need you to tell me who and what my son is."

Emma took notice of Stanton's demeanor. She rose to her feet,

"It's apparent you two aren't going to be civil so I'm going to excuse myself. I have no desire to listen to you insult each other."

The instant Emma was out of the room Stanton zeroed in on Ty, "She doesn't want a virtual stranger telling us about our son anymore than I do."

Stan interrupted, "You do understand I'm sitting right here?"

Stanton didn't bother to glance Stan's way, "Well Stan, maybe you need to know more about the man behind all the bullshit. I'm sure Ty has dazzled you with his Earth shattering opinions coupled with his dark stories of covert actions and conspiracies. Don't ever forget Stan, people who can't do, teach, and people who don't participate, complain."

"You are a piece of work, Stanton. Have you ever noticed why you can't have an intellectual discussion? Because when you disagree you don't debate, you attack. Well go for it. This is your chance to protect your investment before I contaminate his mind with my insanity. I've only offered Stan one small piece of advice so your indoctrination should be safe." Ty grinned at Stan, "Your Dad wants to shock you with tales of my inglorious past."

Stanton's eyes narrowed as he approached his prey, "It has nothing to do with shock. I want to add some truth to the fairy tales coming out of you."

Ty laughed, "You have my attention. You're going to add truth? That's never been your strength, Stanton."

"I'm sure the bullshit stories you've told Stan about me aren't even remotely close to being truthful."

"I haven't told any Stanton stories. If you want your dirty laundry aired you'll have to do it yourself. I agree Stan's future is more important than our pasts but you want to bury yours. At least I own mine."

Stanton sneered, "Don't attempt to spar with me from your high horse. Your whole life is nothing but a series of failures and embarrassments." He turned to Stan, "Did he tell you about him and that giant Indian getting drunk and vandalizing the State Capital. I'll bet you didn't hear any stories about that arrest."

Stan looked at Ty's grinning face, "All true, Stan. We used weed killer to spell out 'Bite Me' on the lawn. It was a thing of beauty."

Stanton roared, "Beauty! They had to returf the whole fucking lawn you lunatic! Are you listening to this Stan? Does that sound like the actions of a sane person? What about that stupid stunt at The White House? This idiot was chaining plastic skeletons in military uniforms to the White House fence. What a brilliant way to affect foreign policy."

"You're not the one to instruct anyone about brilliance. Hell, your bank puts Braille instructions on the ATM machines at the drive up window. Now that's brilliant."

Stan asked, "Did you really do that? Was it during the Vietnam War?"

Stanton cut off any response, "Vietnam, my ass. It was last year. Ty has been a moron for decades. You need the whole story. Not just his lies."

"Hold it! I might be a lot of things but liar is not one of them. Yes Stan, I was chaining corpses to the fence. I still had a dozen more in Brutus when they stopped me. I was pissed. While the government and media were romanticizing the anniversary of the war, I was listening to the testimonies of the Winter Soldiers. Those poor men and women felt totally betrayed by another rich man's war they were sent to fight and die in. I cried my eyes out and then I went to D.C. I've always been a sucker for desperate, futile acts." Ty turned back to Stanton, "Come on Stanton, you're still not shocking him. You want Stan to have truth, give him some. Tell him how scared you are he might see the world differently than you. Tell him how terrified you are he won't accept his legacy like you did from your Father. Tell him how frightened you are he might figure out he has to accept his entitlement to justify feeling superior like you do."

"Don't you dare speak to me about legacy. My Father was a great man. He did whatever was necessary to protect his family. What's your legacy? You gave away the only thing of value you ever had. What do you have left? That pathetic portfolio of stocks? Are you planning on getting four more shares of my bank so you can make a run at me?"

"Careful Stanton. My portfolio is supposed to be confidential between me and my broker. You might give Stan the impression you engage in illegal intelligence activities."

"I monitor your sorry ass for my own entertainment and to protect my family from you. If you want to accuse me of illegal acts, roll the dice."

"I have no desire to attack you. I told Stan exactly how I feel about you. I think you are an elitist and a pompous ass but I respect that you honestly believe in your corrupt world. Your mistake is trying to shelter Stan from anyone who disagrees with you. Power brokers are all the same. You surround yourself with people who agree with you and plot to destroy anyone who doesn't."

"Nice spin, Ty, its called conviction. Men with power take charge because the masses think they are capable of self rule but they're wrong. Great men know what you don't. People aren't capable of self determination. People are sheep and they need to be led like sheep. The illusion is in the eyes of people like you who believe your participation will make things better. I use wealth to create wealth. You throw it away. Who's the fool? Look around, the whole world belongs to the market you despise. Which one of us is in denial?"

"Denial? Are you kidding? I absolutely believe, but that doesn't make it right. There's a fundamental flaw to your perspective. You believe you have the right to decide what is best for others just because you can. You're getting a little sidetracked, Stanton. I thought this attack was supposed to be a character assassination."

"My pointing out your infamous past isn't an attack, it's a history lesson Professor. Oh, excuse me. You quit that job, too. Did you tell Stan about your prison time for aiding and abetting terrorists?"

Ty laughed, "Talk about spin. They arrested me for hiding some people who were trying to stop a mine that was poisoning their water, from reopening. Terrorists attack people. Environmentalists attack machinery. Those people had every right to protect their homes. I'd do the same thing again. If you want to throw down the gauntlet, go for it. Why don't you include your Father's story about his rise to power because of the mines?"

"Fuck you, Ty. You aren't even qualified to speak about my Father. He did what needed to be done. Nothing more."

Stan looked confused, "What the hell are you two talking about?"

Stanton replied, "It was an illegal strike at Colorado Copper in the 1930's. My Father arranged for the removal of illegal squatters so the mine could reopen. Militant strikers only respond to force. My Father was rewarded for doing what was necessary. That's how business works. It takes a man of conviction to make the tough decisions and sometimes people get hurt. That's the way of the world. I will not apologize for my Father's actions and I won't tolerate you disrespecting his memory."

"The truth isn't disrespectful. Trying to call it conviction is the fairy tale. Your Father paid the salaries of the National Guardsman so they would open fire on defenseless men, women and children for John D. Rockefeller. You may call Ludlow good business but I call it contract murder."

"The law saw it differently, didn't they? My Father did everything for his family, no apologies. We make this life possible so bleeding hearts like you can bitch about it. Instead of complaining, you should be on your knees thanking us."

"And there it is full circle. Our rulers deserve to be rulers because their superior breeding entitles them to rule. Poor people don't get a voice because they don't deserve one. You know Stanton, I feel sorry for you. I may have a checkered past but at least in my life I've known people I absolutely trust. On the day you die, you won't know one person. That's sad."

Stanton stood up, "Save your pity. If you're feeling sorry for me then this conversation must be over because that is absurd. I trust but verify. That's why I am where I am and why I am who I am."

"You're delusional. You don't even know what's going on in your own house and you think you have your hand on the pulse of the world."

Stanton glared, "Why don't you go back to the mountains? I told Emma it was a bad idea to bring you here. You can die just as easily in West Virginia as you can here."

Stan spun around, "What's he talking about?"

"I should have told you Stan. I've got cancer. It's not that big of a deal. I don't feel any different."

"Why didn't you tell me?"

Stanton interrupted, "Because Ty only tells what Ty wants known. He wants you to think he's a wise old man when he's nothing but an old fool!"

Stan held up his hand to his Father. His eyes were glued on Ty, "You should have told me. I thought we were friends."

Stanton interrupted again, "Ty doesn't have friends. He has audiences until they tire of his bullshit. Belinda died to get away from him."

Ty exploded out of his chair, "You son of a bitch!"

Stan jumped up and stepped in front of Stanton, "Shut up Dad! That was uncalled for."

Stanton hit Stan with the palms of both opened hands on the chest, driving him back several steps. Stanton roared, "Don't tell me what to do in my own fucking house! I tell you!" His wild eyes glared at Stan, "Don't ever get in my face again unless you want your ass kicked! You hear me?"

This was the moment Stan had always known would come. The entirety of his existence led to this very instant. The threshold to Stan's personal manhood was before him. Stan didn't hesitate. He stepped confidently, putting his chest against his Father's. Stan's eyes bore into his Father's. Stan's voice was a low growl. "You've been threatening me my whole life. If you're going to do it then do it. Otherwise, shut the fuck up! "Stan held his ground and willed himself not to blink while bracing himself for the fury that was sure to come.

Their eyes locked on each other for a tense moment before Stanton stepped back. Pointing at Ty as he retreated to the doorway, "Fuck you old man. Don't get too comfortable because you aren't going to be in my house for long!"

"Don't worry, I don't want to make trouble for Emma and Stan. Look around sometime superstar, your wife is an alcoholic."

Stanton spun around, huffed and stormed away.

Ty looked sadly at Stan, "I'm so sorry Stan. I never meant for it to go this far."

Stan stood facing Ty, "You should have told me, Ty."

Ty looked at the floor, "You're right."

"Did you mean what you said about Mom?"

"I'm afraid so. I noticed it every time I've seen her. Maybe she'll talk to you, Stan. I can't get into her world but you are her world. She's all alone Stan and all the luxury in the world won't change that."

Ty went to the wine rack and opened a bottle, "I'm going out back for awhile."

Stan watched Ty disappear. Stan picked up his wine glass taking it into the atrium. Stan sat down in a resigning cloud of resentment. 'Why can't adults act like adults?' Stan's thoughts drifted, his Dad and Ty had him in an awkward place. He wasn't going to abandon his newfound friendship with Ty and he couldn't turn his back on his Father but why should he have to. They're the ones with the problem, not him. He didn't have a dog in this fight. For that matter, he actually didn't know what the source of Ty and Stanton's distaste for each other truly was. It was definitely well beyond a disagreement over idealism and philosophy. The roots for their disdain were formed deeply and long ago.

Stan stood quickly, with real purpose. "Screw them! I'm not

making any choices! They can both just deal with it!" He picked up a bottle of wine and a corkscrew and headed for the apartment.

Ty was sitting on the bottom stair of the stairway leading to the apartment. Ty held up the bottle of wine when he saw Stan.

Stan drug a lawn chair with him from the patio. He took a seat facing Ty, "How you doing? That got a little intense in there."

"Sorry man. We both went off the deep end wrestling for your approval. That was a lousy position to put you into."

Stan shrugged, "No big deal. This house is too boring. We needed some excitement."

Ty sat silently for a long while, passing the bottle back and forth with Stan. Stan broke the silence, "You're going to leave, aren't you?"

Ty sighed, "Yeah, I am. Emma knows how to avoid being in the middle but you won't have that option. I don't want to put you or her in that situation. Besides Stan, I think you've awakened something in me. I want to write again, I really do. For the first time in a long time and most likely the last time. I'm sorry I didn't tell you about the cancer, but in my defense, I honestly don't think much about it. I mean, I think about death but I'm seventy two so it comes with the territory. You know something, Stan, death doesn't scare me at all. It's just the pits you have to die to get to it."

"I think you were always going to use your conflict with Dad as an excuse to leave. Don't you think that's selfish?"

"Hell yes, it's selfish. You need to understand we're all who we are because of our life experiences. Belle was and will always be the defining experience of my life. The rest of it is filler. I watched the love of my life dissolve in agony right before my eyes. Belle has filtered every breath I've taken in my life. I think about Belle everyday, Stan. Everyday. I watched her die and I couldn't help her. I'll never forgive myself." Ty took a long pull on the bottle. His eyes slumped to the ground. When he raised his head, his eyes were red and swollen with tears of true sorrow. Ty's eyes revealed the lifelong pain beneath, "The last week of Belle's life, she begged me to kill her. Belle was the strongest person I've ever known and she was begging me to kill her, but I'm a selfish son of a bitch. I couldn't do it. Every once in awhile I'd see a little spark in her eyes. There'd be quick little peeks at the woman I loved behind the pain. I couldn't let her go. I wanted every single second I could get. Sometimes she would drift off to sleep and I'd be afraid she wouldn't come back. I'd lie down beside her and hold her so tight she could never escape this world. A person can't be more selfish than me."

"You're WAY too hard on yourself. You've punished yourself for a lifetime over something you couldn't possibly have changed. Even Mom thinks you're too tough on yourself."

"Emma was only ten years old and Belle was so strong. She tried so hard to not let Emma see her pain, but Emma knew. I don't want to impact anyone with memories like those about me. That's my decision, that's why, and that's the way it's going to be."

They finished the first bottle and Stan opened the second. Stan asked, "So what are you going to write about?"

"I think I'm going to try to tie together the only things I know, history and pain. There's no shortage of either. There are so many people with pain filled stories never told. I'd like to give them a voice."

"Do you honestly believe there's been an orchestrated conspiracy causing that pain?"

"Absolutely. I'm not sure conspiracy is the proper terminology, though. It's been the control mechanisms that doomed the majority of people in history into a struggle for survival while a select group enjoyed the luxuries of leadership. Myth, legend, religion, monarchs, governments, empires, capitalism have all exerted influence. They convinced the people the rulers deserved to rule. The faces of power have changed. The mechanisms evolve and transform, but they never go away. They never have. Power vacuums are quickly filled with the new rulers trying to avoid the pitfalls that threatened their predecessors. We live in a world that's been directed by powerful groups who have taken six thousand years to perfect the art of population control. Occasionally a ruling class will claim an unreasonable portion of the resources and wealth, giving life to rebellion. It's happened almost everywhere at some point; France, Russia, China, America. They all rose to confront tyranny. The lesson lost to history is when the overwhelming will of the people confronts a corrupt ruling class, the rulers flee. First and foremost, soldiers and police are of the people so when they see the rulers are unworthy of their support there is no one to protect the rulers. That's the irony of history. The only way a ruling class can survive is with the consent of the people. I think that's why I'm so disappointed with my generation. The social awakening in the sixties gave us a glimpse at a social conscience. We correctly identified the flaw in the system. It was called The Establishment or simply' The Man' but either way it was the truth. The priority of all of man's organizations should be built on the basic premise the people should benefit first. People love to make fun of people like Timothy Leary even though he was right about some things. Tune in for sure, turn on, which is a personal choice, and drop out, absolutely. If everyone recognized the threat and turned away, the rulers would be gone. Power exists because we empower it. If you want to know who is a threat to the ruling class just look at who they persecute. Rulers don't want the people to hear ideas sounding more logical than the ideas of the rulers themselves. The idealism of the sixties confronted some serious issues and then slowly melted into the machine. If the idealism of those times had been mobilized behind a common goal like the IWW did in the early part of the twentieth century, the results would have been extraordinary. The Wobblies were only around as a power for a little over a decade but they scared the shit out of the establishment. Their message was simple enough for all to understand, share the wealth with the workers or the workers will stand united and close down the machine. The IWW had over five million members and was growing when their threat to power was confronted. The assault on the Wobblies was brutal. Leaders were imprisoned, deported, assaulted, intimidated and outright murdered.

The fury that crushed the IWW was unprecedented in American labor history. I admire those people because they fought the righteous fight, even though they lost. My generation identified the threat, roared our disapproval and slowly integrated into the machines of the threat. We didn't make the world better. It's far worse. I'm sorry, Stan."

"No hope, huh Ty?"

"There's always hope. We're all still here. You give me hope, Stan. There are men of power and there are men of conscience. Very rarely are they the same man. I think you could be a different breed and I hope you can leave a better world for your children." Ty took the bottle from Stan, "I'm ramblin'. I've had too much to drink."

He handed Stan the bottle. Stan drained the rest as Ty stood to leave. Stan looked up at Ty, "I want to have passion in my life like yours."

Ty looked down at Stan. The tears again bubbled up. He smiled, turned and headed up the stairs. Softly he said, "Good night, Stan."

# Chapter (17)

Stan knocked on the door to the Queens Wing. It was nine o'clock. His Mother should be up by now. He knocked again.

Emma's voice came through the door, "Who's there?"

"It's me, Mom. Can I come in? I want to talk to you."

The door opened just enough for her to peek through, "I'm not even dressed."

Stan put his hand on the door, "It doesn't matter. Have some coffee with me, please?"

Emma stepped back allowing Stan to enter. He took a few steps into the room before stopping to take it in, "You know, in all these years I've never been in here."

Emma pointed to a table on the balcony, "I'll have Margaret bring coffee." She called Margaret on the intercom before joining Stan on the balcony.

Stan calmly stated, "Ty is leaving. He's probably already gone."

Emma was visibly surprised, "Why? What happened? Where will he go?"

"Dad and Ty really got into it last night. They were both throwing truth bombs. It got pretty ugly. Ty didn't think his living here was going to work. He's probably right."

Emma reached across the table and rested her hand on Stan's, "I'm so sorry. Daddy has always been impulsive. He really cares about you, Stan."

"I know. I think I'm more upset we're not going to hang out together. I don't feel like a kid when I'm with Ty."

"I can talk to Stanton, maybe we can work this out."

"Don't bother. Ty isn't coming back. That doesn't matter now, anyway. I've come to realize I'm going to be leaving soon, too, and I don't know anything about you. I learned more about your life from Ty than I've ever learned from you. I want to know you and not the Rotary Club you. I'm your only son. I'd like to be your friend."

Tears began forming in the corners of Emma's eyes. She took a handkerchief from her robe pocket and dabbed at her tears, "What do you want to know?"

Margaret entered with coffee for two. After she left, Stan asked, "You know Ty was a writer. Have you ever read anything he wrote?"

Emma rose, striding confidently to the end table beside her bed. She removed a thin book from the drawer and brought it to Stan, "It's the only thing I have. I don't know of anything else he published. It's a book of short stories and essays honoring Rachel Carson."

Stan opened the book to the only page with a bookmark. The page contained a short untitled passage. Stan quickly glanced at the bottom to see the author's name, 'Ty Hanstead'. His eyes returned to the beginning:

'His innocence powered hope. The world beyond his vision was his destiny. Man released in black billowing clouds light the Mother had nurtured through the ages. The man child looked trivial upon what should be coveted. The balance of a million sunsets was breeched, benefiting few at a price to all. The hordes looked ever forward, no memory of a road behind. The hordes became masses pondering only what could be but never what truly was. Coronated the chosen child by his own hand, he chose to own. With the Mother's tools he chose to rule. Self proclaimed, he turned away from the needs of the other children. The Mother held us all, the child released his grip on life's touch. He rose to power at the peril of his future. Empty vision condemns his legacy. The Mother's love is no longer unconditional. Darkness is the price of his arrogance. Good night Mother.'

Ty Hanstead

Stan looked up at his Mother. She said, "I think that's how Daddy sees life, dark but elegant. After Momma died, Daddy couldn't reconcile a God. He had nowhere to place his anger or his forgiveness."

"As dark as it is, it's kind of true. This is all you know of Ty's writings?"

"It's the only thing I know that was published. I have a short story he wrote for me when I was a little girl."

"Can I see it?"

Emma returned to the nightstand and retrieved an envelope. She handed the envelope to Stan. He took out two yellowing, hand written pages;

'The villagers fled in horror as the silhouette of the mighty Dragon filled the eastern sky. The Dragon's piercing scream gripped the villager's hearts. They ran from the blistering heat on their backs while they saw fiery death before them. A scorching wind was spawned by the wings of the mighty beast. The monster burned a path of destruction as he dove on the town. The terrified villagers ran mindlessly in frantic chaos. The sinister demon made a sweeping turn, soaring into the western sky. The Dragon's evil, yellow eyes scanned, menacingly, the village below, planning his next lethal path. The villagers screamed in horror, they ran in fear, they knew not where to hide. The monster roared. The frightened villagers covered their ears. The Demon dove on the helpless crowds. At the edge of town stood a lone warrior. Proud and defiant the warrior held forth a shield, mirroring the sun's brightness as a challenge to the mighty Dragon. The champion held high a spear, screaming at the massive beast. The Dragon dove at the lone sentry. The evil monster lowered his head, releasing an inferno that turns men into dust. The flames engulfed the brave soldier but the shield remained high and proud. The menacing head of the creature stayed low to the ground so the monster could swallow the body of the foolish champion. His evil eyes caught a flash of reflected sunlight at the last instant. The warriors spear thrust upward with incredible speed and power. The spear found its mark, deep into the flesh just above the breast plate. The only weakness of a Dragon. The deathly scream drove the villagers to their knees. The impact of the monster crashing to the ground was louder than any clap of thunder. The monster's dying body plowed a deep trench, the length and breadth of the main street. The warrior walked slowly to the head of the dead beast. The villagers slowly gathered around their savior. Only then did the warrior set down the shield and remove the glistening helmet. It was her! It was Emma, the beautiful Warrior Princess! The only hero with the strength and courage to defeat such a powerful enemy. The villagers sang her praises. They screamed her name to the heavens. The brave warrior climbed atop the demon. She held up her hand to silence the crowd. The beautiful Princess looked out at the sea of faces before she parted her lips to share her wisdom, "You can't slay Dragons if you refuse to believe they exist."

Stan looked up from the story, "That is really cool. I can see why you hung onto it for all these years."

"That's the only story Daddy wrote down for me. He could sure tell a great story, though."

Stan paused, "Are your childhood memories good ones?"

"Mostly. We didn't lead what you might call a normal life. We traveled a lot. I remember living in a lot of different places. I'll tell you one thing about my memories which are a little different. I can't picture Momma without Daddy in the picture. I know they were apart sometimes but I can't picture it. In my childhood memories, they were always together."

"I know I've never seen anyone light up like Ty does when he talks about Grandma. They must have gotten along really well."

"They did. Momma could be kind of mean to Daddy, though. I remember them arguing a lot but it never affected them at all."

"What about you and Dad. I don't know any of your story. Why is there so much bad blood between Ty and Dad?"

"I was a sophomore at the university when I met your Father." Emma took the handkerchief from her pocket again. She looked deep into Stan's eyes, "Only truth, Stan. I was hopelessly in love with a boy named Troy Madsen. His Mother and Momma were best friends so Troy and I played together many times when we were kids. After Momma died I only saw Troy a few times until I ran into him on campus. Troy was a senior by that time. We fell in love. It was a glorious time for me. Troy was working as an intern at a downtown bank. It happened to be the bank Stanton's Father sent Stanton to be groomed for his future responsibilities. That's where I met your Father. Stanton began pursuing me from the first time we met. He was relentless. He showered me with gifts and overwhelmed me with his advances. I rejected them all. I was completely in love with Troy. That spring Troy was arrested for his part in an embezzlement scheme at Stanton's bank. Troy swore to me he had nothing to do with it but it didn't seem to matter. The trial happened extremely fast and Troy was convicted and sent to prison. It was surprising to everyone he was immediately sent to McNeil Island instead of a medium security facility. Stanton was there through it all. He convinced me Troy had to have been guilty. All the evidence certainly pointed that way. I accepted Stanton's support and I turned my back on Troy. To this day I feel like I abandoned Troy when he needed me most. Daddy thought Troy had been railroaded but he didn't interfere with Stanton and I. Stanton opened up a world to me I would never have believed existed. I was totally blinded by the brilliance of Stanton's star. We were married the next spring. It wasn't a month after our wedding Troy was killed in prison. Daddy blamed Stanton. They had a vicious confrontation. It was horrible but that was the beginning of their feud."

"Do you think Dad had something to do with it?"

Emma looked out the window into empty space, "I don't know, Stan. I really don't know."

"I heard you say a few times you were in love with Troy but I never heard you say you were in love with Dad."

"It's different with Stanton. Our marriage is based on responsibility and respect. There are parts of Stanton's world which are my responsibility. The appearance of family unity is paramount to someone of Stanton's stature. Everything we enjoy is dependent on an aura of solid dependability. I may not have a perfect companion, but my compensation is I can have whatever I desire."

Stan thought about it before asking, "Is Dad's apartment in the city because there are other women?"

Emma looked directly at Stan, "Yes."

Stan was temporarily stunned. He stared at his Mother before responding, "Doesn't that bother you? Doesn't it bother you that you can't say you love your husband?"

"It used to. You need to understand, Stan. Your Father is good to me. We may lack involvement but we have a commitment. Maybe I settled but I settled for security. Love causes pain. Look at Daddy, he's never recovered."

"Are you kidding? Ty never wanted to recover. He's been celebrating and embracing his love for a lifetime. You can't avoid love just because it might lead to pain. I want to feel like Ty does and I don't care about the pain. Even pain is better than not having emotions. I'm never going to abandon someone again just because it's the easiest thing to do. I made a huge mistake when I left Hannah. I let Dad bully me into losing someone I loved and I will never do that again."

"I can't counsel you on matters of love but I do need to add, you must be careful in picking your battles with Stanton. Your Father belongs to a circle of men who wield power you couldn't possibly understand. Stanton can open any door for you but he can just as easily close them all. Stanton's Father would have crushed Daddy if he had pursued the allegations about Troy. It was me who convinced Daddy to move away to avoid that possibility. I was hoping enough time had passed we could move beyond those times but I guess I was wrong."

Stan looked long and hard before asking, "After all this time if Dad had something to do with it, would you want to know?"

There was no hesitation with Emma's response, "No, I wouldn't. It would serve no purpose. I have to live with my decisions and I've made my peace with it."

"Did you make your peace by drinking?"

Emma sat bolt upright. Her face revealed her shock. Her eyes revealed her shame. Tears instantly filled her eyes, "I'm sorry," was all she was able to get out before her tears became sobs.

Stan reached across the table and took both of Emma's hands in his own, "I'm worried about you. That's all, Mom."

The clock ticked off an eternity filled with regret before Emma's eyes searched out Stan. She released Stan's hands to wipe away her tears, never releasing Stan's eyes, "Maybe I wasn't strong enough. I hope you are. I did what I had to. You know Daddy; he would never have backed down. Stanton relented for me and Daddy moved away. Daddy had no idea who he was challenging. If any part of his allegations were true, Daddy could have been in grave danger." A fire entered Emma's eyes. With a determination Stan had never seen in his Mother, she took a firm hold of his hands, "Stan, you need to listen to me now. There are things you need to know. I married into this world of power but you were born to it. I can live without knowing everything that involves but you can't. I could get out if I cared to but I honestly don't know if you can. You are going to have to face your legacy in that world and there is nothing I can do to change it or to help you. All of our collective pasts will force you to face your own future. That is my sadness, Stan. I can't help you. I hope you are smarter and stronger than all of us."

Stan rose and walked around the table to gently kiss his Mother's cheek. He paused at the door, looking back at his Mother, "I love you, Mom. Thank you."

# Chapter (18)

Stan spun slowly around in his computer chair. His thoughts were a swirling incomprehensible cloud. What does a person do with all the information that had been dumped on him? One day you're a happy go lucky college grad; the next you're the son of a murderer. What do you say when you're told you are being groomed for a seat at the Legion of Doom. The ring of his cell phone shattered his confused daydream, "Stan's phone."

"Stan man. How you doing?"

It took Stan a minute to place the woman's voice, "Georgia, is that you?"

"In the flesh. We're in Monterey. What a cool place."

"I thought you were going to stay in Reno for awhile?"

"We were. Didn't Ty tell you what he did? Man, he slipped five grand in my backpack with a note, said 'For your farewell dance.' You believe that shit? I can't believe he didn't tell you."

"He didn't say anything to me."

"Man, it blew me away. I thought you were the rich guy. Anyway, I wanted to call you because we came down here and we both got jobs at the Marine Center. I met this chick who works on one of the research teams who I think you'd like. In fact, I think you do. Her name is Hannah. She's hot, Stan man. I told you I'd let you know if I ran into her and I never lie to a friend."

"Whoa! Thanks. Thanks a lot. Maybe I should come down to check out the Marine Center. It sounds like that's where all the beautiful people are. How long until your ship leaves?"

"A couple of months but workin' here is gonna be awesome. Man,

I must be livin' under a good sign. The center just got a huge donation from some publishing company so they just made these new jobs. We were in the right place at the right time for a change."

Stan's eyes widened, "A publishing company? It wouldn't happen to be Yellow Feather Publishing would it?"

"Yeah! That's it. You heard of them?"

Stan smiled "Yeah, I have. It all sounds great. I'm really glad you called, Georgia."

"I told you I would. I hope you come down for a visit. I got to get going. Give Ole Ty a big hug for me. You take care of yourself, Stan man. I'll be seeing you."

"Bye, Georgia."

Stan hung up the phone and gave himself a big spin in the chair. Hannah! Stan hadn't thought about Hannah in the real world for a long time. Hannah lived somewhere in the recesses of memory. Suddenly Stan's life didn't seem so structured. There appeared a hopeful light on the horizon, despite all the anger and dissention he had witnessed in the previous few days, Stan's heart was alive. He sprung from the chair and charged out of his room.

Stan sprinted up the back stairs to the apartment. He fully expected to find the apartment empty. Stan knocked. To his surprise Ty called for him to enter. He was sitting idly, bags packed beside him.

"I see you're ready to leave. I'm glad I caught you."

"I wasn't going to leave before I saw you."

Stan sat down, "Georgia just called. They're in Monterey and Hannah is there, too."

"Outstanding! Are you going?"

"I think so." Stan sat quietly until his smile began to fade, "I talked to Mom. She told me about Troy. She also told me about you and Dad."

Ty sighed, "I guess I'm glad you know." He cautiously eyed Stan, "How much did she tell you?"

"Just that you thought Dad had something to do with his death and she convinced you to drop it."

"How much do you want to know?"

"I want the whole story."

"I can't give you the whole story. All I can tell you is my part in it. Stanton has the rest of the story but I doubt he'll share it."

"Do you think Dad set Troy up?"

"Yes, I do but I couldn't prove it. Setting up the offshore accounts with Troy's password was something Stanton could easily have accomplished but only Stanton knows for sure. Troy's murder was a completely different story."

"What do you mean his murder? I thought he died in prison?"

"He did but under pretty bizarre circumstances. They transferred a cell mate in with Troy the day he was killed. The following morning the cellmate was gone. There is no official record of Troy having a cellmate on that date. Whoever it was, he wanted Troy to suffer. The killer bled him out, real slow."

"Are you trying to tell me you think my Dad is a murderer?"

"No. Men like your Father don't murder people but in his world murder is just another tool to get what they want."

"How did you arrive at the conclusion Dad was involved?"

"Are you sure this is somewhere you want to go? Just because it impacted Emma's life doesn't mean it should impact yours."

"That's funny coming from you. I've spent the last few weeks listening to your lectures about how history has been rewritten and now you want to alter my family history with omissions. How about just giving me the fucking truth!"

"You're right, Stan." He paused, "I don't just think your Father was involved, I have the proof. I have the statements of the inmates who were in the cells on either side of Troy's. None of them had ever seen the man who was put in with Troy on that night. I have the guard's testimony saying they were unusually transferred to another unit that night even though the guard's log says they weren't. I have the sworn deposition of one your Dad's bank employee's who transferred a substantial sum of money to a prison official. The man in the cell that night was gone the following morning which means someone on the inside got him out."

"How did you get all the records?"

"I stole them. I saw the cover up unfolding, so I took them. They are the only copies that survived. The rest of the investigation no longer exists. I've had the files hidden ever since."

"Does Dad know you have them?"

"I'm sure he does. He knows most things. I'm sorry Stan. It's not my place to tell you these things about your Father."

"I don't know what to believe. I can't picture my Dad doing something like that. He's tough but I can't see him being that ruthless. Why did Mom think she had to protect you?"

"Stan, I want to tell you what I know about Stanton's world. You know your Father is a powerful man but I don't think you realize how that power is retained or exercised. Stanton is a cog in a machine that has been directing civilization for centuries. You need to understand about wealth and power, not just economics. And I mean wealth, real wealth. Real wealth isn't Wall Street or any other public institution. Real wealth is private. Through the ages the names may change but the system protecting the wealth always remains. Think about it, when an empire falls or a country fails the property and the machinery representing actual value continues to exist and someone controls it. That control has persisted through Revolutions, Inquisitions and World Wars. Have you ever wondered why Washington DC, London's financial city center and the Vatican are not part of the countries where they are located? Those three city/states represent the three power structures that have dominated the planet for the past sixteen hundred years. Do you think that's a coincidence? The Roman Catholic Church was devised to ensure the survival of the wealth of the Roman Empire. Try to imagine the wealth that was accumulated by the church for over a thousand years while they ruled the Western World. The British Empire ruled the next three hundred years until they passed the baton to the United States a hundred years ago.

Currency is merely a tool to transfer wealth upward. Failing economics and currencies mean nothing to these men. The only thing that matters is who owns and controls actual value. These powerful men manipulate wars and revolutions to eliminate opposition and advance their holdings. Both sides of every conflict are indebted to the same people. I'm afraid I have centered my anger at Stanton because I don't know the names of the power elite. They are the names on the charters of the private banks making up the Central Banks of the world. They are the names on the deeds of the private foundations. They are the names behind the enormous private equity funds. Doesn't it seem strange a corporation can show huge profits for decades but face bankruptcy after a couple of unprofitable quarters? It happens because profit doesn't remain in the economy of ordinary people. It moves upward into great pools of accumulation. Corporate globalization is a tool, politicians are pawns, and militaries are enforcement machines all serving the same masters. Most people refuse to believe this power exists but the truth is there for anyone who wants to see it. There are researchers who believe there are fewer than three hundred families controlling sixty to seventy percent of the world's wealth. The House of Rothchild is estimated to be worth between three hundred and five hundred trillion dollars by themselves. After every crash, war, or disaster that concentration of wealth grows. All of the great events in history play out in the exact same way. Look what happened around World War I. Philosophically, there was no reason for the war to be fought. The outcome tells the story. A quarter of the countries on Earth were invented after the war. Two things were happening: We were coming to the end of colonial expansion and oil was replacing the coal England had burned to power their empire. Cecil Rhodes and other European industrialists had created a power struggle for the resources of the African continent. The colonial powers were all establishing foot holds in the oil rich Middle East. The boundaries for the countries of the Middle East and the African continent were all drawn after the war. Twenty million people died in that war to decide which powers would control the value of the resources of those areas. You might have noticed the struggle, sadly, goes on to this day. The point is the instigators and the financiers are always the same. The names change, tactics and techniques change, but the game remains the same. That is Stanton's world. His Father secured him a seat at the big table and he will never relinquish it. That is at the core of your existence. That seat is yours if you accept your legacy, unconditionally, like Stanton did. Those people don't personally kill but history is a testament to the fact that there is no limit to what they will do to increase and protect their interests. That system supersedes country, religion, or even family. The system is protected at all costs even if an insider has to be sacrificed. If there are no men behind the curtain we are in the middle of the intrigue of the ages because the bulk of the wealth created in the last two thousand years is missing. Troy was a minor obstacle but that didn't stop Emma from falling in love with him. The only mistake Troy made in his short life was to fall in love with a woman who was desired by a powerful man. Emma was right. I was in over my head. Stanton's Father would never have allowed Stanton to be hurt by something as inconsequential as the murder of a nobody."

"Why are you holding onto the files if you dropped it? Is that your insurance policy?"

"Maybe. I'm not sure. I guess I've never given up on the concept of justice."

"What are you going to do?"

"I don't know. What about you?"

"I don't know what I think about anything anymore. What I do know is every member of my family is unhappy and I don't want that to happen to me. I think I'm going to Monterey to see if Hannah will forgive me. I don't want to live a life of regret like all of you."

"That sounds beautiful, Stan. I hope you can pull it off. Big Stan isn't going to like it."

"I don't care. I'll talk to him before I leave. I want his side of this story."

Ty paused, "Do you want the files? I won't use them. I planned all along on giving them to Emma but I think you should have them."

"Is Dad simply implicated or is he actually named?"

"He's named a few times along with a few other names I didn't recognize."

Stan thought about it, "I think I would like to have them. I might need a little leverage someday."

Ty reached into his pocket and pulled out a key ring with two small keys, "The files are in a private security vault."

Stan took the keys and held them up for inspection, "I don't know how to feel about any of this shit. Yesterday I was a spoiled little rich kid, today I'm the Spawn of Satan. Dad might be hard nosed but I can't get my head around him being tied to a conspiracy."

"Quit trying to frame it as conspiracy. It's the reality of our existence. The cause and result of every event of major consequence in our time is the same. Those who control the wealth. Capitalism took the baton from Religion and they hold that leadership role to this day. The world and her people are financial puppets. I have a good one for you. What has been the measure of wealth until Capitalist currencies came along? Gold! Do you know why there has never been an audit of the people's gold at Fort Knox? Because since the dollar was removed from the gold standard the gold has been paid to the banks of The Federal Reserve to pay off the country's debt. There is no gold. That leaves value as the final wealth frontier and what is of value? What has actual value? Commodities and resources, property, and labor. That's it! The industrial and corporate world control the planet's commodities and resources which are financed and securitized by the financial industry and are valued in currency. Property is represented by deed contracts and is valued in currency. Labor is the people's contribution of value which is also valued in currency. Do you see a common denominator? That's why it doesn't matter who wins the wars or which corporations fail. Power and representations of value always end up together. The only thing that matters is who holds the deeds, mortgages, securitizations and who controls the labor. That's everything there is to own and it will all be purchased with worthless paper. Free Market Capitalism is neither free nor is it capitalism. It's a rigged game which can have but one winner. Big Stan is not the driving force, he's simply a piece of the evolutionary cabal that has the means to control entire civilizations. When economic collapse comes to America, and it will, Stanton will find out his standing in the system because it will be the system that survives. Stanton doesn't know who the ultimate rulers are any more than I do. He knows he has a seat at the big table, he just doesn't know how much bigger it gets. Stanton didn't invent the game, he just embraced it."

"You're getting way beyond my pay grade. If what you say is true, I can't do anymore about it than anyone else." Stan's face reddened, "What I want to know is why it was necessary to blackmail my Father! I want to know if my Father is a contract murderer! I want to know if I fucked up and doomed myself to a life of resentment like you and Mom. I want some fucking answers!"

Ty kept a solemn eye on Stan, "And you deserve answers."

Stan held out the keys, "If Dad has so much power why didn't he just take the keys from you?"

"Because someone else had one of the keys and neither one of us knew where the safe deposit box is located."

"How could it be of any use to you then?"

"I said I didn't know where it is. I didn't say I couldn't find out. Darnell gave me the other key when we were there."

"This cloak and dagger stuff is bullshit. I may just destroy the files so it's over."

"You do whatever you think is best, Stan, it doesn't matter to me anymore."

Stan stood to leave, "You mentioned Darnell and that reminds me. Georgia said the research center just received a sizeable donation from Yellow Feather Publishing. She also said you put five thousand dollars in her pack. That can't be a coincidence."

Ty grinned, "No, it's not."

"What's the story? Why is everything a damn secret? Don't you people ever do anything in the daylight?"

"Good point. The story is easy. I wrote a few books under a name-de-plume and Darnell publishes and distributes them. I've never known what to do with the money and the research center sounded like as good of a cause as any."

"What name did you write under?"

The patented Ty grin appeared, "Hi Stan, I'm John Done."

Stan looked intently for a moment, "You know what Ty? You're just like Dad. You expect people to trust you but you don't trust anybody." Stan turned and started for the door.

Ty asked, "Don't you want to know how to get the location?"

Stan smiled at Ty, "You take care of yourself old man. I'll be seeing you." He closed the door behind him.

Stan's thoughts were filled with nothing but conflict. He marched purposefully to the main house. Stan knocked boldly on the door to the Queen's Wing. Emma answered the door quickly. She immediately spotted the intensity in Stan's face. He held up the two keys for Emma to see. Her eyes widened with surprise and slowly with recognition. She looked deep into Stan's eyes. Emma leaned forward, lightly kissing Stan's cheek. Emma's lips went to his ear and she whispered into it. Emma stepped back. Stan nodded, acknowledging he had clearly heard her. He smiled at his Mother, turned and walked away.

Stan got off the elevator at his Father's executive suite. He stopped at the assistant's desk, "I need to see my Dad."

The assistant reached under her desk and pushed the release button, opening the door into his Father's office, "Mr. Wainwright is expecting you."

Stanton was seated behind a large desk, very similar to the desk in his home study. He watched Stan stride towards him, "Have a seat. What's on your mind?"

Stan sat down, "How did you know I was coming?"

"Surveillance cameras. Have you spent so much time with Ty you're paranoid, too?"

"I need some answers. It sounds like everyone has dirt on everyone else. I just want the truth. Did you set that man up?"

Stanton gave a slight nod, "Right to it, huh? Well the answer is no. Is that all?"

"Why should I believe you?"

"Are you serious? Why should you doubt me? Do you doubt I have always acted in your best interest? You spent two weeks with a burned out old man and now you're questioning my loyalties. Even you have to see the irony in that."

"Ty said he has proof of your involvement in that man's death. I don't know what to believe."

Stanton remained calm, "You've seen how Ty feels about me. Don't you think if he had damning evidence against me he would have used it long ago? If you haven't noticed, Ty has a propensity for making unsubstantiated claims. Everything is a conspiracy to that old man. Consider the source and move on, Stan."

Stan sat silently processing what his Father was saying. Stan had so many questions he was momentarily dumbstruck.

Stanton calmly continued, "That story is ancient history. It doesn't matter anymore. That's not what you're here for, now is it? You want to know if your Father is an evil man who lives in a shadowy, ruthless world. Am I right?"

"Well, yeah, kind of." He paused, "I know who you've been in my life but I never took the time to see who you were to Mom or anyone else. A lot of what Ty says seems to fit the facts."

"I believe you have that reversed. Ty fits selective facts to support his misguided opinions. You can't honestly believe there are men meeting in secret to plot the destiny of mankind? Ty reads too many stupid novels. What Ty calls a conspiracy, I call a board meeting. Creating wealth is not a sinister pursuit, it's a full time job. Everyone can't benefit from every business transaction. There are always winners and losers. I like winning and I won't apologize for that. Ty believes the world is idealistically flawed. He might be right but it doesn't matter. I'm not a philosopher so I deal with reality. That's why I prosper while others spend their time complaining. Maybe Capitalism is jaded. I don't care either way because the fact is, Capitalism exists. That is our reality. You can't paint the world just in the colors you agree with. Let the scholars argue ethics and morality, I live in the world as it exists."

"So you don't believe there is anything sinister behind International Banking? It's just business as usual."

"Exactly! Every corporation holds closed door meetings. That does not comprise a conspiracy, it's simply good business. I don't make public every decision I make, my competitors would crush me. It's all a simple matter of perception. Bleeding hearts like Ty preach about the abuses of our Capitalist system because they don't participate. People like myself who do participate are the only ones grounded in reality. Capitalism, right or wrong, is the driving force in the world. You can't ignore that fact simply because you don't agree with it. It's human nature to ridicule what you don't understand. Ty is correct about one thing, I don't know the names behind the world's great institutions."

Stan's eyes widened, "You! You bugged the apartment!"

Stanton sat quietly, assessing Stan's reaction. The similar genetic veins began to appear on his temples, "So What!"

"So what? Are you kidding? Is there anyone you don't spy on?"

Stanton leaned forward in his chair. His eyes narrowed, "I monitor everyone and everything that concerns my business and that crazy old man concerns me. Look what he's done to you. In two weeks time he's pushed you to question your own existence and you think that's normal. Well Stan, I'm here to tell you, you're heading down roads you have no business being on. It doesn't concern you, it only diverts your attention from where it should be."

"You mean my future? It's never been my future. Everything I've ever done has come directly from you. You even told me who I can love! You don't trust anyone, certainly not me."

"You weren't in love with that little tramp…"

"How do you know? You don't know anything about me! You didn't know anything about Hannah. She wasn't right for you. You couldn't possibly know if she was right for me."

Stanton's face reddened, "I do what I do for you! I'm the only one protecting you. You're too young to know. That little girl would have latched on to your money, nothing more. Damn it, Stan! You need to get it through your head, you're not like these other people. You are a Wainwright and that means something. Ty's right, there is a ruling class and you were born into it. Ty is just another in a long line of pseudo intellectuals who believe the masses deserve to share in the wealth. He's delusional. People can't share in the wealth because they aren't capable of it. I'm sure the Professor has dazzled you with stories of his liberal history. What he doesn't know is people live in poverty because that's the only way civilization can advance. If the last six thousand years have taught us anything it's anytime the people have been given any degree of self determination, they have squandered the opportunity. The best of men figured out long ago that people are weak and they need to be herded and led like sheep. People are where they deserve to be. You, Stan, are descendant of those great men. For all of civilization the best of men have directed the evolution of the system we have today. Don't be naïve, Stan. The world bows to the rulers because there is no other way it can be. It doesn't matter if everyone despises the ruling class because they wouldn't exist without them. That's why you need to think seriously about the decisions you make now because you either except the privilege of your station or you're one of them."

"You honestly think you are better than everyone else?"

"I don't think it, I know it. I live it! And so are you. That's why I didn't want you with that girl. I know what is best for you. You're the one who needs to develop trust. You need to trust me. I'm the only one who can open doors for you. I can open doors to places that are beyond your wildest imagination. The power and wealth within your reach is incomprehensible to normal people. If it's beautiful women you want, you can have as many as you desire in any manner you desire. There are no limits where I can take you." His eyes gave Stan the once over, "Look at you. You're so full of yourself right now. You think because you hold those two keys and a location you have real leverage against me."

Stan rose to his feet, "No one is safe from your spies. You know what the difference between you and Ty really is? You want to make up my mind for me. Ty wants me to make up my mind for myself." He started for the door.

Stanton stood up behind the desk, "Stan, don't make rash decisions you can't rescind. If you turn your back on me, there is no second chapter. I deal in absolutes and I can't abide having doubts. Why don't you just give me the keys and get on with your life."

Stan stood at the door silently appraising his Father, the man who had always been larger than life. Stan recognized the confident posture but there was something new in the eyes. The dark, commanding power that had cowered Stan forever had given way to a flicker of fear. If Stan hadn't known better, he could swear there was the faint beginning of a tear in the corner of his Father's eyes.

Stan asked, "Are you happy?"

Stanton's face contorted with confusion, "What kind of fucking question is that? Just give me the keys."

Stan flashed his best Ty grin, "I'll let you know."

Stan closed the door. His mind was in supernova by the time he reached his car in the underground parking garage. Stan stared aimlessly through the windshield. 'What now? What do I do next?' This was too much. Two weeks ago he was a college graduate preparing for a road trip through Europe. He should be getting stoned and getting laid not dealing with this shit. He was only twenty one, he shouldn't be thinking about the hate, discontent and malice of mankind's spirit. Stan felt like he should make a decision, right now, in this time and place. This could be one of those crossroads moments where everything from this moment forward would be different. He thought about his road trip with Ty. That trip had changed him. He had left as Stan the obedient son but he had returned as Stan the man, Stan the individual. He was no longer merely in the world, he was of the world. Ty may be hurt and frustrated but he was sincere. Ty honestly cared. Emma had opted, for reasons of her own, to be an observer of her own life. What of Stanton? Did he have to reach a conclusion about his Father's morality right now? What to think? What to do?

Stan sat for a long time, replaying the conversations and confrontations of the previous few days. Everyone close to him had mountains of burdening baggage they carried around with them. Their lives were shadowed by secrets, regrets, grudges and judgments.

"Screw it!" Stan slammed the steering wheel. Let them all deal with their own. Stan was going to write his own story! He began plotting his moves. First, he would tap his trust fund. Once he had money in his pocket, he would go home, pack some clothes, say goodbye to his Mother and go to Hannah. He would beg her to forgive his cowardice. He would plead with Hannah to share her life with him. The open road had given Stan a glimpse of a life beyond his own. A world where Stan's hopes and dreams reigned supreme. The class wars could be waged without Stan's help. The battle between good and evil had raged for millennia and it would be fought long after he was gone. Stan had, willingly and compliantly, donated the first twenty one years of his life to someone else's vision and now, at this very moment, Stan was claiming the right to his own vision. From this day forward was the time of Stan.

Stan started the Acura and left the garage. He pulled into traffic with a new design for life, his own.

A beige Crown Victoria pulled into traffic behind Stan. The two men inside the car were known to each other although they had been brought together just this day. The passenger sat his pistol on the seat and picked up the folder provided by the driver.

The passenger said, "I'm surprised they brought you in on this. There must be some real players mentioned in that file if they want you on it. How far can we go on this?"

"Our primary interest is to secure the files. Ideally we can just take them from him after he retrieves them. Failing that, we'll grab him and get the keys and the location from him. Worst case is we grab the girl to coerce his cooperation. There's someone watching her now. The principle wants to spare the kid if possible but the files are paramount. There are names in those files that can't be made public."

The passenger looked back at the folder in his lap. He shook his head, "Welcome to the real world, kid."

## The End

Printed in the United States
217060BV00001B/38/P